Edwin Abbott Abbott

Onesimus

Memoirs of a Disciple of St. Paul

Edwin Abbott Abbott

Onesimus
Memoirs of a Disciple of St. Paul

ISBN/EAN: 9783337092887

Printed in Europe, USA, Canada, Australia, Japan

Cover: Foto ©Raphael Reischuk / pixelio.de

More available books at **www.hansebooks.com**

ONESIMUS

MEMOIRS

OF

A DISCIPLE OF ST. PAUL

BY THE AUTHOR OF "PHILOCHRISTUS"

Νυνὶ δὲ μένει πίστις, ἐλπίς, ἀγάπη, τὰ τρία ταῦτα·
μείζων δὲ τούτων ἡ ἀγάπη.

London
MACMILLAN AND CO.
1882

Art thou a slave, as I was? Or an orphan, as I was? Or wanderest thou still, as I long wandered, in the wilderness of doubt and sin? Then for thee is written this story of one that was made free in Christ, and adopted to be the child of God, and in the end brought safe out of the deep darkness of Satan into the Light of the Eternal Truth.

THE TABLE

THE FIRST BOOK

THE SECOND BOOK

THE THIRD BOOK

THE FOURTH BOOK

THE EIGHTH BOOK

AN ADDITION CONTAINING

ONESIMUS

Memoirs of a Disciple of St. Paul

ONESIMUS

THE FIRST BOOK

§ 1. OF MY CHILDHOOD.

IN the last year of the Emperor Tiberius I and my
twin-brother Chrestus were found lying in one cradle,
exposed with a great number of other babes upon the
steps of the temple of Asclepius, in Pergamus, a city of
Bithynia. Sign or token of our parents, whether they
were free-born or slave, there was none; but only a
little silver seal hung round my neck, and on the seal
these words in Greek characters, I LOVE THEE, and
on my brother Chrestus another of the same fashion,
bearing the inscription, TRUST ME. Many a time
during the days of my wandering have I spoken reproachfully in my heart, saying that our parents gave
us small cause for trust, and that it was poor love to
send out into the rough world two innocent babes with
no other equipment against evil than these slight toys.
But the hand of the Lord was in it, to turn this evil
into good in the end.

B

Ammiane the wife of Menneas was the name of our new mother. Her own son Ammias was but lately dead ; and that which drew her kind heart to us more than to any other among so large a multitude of poor babes there pitifully lying on the temple steps, was that in my brother Chrestus she seemed to discern a likeness to her lost one.

Menneas took us, together with Ammiane, to his house in Lystra, a city of Lycaonia, where was the better part of his estate ; and soon afterwards he died. But his widow, the good Ammiane, to whom old Menneas had left all his possessions, treated us as if we had been her own children, and taught us to call her mother ; and we had no thought but she was our mother indeed. Yet as there had been no formal adoption of us according to law, we were still in the eyes of the law not free, but slaves ; for so runs the law, that whosoever is exposed as a child and saved and reared, becomes the slave of them that rear him. For our enfranchisement had been first delayed, and then forgotten in the sickness and death of Menneas ; and by that time we were so established in the household that none questioned but we had been enfranchised, and all thought of it was laid aside. Therefore according to the law we were still Ammiane's slaves, and not her sons, and in danger to be sold whenever our dear foster-mother might die. But of all this neither I nor my brother Chrestus knew anything ; but we rejoiced in the love of her whom we called mother ; and all the household loved us for her sake, and some for our own. And so the days rolled on in happiness till I had come to my tenth year.

§ 2. HOW I FIRST SAW THE HOLY APOSTLE PAULUS.

It was in the spring, as I remember, of the fifth year
of the emperor Claudius that I first saw the Holy
Apostle, whom I saw not again till many years had
passed away; and though I was at that time but a child
of ten years or thereabouts, yet every circumstance of it
is imprinted upon my memory.   It was the cool of the
evening, and I was without the wall, hard by the Iconian
gate, on one of the smaller hills that look down upon
the town, a little to the north of the Iconian road.
Hermas, our herdsman, was playing upon his pipe some
song to the god Pan, and the goats were gambolling
around him.   But I—being wholly taken up with
teaching a little kid to dance to the sound of the music
—paid no heed to the chidings of our nurse Trophime,
who would have had me go back with her to the city
because it was now near sun-down.   So lifting up her
eyes and seeing some dromedaries and a dust on the
Iconian road, "Look, dear child," said she, "yonder come
merchants from Iconium; if therefore thou wilt go
with me without delay, thou wilt see their stores of
pretty things, and perchance Ammiane will buy thee
somewhat."

Hearing this, I willingly ran down with her to the
city gate; and arriving thither before the travellers, I
waited till they should enter.   But when they were now
nigh, I perceived that they were no merchants, and I
would have turned away.   Yet I did not, for somewhat
in the face of one of the travellers held me fast, I know

not how, so that I fixed my gaze on him perforce, even as a bird fascinated by a serpent ; and indeed I thought myself to be bewitched and spat thrice ; but yet I stood still gazing upon him.   At that time he was not yet bald, he had a clear complexion, a nose hooked and somewhat large ; he was short of stature, and as he walked he bent his head a little forward, as if not able to discern things clearly ; his eyebrows were shaggy and met together ; but what most moved me was the glance of his eyes which were of a penetrating brightness, as though they would pierce through the outside of things even to the innermost substance.

When the travellers were entered into the city, I stood still in wonder, as one who had seen a dream betwixt sleeping and waking.   But soon, coming to myself again, I chid my nurse that she had drawn me away from the flocks by stratagem and I persuaded her to return for some short space, that I might continue my sport.   But my heart was no longer in it, and presently, it being now sunset, I came down with Trophime to go into the town.   Scarce were we come within the gates when we perceived a great concourse of the people near to the market ; and running thither we entered with the rest into a courtyard and there found a great multitude assembled, and the travellers, in the gallery above, discoursing to them.   What touched me (as being a child) more than all the words that were spoken, was the marvellous stillness of the multitude, who all listened as if the speech were about matters of life or death, so that herdsmen and ploughmen and litter-bearers and water-carriers and others of the lowest and meanest sort, coming into the courtyard with shouts and scoffings, no sooner passed into the circle of the hearers than they were at once subdued and tamed like the rest; among whom, most earnestly listening, as I noted, was a poor creature, part demented and part buffoon, whom, having been lame for thirty years and more, we were wont to call "lame Xanthias." This man, when the traveller had made an end of his discourse, said some words that I could not clearly understand; whereupon he that had been speaking came straightway down from the gallery and drew nigh to the lame man, and fixing his eyes upon him he took him by the hand. If there had been a silence before, there was a tenfold silence now, even such a silence as one seemed to feel in one's flesh. But the stranger first lifted up his eyes to heaven and then gazing fixedly on the lame man he cried in a loud voice, " In the name of Jesus of Nazareth, rise up and walk ; " and behold, Xanthias,—this man who had been thirty years lame,—rose and walked and leaped, and wept aloud praising and magnifying God. Then there was a great shouting, and all rushed forth into the market place, some crying " a miracle," " a miracle," others holding up Xanthias in their arms to show him unto the people, others magnifying the new god whom the strangers had revealed to us, others crying out that the strangers themselves were gods, namely Zeus and Hermes, come down from heaven as they had come down in the old days; and saying these things, some sped away to the priest wishing to offer sacrifice to the strangers. But suddenly there was a deep silence again, and we perceived that the traveller, he I mean who had healed Xanthias, was once more speaking to the people. What he said I could not clearly understand, being

more busy with noting his countenance than the
meaning of his words ; but I gathered so much, that
he said that he and his companion were not gods
but men, and that indeed there was One God above (not
many gods) who gave all good gifts to mankind and who
now called all men to come unto him. When he had
made an end of speaking, the women pressed close to
him with their babes and children that he might touch
them ; and so it was that Trophime pushed me forward
with the rest. Then he laid his hands on me and
looking kindly on me asked Trophime whether I was a
native of these parts and who was my father. What
Trophime replied I did not hear, except that my father
was now dead ; but the stranger looked on me more
lovingly than before and said, " The Lord be unto thee
as a Father, little one " ; and laying his hands on me a
second time he blessed me.

§ 3. OF THE STRANGER, AND OF DIOSDOTUS THE PRIEST OF ZEUS.

When we were come home to Ammiane, I spoke
freely to her as I was wont, concerning all that I had
heard and seen ; and I asked her which of the two she
judged to be the wiser and the mightier, the hook-nosed
prophet—for so I called the stranger—or Diosdotus.
Now Diosdotus was the priest of the city, a man of
noble birth and very wealthy, having rebuilt the baths
at his own expense after the earthquake, as also his
father before him had rebuilt the amphitheatre. He
was also tall of stature and of a gracious and

commanding carriage. Yet now I could not help making comparison between him and the stranger of mean presence and short stature ; bethinking myself that Diosdotus had lived for thirty years in the same city as poor lame Xanthias and yet had suffered him to be still lame, whereas the strange prophet had healed him on the very day of his first coming in. However Ammiane laughed and chid me for my question, saying that I did ill to compare an obscure vagrant soothsayer with the high priest of Zeus ; for that there were many travelling priests of Cybele and Sabazius and jugglers and necromancers that would work signs and wonders in the eyes of the common people, and all for a drachma or two ; but Diosdotus was none of these, nor to be mentioned along with them. Nevertheless, when the report came in from all sides that the lame man was wholly cured, she said she would send for Xanthias, as soon as might be, that she might see him and learn the truth of the matter, and what charms or herbs the stranger had used. But about the fourth or fifth day afterwards—my foster-mother having in the meanwhile, upon one cause or other, delayed to send for Xanthias, but many rumours coming daily to our ears of the great wonders which the magician was working—word was brought that the stranger had been slain ; others said that he had ascended to the sky, others that he had been swallowed up in the earth ; but all agreed that he was not now in the city. Then we found that there had been a great conflict in the Jews' quarter ; for certain Jews had come over from Lystra to Iconium pursuing after the enchanter (so they called him) and accusing him of many grievous crimes. Now it happened to be a time of drought, and the rain, which had begun to fall on the day that the stranger came to Lystra, ceased on that same day, about the time of his entering in, and fell no more for six or seven days, though all the crops were perishing for want of it. So the Jews said that this plague was fallen upon the city of Lystra because we gave shelter to an accursed necromancer; and having persuaded the people they stoned him. But his body could not be found; wherefore the people were the more persuaded that he was a necromancer, insomuch that all now (except Xanthias and a very few others) believed him to be no prophet but an evil-doer and a deceiver of the people.

But on the very day after these things the sun was darkened, and still no rain fell; and on the third day after the stoning of the stranger, came a great plague of locusts so thick together that they lay two inches deep in the race-course; and not many days after that, came the shock of an earthquake; and ten houses in the Jews' quarter were wholly thrown down (besides others sorely shaken and shattered), insomuch that some four-score of the Jews were slain, and their synagogue was utterly destroyed. Upon this the people began to change their minds again, and some made bold to say that the god of the new prophet had sent these evils; and so the city was divided, and part held that the stranger was a deceiver and an enchanter, but part that he was a teacher of the true God and a prophet. At last when the customary sacrifices seemed of no avail, but the drought still endured, and by intervals there came ever and anon shocks of earthquake, it seemed good that there should be a solemn procession of all the city to avert the wrath of the gods, one for Pessinuntian Cybele, the other for Asphalian Poseidon and the third for Zeus Panhemerius. This last far surpassed the other two in splendour, and amidst the whole procession most of all to be admired was Diosdotus the chief priest, himself most like to a god, clad in white linen with a purple border, and a garland on his head, and attended by the inferior priests, and by ministers bearing incense and scattering flowers and perfumes; and after them, the white oxen with their horns gilt for the sacrifice, and then the choir of boys, with laurel branches in their hands, singing, to the accompaniment of the lyre, the hymn which had been chosen by Onomarchus the secretary of the senate. Beholding all this splendour (exceeding anything I had ever before witnessed) I inclined now to prefer Diosdotus to the strange prophet; and all the more because Ammiane was clearly on the side of the former. Moreover on the second day after the procession there fell rain in abundance. So all the people now turned to magnify Zeus Panhemerius; and the drought and the earthquake were forgotten, and with them the memory of the stranger faded away.

Yet in my dreams sometimes, both then and for many months afterwards, methought I saw the strange prophet who had healed Xanthias, standing over against Diosdotus and contending against him; and I heard his voice again and again in the darkness, saying, "The Lord be unto thee as a father."

§ 4. HOW WE GREW UP AT LYSTRA.

Six or seven years passed smoothly away for me and
my brother Chrestus.   Our dear mother Ammiane
caused us to be taught singing and dancing, as well
as riding and the exercises of the gymnasium; and
partly because of our beauty and partly because we
were regarded as the adopted children of one whom all
the citizens loved and honoured (for there are still extant inscriptions in Lystra praising our benefactress and
calling her the MOTHER OF THE CITY, on account
of her many gifts and benefactions to the people of
Lystra) we were chosen among the choir of boys who
were to sing songs year by year in honour of Apollo
and Ephesian Artemis in accordance with the recent
decree of the senate; and in all our riding-lessons and
wrestling-lessons we took part with the well-born youth
of the city; for all knew that Ammiane intended us to
be her heirs after her death.   But in my fourteenth
year it happened that, while seeking for a goat that
had strayed in the mountains, I missed my footing
and fell down a steep place, where I was taken up
for dead; and Hermas brought me home wounded
well-nigh to death with two deep gashes on my fore-
head and left cheek.   In a short space I was recovered
of my wounds; but I was grievously disfigured with
the scars upon my face, and when I went with my
brother, as I was wont, to the choir-master, he plainly
told me that I was no longer fit to dance nor sing
with the choir, for the god required comely youths to
minister to him.   Hereat I was sore vexed, and yet

more when I perceived (or thought that I perceived) that
in the palæstra also and in the riding-school I was no
longer so welcome as of old ; for some openly jested
at my disfigurement, and others, who had before
courted my company, now avoided me ; at least so
I thought, misconstruing perhaps and aggravating
little slights, in my discontent. However it was, I
became morose and lost my former cheerfulness ; for
the world seemed changed and turned against me. But
the kind Ammiane, discerning what was amiss with me,
persuaded me to apply myself to letters ; and she
bought for us one Zeno, a Greek, to be our tutor.
Now Chrestus, being the leader of the choir and the
favourite in the palæstra, by reason of these distractions
cared less for learning ; but I, withdrawing myself from
my former pursuits and devoting myself to letters,
made good progress in my new studies, so that I soon
became skilful at transcribing Greek characters ; and I
took a great delight in the reading of Euripides and
others of the Greek play-writers, but most of all in the
poetry of Homer. And in these pursuits I continued
till my sixteenth year, finding pleasure in many things
but most of all in the love of my beautiful brother
Chrestus.

§ 5. HOW AMMIANE DIED AND MY BROTHER AND I
WERE SOLD FOR SLAVES.

But now indeed our trouble was at hand. For toward
the end of my sixteenth year, our dear foster-mother
died, and whether it was that she had made no will, or
that the will had been stolen or lost, certain it was that

no will could be found. It was commonly said, in the household, that a will had been made and deposited with one Tertullus, a banker of Iconium, but that he had destroyed the will, being persuaded by Nicander of Tyana the heir-at-law, and the two witnesses being both dead. Diosdotus the high-priest of Zeus affirmed that Ammiane had deposited a will with him fourteen years ago in the presence of two witnesses, immediately after the death of her husband, but that she had received it back in the presence of the same witnesses, two years afterwards, and had deposited no other will in its place. Whatever the truth may have been, when Nicander arrived on the second day from Tyana, there was none to dispute his claim; so, though he was known by all to be hateful to Ammiane and had not set foot on her threshold for fifteen years, he now took upon himself to give orders for the funeral and to dispose all things according to his pleasure. Hereupon arose a great wailing and lamentation among the household, that is to say all that were old enough to know what it was to be a slave. For many of them had looked to be made free by Ammiane's will; and to some she had in express terms promised freedom : and others, who had not been long with us, knowing the kindness of their mistress, expected that they should not be sold, or that after four or five years of service they should be made free. For so much as this was customary with all the wealthy townspeople of Lystra, those at least that had large possessions in land and many household slaves; and how much more might have been expected from one who had been publicly praised as the "mother of the city"! But now all these hopes were dashed to the ground ; and

. all were at the mercy of a new master, of whom we knew nothing by hearsay except that he hated our dear mistress, and from our own knowledge we had begun to suspect that he was greedy, cruel, violent and tyrannous.

For a few hours Chrestus and I remained weeping bitterly in the room where we were wont to sit with Zeno ; but when Nicander entered and, in answer to his question why we wept, we made answer that we were weeping for our mother, he reviled us as beggarly brats, slaves seeking to escape from our condition ; and spurning us from the chamber bade us be gone at once to the slaves' apartments. Going thither we found all faces full of sorrow ; yet none so sorrowful as not to be able to spare some little further sorrow for our case ; all pointing to us and exclaiming at our ill fortune because yesterday we had been free and heirs to great possessions, but now we were slaves and a second time motherless.

I suppose that our cruel master foresaw that some of the friends of Ammiane would, in all likelihood, interfere in our behalf, if not by appeal to the courts of law, at all events by offering to purchase us from him ; for he gave command that on that very day, immediately after the performance of the funeral rites, we should be sent to his estate at Tyana. A miserable procession was that, wherein Chrestus and I walked for the last time together, following our dear Ammiane to the grave ! The whole household filled the air with lamentations, for themselves even more than for their mistress, so that there was little need of the hired mourners.

But when all was over, and the funeral line moved back homeward, Chrestus and I for a short space turned quietly aside and betook ourselves to a new-made tomb cut in the side of one of the hills that look down upon the city; and there we sat down and wept and poured forth all our sorrows in one another's arms, beseeching the gods to have mercy upon us. For we began to see that we could expect no pity from Nicander, and that he would not hesitate to sell us and to part us asunder if he could thereby make more profit from us; and our hearts swelled to bursting at the thought that we, who had never been divided, should now perchance be parted, each to live lonely and desolate till our life's end. As we wept, we looked down upon our dear home. The fields beneath us had been the fields of Ammiane; we could call by name the sheep and goats that were leaping and bleating in the valley at our feet; the temples in which we had worshipped, the shining roofs of the houses of many well-known friends —all reminded us of past happy days, happy most of all because we had enjoyed them together. At last we rose up to go down to our new life of slavery. But because our minds misgave us that we should be parted on the morrow, we determined to take our last farewell there alone, and not in the presence of Nicander nor before the eyes of the household slaves. And Chrestus said that we should interchange some token, whereby we might recognize each other in days to come, if ever the gods should bring us together again. So we took from off our necks the charms which we had always worn from our infancy and I received from Chrestus his seal with the inscription TRUST ME, and he mine with

the words I LOVE THEE. Then we bade one another
farewell, no longer able to constrain ourselves, but with
piercing cries falling each on the other's neck and
weeping and calling on Ammiane to help us because
the gods helped us not ; and then, drying our tears,
without another word we went down into Lystra. Here
Nicander, rating us for our delay, gave command that
we should be at once placed on separate camels and set
out for Tyana.

§ 6. OF THE DEATH OF CHRESTUS.

On the third day after we were come to Tyana, being
summoned to the presence of Nicander, we found with
him certain of Ammiane's household slaves, and by the
side of our master a smooth-faced Greek from Delos
who seemed to be inspecting and appraising the slaves ;
who, looking at my scar, laughed and said that he
should not need to ask Nicander to name a price for
me ; but he praised the beauty of Chrestus and caused
him to be stripped and to walk up and down the room,
and to sing and to go through the steps of two or three
dancing-measures ; and finally he declared with an oath
that he was more beautiful than Nireus and that he
would buy him at Nicander's price. When we heard
this, we both of us fell down at the feet of Nicander
and of the slave-dealer, beseeching them in the name
of their parents and their brothers also, if they had
any, that at least they would not part us, but that the
Greek might buy us both ; and at the same time I told
the slave-dealer that I could read and write Greek

easily and rapidly, so that I might fetch a good price
as an amanuensis; and even the rest of the slaves of
Ammiane fell on their faces before our master and
joined in our petition.

But Nicander angrily spurned us, and the Greek said
to Chrestus that he must go to Rome where he would
fetch ten times as much as a paltry amanuensis or
grammarian because he was as lovely as Ganymede
and sure to please some great nobleman or perchance
the Emperor himself; but added he, "Your brother is
of no worth to me, for I deal in none but pretty boys;
and therefore, my beautiful one, thou must needs make
ready to be my companion at once, for I should be by
this time well on the road to Tarsus." Hereat Chrestus
arose and following the Greek his master he would have
gone forth without a word more from the chamber.
Nicander, scoffing at his misery, called him back to say
farewell to me, "for," said he, "it may be some time
before you see your brother again." But Chrestus remained silent; only, as he went out at the door, he
turned round to me and held up the little token round
his neck. But that silence was better than many words,
and the memory of it abides with me unto this day.

So long as Chrestus was in the chamber I restrained
myself for his sake lest I should break his heart with
my weeping and passion; but when he was gone forth
I again attempted to bend Nicander with prayers and
entreaties. But finding all in vain, I leaped up from
the ground in fury, and invoked curses upon him
threatening that I would slay him if ever I found occasion. At the word he clapped his hands and calling in
the slaves of his household, "Take this young rebel," he

said, " to the upper quarries, and put him to hard labour with the lowest class, till the brat understand his condition, and learn to be a slave and to submit himself to his betters." So while Chrestus was being carried away to Tarsus, I was dragged to the quarries, which were in a wild place, void for miles round of all human habitation, about twenty miles north of Tyana. In these quarries there laboured a large gang of slaves, with scant food and scanter clothing, forced to work in chains under the burning sun all day, and at night locked up like sheep in a foul den underground ; and if any died, little heed was taken of it, for it was cheaper to buy new slaves than to treat the old slaves well. But I doubt not that Nicander, who had good reasons for wishing to be rid of my brother and me, did what he did wittingly and with forethought, supposing that I should soon have succumbed to the hardships of the place and the life, and that the quarries should have been my grave and his deliverance.

On the morrow I began my labours amid a new sort of companions, creatures to all outward appearance resembling apes and dogs rather than human beings, some stamped and branded on their foreheads with T for " thief," or M for " murderer " ; others having their backs discoloured with the weals of the lash or torn and bleeding with the marks of fresh punishment ; others with collars round their necks, or clogs and fetters shackling their legs and feet ; others labouring beast-like under a kind of fork or yoke ; all were chained in some fashion, and all had one side of the head shorn, so that they might be recognized at once if they should break away and escape any distance. Speech was not

allowed among us; and as we toiled on from sunrise to
sunset amid the heated rocks, the only sounds that
could be heard (beside the clinking of the tools upon the
stone) were the threats and curses of the overseers
and the crack of the whip followed by the scream
of some stricken slave. All the more leisure was
there for thought of Chrestus, whose fate was infinitely
worse than mine, because he was to go to Rome and
there to be sold for his beauty; and I knew well the
saying of the philosopher that "What is counted impurity in the free-born must be counted a necessity in
slaves." Thinking on these things I felt such an agony
that neither the heat nor the parching thirst could
be compared with it; and even the first feeling of the
slave-whip upon my shoulders, though it maddened
me for the moment, could not drive out the thought of
Chrestus. But hatred and thirst for revenge and distrust of the Gods began to blend themselves with my
love of my brother; and whereas at first I had prayed
to Ephesian Artemis to preserve him, now I began to
doubt whether prayers availed anything.

I had been scarce a week in the ergastulum when, as
we came forth in the morning to be marshalled and
numbered, according to our wont, before going to our
several places in the quarries, I heard the voice of
Hermas behind me giving some message to Syrus our
overseer. But when I leaped forward to embrace him,
he spoke roughly to me, calling me a fool and a rebel,
and saying that he would have no speech with me till I
had submitted myself to the worthy Nicander. I shrank
back quickly to my place, feeling myself friendless
indeed now that Hermas had turned against me. By

this time we were on our way from the ergastulum to
the quarries, and I with the rest in my place in the rear.
But when the crack of Syrus's whip showed that he was
at some distance in the front of the long column, I heard
my name called in a low voice and Hermas was by my
side.   He told me in few words that he had accompanied the slave-dealer to Tarsus, but that on the way
Chrestus, either slipping or casting himself down in a
narrow and precipitous part of the road, had fallen down
a high cliff and had been taken up sorely gashed and
wounded, and within two or three hours afterwards he
had died.   In my heart I knew that Hermas spoke the
truth, but I refused to believe his tale, saying that he
was in league with Nicander to deceive me; else, why
had not he brought some token?   But the old man
with tears in his eyes, declared that he would have
brought me the charm that hung round my brother's
neck, but one of the slaves had stolen it; however, in
his last moments Chrestus had written some message on
his tablets for me; and so saying he produced the
tablets which I knew to be indeed my brother's.   Now
all my hopes fell, and I knew that I was alone in the
world; yet could I neither speak nor weep but walked
on without a sign; but the old man looking anxiously
in my face bade me trust in him, and seeing Syrus
approach, he pressed my hand and departed.   For almost
all that day the overseer—perchance because he suspected something amiss, having caught sight of Hermas
stealing away—would not depart from my neighbourhood but kept his eyes so fixed on me that I dared not
stop my work for an instant to pluck the tablets from
my bosom where I had thrust them; and what I did I

knew not, but I could neither think, nor weep, nor do anything but toil on, like some machine. But toward sun-down, a little before we were marshalled that we might go down into the ergastulum, seizing my occasion I plucked out the tablets and upon the first leaf of them I found traced in faint characters, as if by a feeble hand, the words on the token which I had given him, I LOVE THEE; and when I read them, the tears delayed no longer.

§ 7. OF MY LIFE IN THE ERGASTULUM.

If it was a marvel that my body held out against the hardships of the quarries, it was much more marvellous that my soul perished not. Nor do I speak now merely of the words and deeds of darkness wrought by the slavish herd in their underground den, from which the grace of the Lord preserved me; but I speak of the trust in any divine governance of the world which seemed at this time to be in danger to be utterly extinguished, or even to be replaced by a belief in evil. For not only was I becoming day by day more like a brute beast in mind and soul as well as in body, listening with less horror to the obscene jests and tales of my companions and learning to take all evil as matter of course and to expect no good in the world; but also I began to think that, if there were gods indeed, they could not be such as the Epicureans would have us believe, " idle gods that take no thought for mortals," but they must be bad gods to have made, and to endure, so bad a world.

Now I knew that Ammiane had believed in witches

and necromancers and the like ; yea, and even Zeno our
tutor, though he were a philosopher and of the Stoic
sect, had freely confessed that he himself would be
unwilling to be persecuted with the charms and incantations of witches. As often therefore as my companions turning from their obscenities and filthy tales,
began to tell of witchcraft (which they were wont to do
more especially after earthquakes, when they were under
some influence of fear) and stories about Empousæ and
blood-sucking monsters, and the raising of spectres and
the drawing out of the hearts of living men, at such
times I would give an eager ear to all their sayings ; and
although Zeno had taught me to believe that these
superstitions of the common people were no better than
old wives' fables, yet now I began to incline to the
opinion that these stories were true. And in my present
condition the gods of darkness, such as Hecate and
Gorgo and the like, seemed to have more substance and
real power than the greater gods Zeus and Poseidon, who
were worshipped in processions by noble priests in fine
raiment with perfumes and flowers and offerings of fat
victims, but did nothing for their worshippers. When
therefore I heard how one witch had drawn forth oracles
from a little babe whose throat she had cut and enslaved
its spirit ; and how another had obtained vengeance over
her enemies by means of the marrow of a child whom
she had buried up to the midst in the ground and then
left to starve in sight of abundance of food ; and others
had caused their enemies to pine away by making
waxen images to be pierced with needles or melted at
slow fires, and the like ; then came the thought of
Nicander in my mind, thus caused to waste away and

to live without a heart and suddenly to drop down dead, and I prayed that I too might learn these mysteries.

One evening more especially I call to mind, when we had been driven earlier than usual into our dungeon because of a great storm and earthquake, and all the earth seemed in a flux—the crags from the hill sides falling on this side and on that, and whole cliffs swaying to right and left as if we were on sea and not on solid earth—and nine or ten of my companions had been already crushed by the rocks or by the falling in of the sides of the quarries. When we were thrust into our dungeon, sitting in darkness, we could still feel the ground moving beneath us and ever and anon such rockings and rumblings as made the more timid cry out that some gulf would open and swallow us up alive, others, that the sides and roof were falling in upon us. But, of a sudden, amidst the din and tumult of so many voices, a few weeping, but the most part shouting and yelling and blaspheming and cursing the gods, we heard one of the slaves speaking out clearly above all the rest and commanding silence. His name was Nannias, a Colchian by birth ; and he bade us desist from our fears and take heart, "for," said he, " I myself have brought about this storm and earthquake, and as I hope, we shall soon learn that our master has miserably perished in it."

Then all held their peace and listened to the Colchian who continued thus. "From my earliest years I was instructed by an old witch (who bought me as a babe) in all the arts of magic ; and from her I learned how to raise the winds and how to lull them, and how to

make away with a man though he be miles distant, in
such wise that none may know the causer of the mischief.   From my infancy I have ever taken a delight
in all evil.   For why not?   The cross has been the
tomb of all my brothers, my father and my grand-
father; nor will I degenerate from my ancestors.   The
world is against us; let us also be against the world."
At this all shouted in assent; but the Colchian im-
patiently continued, "My first master in Laodicca I
destroyed by placing bones and blood, and nails from
a cross, together with certain herbs which I will not
now mention, beneath the floor of his bedchamber, so
that he wasted away and died in less than a month to
the astonishment of the physician.   And what was best
and sweetest of all, I caused the suspicion of the deed
to fall on the overseer of the slaves, a tyrannical wretch
like Syrus, who was condemned to the wild beasts on
the charge of having made away with our master by
slow poisons."   Hereat all shouted and applauded even
louder than before; and then though the earth still
rocked and groaned beneath us, and the sides of the
ergastulum swayed in and out more violently than ever,
yet every one sat silent in the darkness waiting to hear
what project the Colchian might have in hand so as to
take vengeance on Nicander.

While we all held our breath he cried aloud on
Hecate the goddess of darkness and hater of light, who
delighteth in blood, to come and seize Nicander, at the
same time appealing to other horrible-sounding and
unknown gods, and invoking on Nicander the most
direful curses.   When he ceased, behold, up from the
ground (as it seemed) there came a thin voice, not loud

but very piercing and such as made my very flesh to creep, saying, "I come, O master, I come, I come." Hereat we all leaped to our feet and some shrieked aloud that the demon was upon them, and then all rushed this way and that, and many fell in a heap wallowing together on the floor, and such a hubbub as if hell itself were let loose; and methought if the uproar had continued but a few moments longer, many of us would have been made mad; but at the instant the guard came in with one bearing a lamp, and nothing could anywhere be seen; and they smote on all sides with their whips till the clamour had well nigh abated; and then they went out leaving us in the darkness as before.

Now during all these many years I had had few or no thoughts of Him in whose name Xanthias had been healed; but on this same evening of the earthquake, while I was musing whether there were gods or no, it came into my mind that besides invoking Hecate and Gorgo and the rest, it might be wise to offer up prayers to the God of the strange prophet whom I remembered in my childhood, that He also might join in destroying Nicander. But blessed be the Lord, He hindered me from thus blaspheming His Holy Name; for whether it was that I remembered that the prophet had said that this God was a God of mercy and would be as a Father to me, or whether it was the memory of the pure and holy face of the prophet which seemed not to agree with my impure and unholy prayers, certain it is that the Lord closed my lips and restrained my tongue that I should not take His name in vain. But when all the rest were at last asleep I lay a long while awake and

musing upon the words " the Lord be unto thee as
a Father" and wondering what manner of god this
" Lord" might be.

§ 8. HOW I WAS SOLD TO PHILEMON OF COLOSSÆ.

Not more than three or four days had passed since
the prophecy of the Colchian, and it was the 8th month
or thereabouts from the time of my first being brought
to the quarries, when behold, one morning, coming out
of the ergastulum to our work according to custom,
we found, in the place of the usual overseers, a band
of soldiers; and instead of being drafted off to our
several stations in the quarries, we were caused to
march in one column through Tyana. As we passed
through the town, we heard the reason of our journey.
Nicander was dead. However he had not perished, as
the Colchian had prophesied, in the earthquake; but
having committed an outrage on the wife of one of his
slaves, he had been mortally wounded by the man in a
fit of passion. Yet had he lived long enough to revenge
himself by causing the whole of his household to be put
to death, three hundred in all, including those who had
been of the household of Ammiane, among whom perished our faithful Hermas, and our old nurse Trophime.
On the morrow he died, and the heir, entering on the
estate, had ordered all the slaves that were in the
quarries to be sent to Tarsus and there sold. So brutal
had I become and so hard of heart during my stay in
the ergastulum, that even the news of the death of
Hermas and Trophime did not greatly move me, and

the pain of it was not so great as the pleasure I took
in hearing of the death of Nicander.

When we were come to Tarsus and set up on the
slave-platform, and there caused to leap and dance and
carry weights and to proclaim aloud what arts and
accomplishments we knew, I felt little shame, but only
some faint desire to know who would be my master, and
at the same time a rebellious hatred against gods and
men, as being all alike unjust, and a determination to
be avenged on mankind. At this time my knowledge
of letters and my skill in transcribing stood me in good
stead. For when one of the slave-dealers had seen me
give proof of my skill upon tablets, he bought me at a
higher price than the rest, and after taking me to the
baths and using medicaments to remove or lessen the
marks of my stripes, he clothed me decently, and
placed me with a Greek teacher to increase my skill in
letters ; and after two or three months thus spent in
Tarsus, I was sold to one Philemon, whose step-son
Archippus had been studying rhetoric in the schools.
My new master was a wealthy citizen of Colossæ and a
man of learning, devoted at that time to Greek literature,
and he had come to Tarsus to take note of his son's
progress in the schools there and to conduct him home ;
and by reason of a growing infirmity of sight he
desired to buy some slave who could read Greek with
understanding and take short notes of such things as he
dictated. So he bought me for four minæ, and I
accompanied him to Colossæ.

I was now in my eighteenth year, being the last year
of the emperor Claudius ; but though young I was not
so pliant or supple of nature as might have been

expected from a youth. For I was, as it were, old and stiffened with suffering ; and however the kind Philemon might shew me favour and allowance, yet would my mind still harp on this, that, if I had my rights, I should be free, and whosoever was my master possessed me unjustly. Moreover the terror of my recent life in the quarries never forsook me ; and each night I said to myself, " I am pampered and made a plaything to-day, but I may be cast into the ergastulum to-morrow." This bitterness of distrust spoiled all the pleasures with which the good Philemon would have gladdened my new life at Colossæ ; and indeed my present freedom from oppression and my very leisure, giving me increased occasions for brooding over my loneliness, made me more morose than ever. Sometimes when I looked at the little token which my brother had given me and bethought myself of the token that I had interchanged with him, I would declare that I had not only bestowed on my poor Chrestus the legend I LOVE THEE but at the same time I had parted with my very faculty of love—so barren and dry of all affection did my heart now seem—and as for the other legend TRUST ME, I would inveigh against it as idle and deceiving. For whom had I on earth to trust ? My parents, who had forsaken me ? Or Chrestus or Hermas or Trophime, who were now but dust and ashes ? But if I looked elsewhere, to the gods in heaven above, or to the gods beneath the earth, behold, I saw none save beings that either rejoiced in evil or at least had not power to destroy evil ; which therefore were either too bad or too weak to claim trust from men.

But herein is thy hand manifest, O Lord Jesus ; for

through the loss of earthly love and trust thou wast leading me to thyself, the fountain of all goodness, O thou whom to love is to trust, and to trust is to love, and in the loving and trusting of whom is Life Eternal. Blessed art thou, who dost free the oppressed and guide the wanderer! Blessed art thou, Lord of all Love, who didst take from me unto thyself the earthly love of my dear brother that thereby thou mightest guide me to a better and higher Love, even to thyself, in whom, long afterwards, I found my brother once again.

THE END OF THE FIRST BOOK

THE SECOND BOOK

§ 1. HOW I RETURNED TO THE WORSHIP OF FALSE GODS.

PERCEIVING that my mind was under some trouble or disturbance, my master often turned the discourse to matters of morals and philosophy, and especially to the belief in the gods and the divine government of the world ; and I told him plainly that I had no such belief, for that the world seemed to me governed by chance, or by fate, or by evil gods, but in no case by good gods, seeing that ill-doing prevailed in the world. Upon this Philemon, being grieved because of my unbelief, asked me whether I had had much discourse with his friend Artemidorus, the Epicurean, on these matters. When I said no, not much, but that my unbelief arose from my own experience of things, because I had seemed to discern more proof of the power of evil than of good, he bade me take comfort; for he would in due course emancipate me, and meantime I should be to him as a friend. After this he advised me to study the books of Plato and of Chrysippus, if perchance I might thus frame myself to a better mind. But when I urged (which indeed was not my own argument but I had heard it

lately from Artemidorus) that the stories concerning
the gods were full of all manner of myths, and fables
containing portents, and metamorphoses, such as no sane
man could believe, to this he replied that the whole
world was full of no less wonders, if a man rightly
considered it; for that summer should follow spring,
and autumn summer, that storm should follow calm,
and calm storm, and that the whole world should be so
orderly and evenly governed as it was, this, he said, was
a far greater wonder than the metamorphoses of which
the poets speak. In particular he pointed out the
wonderful things past all common course of nature,
which were to be seen in that very neighbourhood of
Colossæ and Laodicea; and taking me with him up and
down the valley of the river, called Lycus, which flows
through that region, he shewed me how the water is
there changed into stone of a dazzling brightness, so
that the hills are in many parts covered with the
appearance of snow, and cataracts abound of the same
substance, and how other mountains vomit forth smoke
and fire, and others have wells and springs bubbling upward hot from the earth. Again on another day he
brought me to a certain pool sacred to the goddess
Cybele, and bade me mark how sheep and goats and
cattle, driven into this pool, straightway fell down and
perished, but the priests of Cybele, entering into the
same waters, stood upright and unhurt in the presence
of many spectators; and upon this he asked me what
more proof was wanting of the power of the goddess
to protect her votaries? When I could make no
reply, he affirmed that all these wonders were placed
at hand to convince them that disbelieved in the gods;

for if we were forced to believe in these wonders, being as they were before our eyes, why should we be so loth to believe other wonders that our eyes had not seen ?

In course of time the words of Philemon and still more his kind deeds and the kindness of his wife Apphia, had power to quench that rancorous spirit which had inflamed my heart. Other friends also, both at Colossæ and in Hierapolis, moved me in the same direction, I mean towards a belief in the gods. Among these was the good Epictetus (a slave like myself and at that time a very young man) concerning whom I shall have much to say hereafter ; and a certain Nicostratus of Laodicea, full of zeal for learning, but devout and liberal, and of a gracious nature. Nor must I forget Heracleas, a great reader of the works of the ancient poets as well as of the philosophers, who had studied for some time in Alexandria. These three, being of the acquaintance of Philemon, treated me with exceeding courtesy, seeking my society and willingly conversing with me ; and I soon perceived that almost all the rest of our acquaintance though in no respect given to superstitions, nevertheless agreed in believing that the world was governed by good and divine powers.

§ 2. HOW SOME OF PHILEMON'S FRIENDS AVOWED A BELIEF IN ONE GOD.

I soon found that, although the philosophers whom I have mentioned above, believed in gods, yet their belief differed much from that of the common people ; for the latter believe in many gods, but the former inclined to acknowledge one god under many names. It was at a symposium, during a public festival in honour of Artemis, that I first heard this opinion broached by Nicostratus who said that " there was in reality but one Power, however He may manifest Himself to mortals by many different shapes and names in several lands and nations, speaking also through different prophets, a Delphic woman in Pytho, a Thesprotian man in Dodona, a Libyan in the Temple of Ammon, an Ionian in Claros, a Lycian in Xanthias, and a Bœotian in Ismenus." I looked that he should have been reproved and put to silence by my master; but Philemon said nothing except that this doctrine was not fit to be taught in that shape to the common people; and the rest seemed to assent to Nicostratus. Heracleas, in particular, said that " though the number of gods and demons, or demoniacal essences, be far more than the 30,000 whereof Hesiod makes mention, yet the mighty King of all this multitude, seated on his stable throne as if He were Law, imparts unto the obedient that health and safety which He contains in Himself." To me also, in our private and familiar discourse, the young Epictetus would always speak, not of many, but of One, who guides all things and to whose will we must conform ourselves. As for idols and statues of the gods— of which I had always been wont at Lystra to speak as being themselves gods, so that I could scarce think of the gods apart from them—Nicostratus said openly at this same feast, that it was no marvel if the immortal powers preferred to inhabit beautiful shapes of gold and stone and ivory; which nevertheless were of course to be distinguished from the gods themselves, as being but the integuments of the divine senses; but Heracleas went yet further (and Epictetus with him) saying that one should no more accost an image than a house (instead of the householder) ; and that images were not needful but only helpful for the forgetful souls of men.

When Heracleas avowed his belief in the myths and metamorphoses and fables about the gods I said to him, " Why, O Heracleas, are there no metamorphoses in our days ? "   " Because," replied he, " men have degenerated from their progenitors of ancient date. Therefore it is no marvel that the gods refuse to perform such wonders as of old for mankind upon earth. But in the former days the pious were naturally changed from men into gods, and these are even now honoured, such as Aristaeus, Heracles, Amphiaraus, Asclepius, and the like.   Having regard to these facts, any one may reasonably be persuaded that Lycaon was changed into a wolf, Procne into a swallow, and Niobe into a stone. At present, however, now that vice has spread itself through every part of the earth, the divine nature is no longer produced out of the human, or, in other words, men are no longer made gods but only dignified with the title thereof through excess of flattery, as some among us call the emperors gods even while they yet live." To this Nicostratus assented, but added that " the lies of the multitude are sometimes to blame, pouring contempt upon undoubted facts in the attempt to adorn and exaggerate them, as for example, asserting not only that Niobe was changed into a stone, which is true, but also that Niobe on Sipylus still weeps, which is not true." More passed between them ; but this I discerned clearly that both they and many others, while acknowledging

D

one god under many names, agreed with Philemon
(and not with Artemidorus the Epicurean) in believing
without doubt the myths and fables about the gods.

§ 3. HOW NICOSTRATUS URGED THAT, WITHOUT THE BE-
LIEF IN THE GODS, THE LIFE OF MAN WOULD BE VOID
OF PLEASURE.

It happened about this time that there was a great
feast in honour of Artemis, and the customary processions and dances, and games also and chariot-races and
plays exhibited in the theatre. Being sick at this time
and not able to go abroad, Philemon besought Nicostratus to take me with him to the theatre, and to show
me the pomps and shows of the festival, which far ex-
ceeded anything that I had ever seen in our little town
of Lystra. So on the morning of the festival, early before
sunrise, I went to the house of Nicostratus ; who had
no sooner saluted me than he began at once, after his
manner, to take occasion of the festival to commend, in
a long discourse, the belief in the immortal gods. " For
seest thou not," said he, " how to all men, poor as well as
rich, slaves as well as masters, the festivals of the gods
bring round brightness and gladness ? " Methinks he
noted that my countenance was altered when he spoke
of " slaves," for he hesitated and was silent for a moment ;
but anon, collecting himself, he continued cheerfully
thus : " When I speak of slaves, I mean not such as
thou art, being already half emancipated and rather thy
master's friend than his servant ; but I mean rather the
poor wretches toiling in chains or grinding at the mill,
to all of whom the festival brings relief and some gleam

of joy. For five days ago, before the feast began, sawest thou not how even at the approach of the holiday all was astir within the city, yea and without too; food and wine and fruits and oxen and sheep for sacrifice being brought in from the country; old garments purified and freshly decked out, new ones bought or borrowed from friends; the statues of the gods taken down and carefully cleansed and polished till they glitter." At this point he was interrupted by a slave who had been waiting to tell him that it was time to go forth to the temple. Descending to the court-yard we found all the household awaiting us, clothed in their best attire, the little children bearing frankincense in their hands and the victims adorned for sacrifice. Regarding them all with a glad countenance and saluting many of them by name, Nicostratus bade me remember that at this same moment every householder in Colossæ, however austere or miserly by nature, was constrained by the observance of the gods to go forth in like manner to offer sacrifice. "And now," continued he in an unbroken discourse, "we shall all go to the great temple. Prayers will be offered up; none but words of good omen will be uttered; no sound of quarrel or abuse or even of ribald mirth will be heard in the whole of the vast assemblage. After this, some offer sacrifice; the rest stand by as spectators. Then begins the feasting, some feasting in the temples, others at home where you and I will make merry together. And as for the rest of the day and the days following, thou shalt see how pleasantly they will pass. Yet all this is but a copy of that which happens at every festival in every city where the gods are rightly reverenced. For during the

feasting, the whole city resounds with singing, some
chanting hymns in honour of the god, others odes and
songs, serious or merry, according to each one's pleasure. I omit to speak of the processions and shows, all
full of beauty and delight, but not more beautiful here
than in a thousand other cities of Asia and Europe."

Here he broke off, to salute some of his acquaintance.
"Hail, Charicles! and you too, Charidemus! I rejoice to
see you in the city, and forget not that to-morrow you
are bespoke to dine with me." Then turning again to
me, "Note, I pray you," said he, "how all the people,
both citizens and country-folk, are knit together in concord on such days as these. For there is scarce one
citizen in Colossæ but has invited some stranger or some
acquaintance from the country to partake of his good
cheer. Amid the drinking old friendships are drawn
closer, new friendships are begun. After dinner some
shew strangers about the city; others sit down in the
market-place and talk pleasantly together. Throughout
the day no law courts are open, no execution is allowed,
no debtor need fear arrest, no slave dreads the lash; all
quarrel, all strife receives at least a cessation, which
sometimes brings about a permanent peace. In the
evening the feasting begins again, and all sit down to
sup; so many are the torches that the whole city is
filled with light; each street resounds with the flutes
and the joyful songs of the revellers. Austere sobriety
is laid aside for once, and to drink a little to excess in
honour of the gods is esteemed no great disgrace. Thus
for three days the feast continues; and when it is over
we part with vows of friendship, in peace and good will,
praying that we may live long enough to see such

another feast come round again. Now," concluded
Nicostratus, "take away the gods from out of the
world and what cause remains why men should thus
meet and rejoice together? For where there are no
gods, there are none to be thanked, and therefore no
thanksgiving; but thankfulness is the salt of life.
Whosoever therefore takes away the gods from the life
of man takes away the prime cause of human joy, and
must be esteemed the enemy of all mankind."

I felt in my inmost mind that a keen and subtle
disputant, such as Artemidorus, might have had much to
urge against these arguments of Nicostratus; yet at
that time many things joined together to incline me to
accept his reasonings. For having been now nearly a
year at Colossæ I had received on all sides such tokens
of goodwill, and I may almost say of affection, as had
already well nigh won me out of my first condition of
distrust; and although it were not according to reason
to argue that whatsoever things are pleasant must needs
be also true, yet did it appear beyond doubt that life
without the gods would be full of dulness and gloom,
all men being everywhere wholly given up to cares and
self-searchings. And I reasoned thus with myself, "If
indeed there be gods, then it were wrong not to
acknowledge them; but if there be no gods, why even
then it seems happier to believe that gods exist, and, in
that case, how can 'no gods' deem belief in gods to be
a sin?" So for my part, being at that time recovered
from my melancholy, and young, and in good health,
and taking pleasure in the pride of life and the pleasure
of the flesh, I concluded to take the happier side and to
believe that there were gods ruling the world to good ends.

§ 4. HOW PHILEMON, FALLING SICK, INCLINED TO SUPERSTITION.

About this time Philemon falling sick, turned to a melancholy, and becoming wholly changed from his former disposition, gave himself up to all manner of superstitions. Resorting in vain to all the physicians of the place, he was led at first to try charms and amulets, and then to consult soothsayers and astrologers and the priests of strange gods ; and thus, little by little, partly by the burden of his disease enfeebling his understanding, and partly by reason of the company which he now frequented, he became daily more timorous and superstitious. He offered sacrifice almost every day, and anxiously awaited the report as to the entrails ; he resorted often to the priests of all kinds of gods more especially Isis, Serapis, and Sabazius, and sometimes he would invite them to his own house, so that our house became a kind of temple in Colossæ ; he purified himself many times a day both with the lustral waters and with other strange purifications ; he would wear naught but linen, and abstained from many kinds of flesh, and in the end from all flesh ; if he saw a sacred stone he would fall down on his knees before it and anoint it with oil. Nay, once, during this melancholy fit of his, when we had set out after much preparation upon a journey to Ephesus, the sight of a weasel— though we were now fully a mile past the city gate— made him turn back and give up the journey altogether. At last, when no remedies and no charms availed anything, supposing himself to be under the special displeasure of some unknown god, he took to his bed and could not be persuaded to leave it.

My master having been about a month in this case, growing daily weaker, there came to him one Oneirocritus of Ephesus (the same to whom he himself had been intending to journey) who also himself had been sick of some disease insomuch that the physicians had despaired of him; but he was now quite recovered. This man coming into Philemon's chamber questioned him concerning his condition and symptoms, and the sacrifices he had offered, and the gods he had propitiated. Then he spoke concerning himself and his own deliverance, how after he had been sick nearly twenty years, he had been healed by Asclepius at the famous temple in Pergamus; and he very earnestly exhorted Philemon to go thither with all speed. At the same time he described the wonders wrought by the god on those that believed in him, and the punishments he had inflicted on the impious and unbelieving. Upon this Artemidorus the Epicurean—whom, because of his exact knowledge of medicine and his skilfulness in noting symptoms, Philemon would never exclude from his bed-chamber, even in his most superstitious moods—once more recommended Philemon to try the baths of the neighbouring city of Hierapolis, saying that it was not wise to despise remedies merely because they were near and easy and familiar. "For this disease," said he, "arises from no anger of the gods or any such matter, but from some disorder of the liver which may not improbably be removed by the hot baths of Hierapolis." "But if the liver be disordered," replied Oneirocritus, "truth compels

me to speak of the virtues of a certain sacred well in the
precincts of the temple at Pergamus, availing for the healing not of one disease, but of all; for great multitudes
of the blind, washing therein, have obtained their sight;
others have recovered from lameness; others from asthma
and pleurisy; nay, to some even the mere drawing of
the water with their own hands, (it being so prescribed
by the god) has restored soundness and health."

Then others of the companions of Oneirocritus added
other stories all tending to the honour of Asclepius;
some indeed possible and deserving of attention, but
others absurd and fit only to move laughter; how, for
example, a sculptor in Pergamus had been punished with
immediate disease for making a statue of the god with
inferior marble, but having atoned for his fault by
making a second statue of fit material, he straightway
recovered; also how a fighting-cock, wounded in one leg,
chancing to take part in the procession of song in honour
of the god, extended his leg, no longer wounded but
whole, and hopping onwards crowed in harmony with
the songs of the choir; and lastly how a certain rich
Epicurean having had a dream in the temple of the god,
forthwith obeying the heavenly vision, burned the books
of Epicurus, and having made a paste of their ashes
applied a poultice to his stomach and thus was perfectly
healed. This last story seemed to touch Artemidorus
(because of the contempt, as I suppose, which it cast
upon the doctrine of his master Epicurus) and he was
on the point of making some rejoinder, when Oneirocritus, like one inspired with a divine enthusiasm, broke
out into a long and passionate discourse concerning the
benefits that he himself had received from the god

Asclepius : "For seventeen years," he said, "I had kept my bed through disease, and for many more years I had been ailing and infirm, troubled with the falling sickness ; yet such hath been the favour of the god toward me, manifested by continual tokens of his presence during my sickness as well as at my recovery, that I would not exchange my state for all the health and strength of Heracles. For I am one of those who have been blessed, not once only but many times, with a new life, and who, for this cause, esteem sickness a blessing. Many a time, half awake, half asleep, have I found myself not indeed seeing the god but conscious of his presence, my eyes full of tears, my hair erect, and a savour of divine odour in my nostrils. Thus have I received the most helpful manifestations. It was thus that the god revealed to me that I must go forth from Apamea, the day before the great earthquake ; it was thus, half in a dream half in a vision, that he also shewed me how Philoumene the daughter of my foster-mother had devoted her life for mine ; and behold on the eighth day she died and I recovered from my disease. Moreover at one time the god appeared to me in no dream but in a vision, having three heads, and his body wreathed in flames ; and at another time not Asclepius only but Athene herself also appeared to me and held converse with me. A sweet odour exhaled from the ægis of the goddess and she bore the shape of the statue of Phidias. My nurse and two other friends, who happened to be sitting by my couch, stared and were astonished, and at first they deemed me to be beside myself; but presently they also understood the discourse and were aware of the divine presence."

While Oneirocritus was saying these words, his eyes kindled and his voice trembled, and he seemed ready to weep for joy and gratefulness; and there was not one present except the Epicurean who was not somewhat moved to sympathy. But after a pause Artemidorus praised the priests of Asclepius, saying that it was well known that they were wise physicians and prescribed wise remedies, but that their cures might well be believed to be according to nature. To which Oneirocritus replied with exceeding vehemence : "Nay, but let any one consider how strange and past all natural invention, yea, how contrary oftentimes to all the rules of art are the prescriptions of the god, some being bidden to swallow gypsum, others hemlock, others to strip naked and to bathe in cold water, (and these so weak and puling that their own physician durst not prescribe to them to bathe even in warm water) and assuredly, when all this is considered and the great multitude of them that are healed, beholding the sides of the temple all covered with the votive tablets of them that have given thanks for their recovery, surely the veriest atheist will cry out 'Great is Asclepius, and holy is his temple.' Therefore, O most excellent Philemon, my counsel is that you also, despising all other waters, whether they be of Cydnus, or Peneus, or Hierapolis should resort to the sacred well in Pergamus ; and, if you do this and the god so will, you shall assuredly return healed of your disease."

To this the greater part of those present gave assent. Only Artemidorus, when mention was made of the votive tablets of those that had recovered, whispered

to me : " But where, O Onesimus, are the votive tablets
of those that have not recovered ?　Or perchance the
temple could not find room for so many ?"　And when
Oneirocritus had departed, he did not conceal his
judgment that of the things that he had related, some
were according to nature, but others only the dreams
and imaginations of one that was scarce master of
himself.　But the rest were entirely against the
Epicurean and on the side of Oneirocritus.　And so
I found it both then and afterwards in most places
whereof I had experience, not only in Asia but also
in Greece and Italy : those that believed in the gods
were many ; and those that believed not were men
of culture and learning, but very few.　And with the
multitude in some places to be an Epicurean or an
Atheist (for it was all one with the common people)
was deemed a crime sufficient to bring down the wrath
of the gods in shipwreck, famine, pestilence, or earthquake.　The magistrates also everywhere dissembled,
even though they were atheists ; and they not only
offered sacrifice and kept holidays, but also of their
own free will, and at their own cost, they built and
repaired temples, and set up statues to gods in whom
they disbelieved, esteeming this kind of dissimulation
to be a sort of piety.　But as for myself at this time,
I was in a strait between two opinions ; for on the
one hand I had begun to despise the excessive and
unreasonable superstitions of Philemon, but on the
other hand while I respected Artemidorus as an honourable man and a seeker after truth, I shrank from his
philosophy as void of hope and happiness.　So with
my mind I inclined towards Artemidorus, but with

my heart not indeed towards Philemon as he now was,
but as he had been ; and I believed in the gods with
my wishes, but I disbelieved in them with my reason
and understanding.

§ 5. HOW I ACCOMPANIED PHILEMON TO PERGAMUS.

On the morrow Artemidorus came again and would
have dissuaded Philemon from going to Pergamus,
maintaining more fully than before that he had spoken
with many to whom the god had revealed prescriptions
and that there was nothing divine in them : " for to
some " said he " being of a melancholic temperament
the god prescribes the hearing of odes, hymns and
other music, or sometimes even farces ; to others riding
on horses ; to others bathing in cold water ; to others
walking or leaping ; to others frequent rubbing and
careful diet ; thus the god gives in each case wise and
exact prescriptions such as a skilful physician would
use ; but in all these, and in the cures that issue, there
is nothing of the power of a god." Philemon listened
patiently enough, but replied (not without sense as it
appeared to me) that if this were so, or were not so,
in either case one of two good results might be expected ; for if it were a god that prescribed, then he
should receive benefit from a god's prescriptions, but
if it were not a god but only the priests, even then
he should have the prescriptions of physicians so skilful
that they obtained the praises of Artemidorus and were
esteemed by the multitude to have the wisdom of a
god. So it was settled that to Pergamus we should

go, and in the autumn of that year we came thither.
There was much in the place to delight a youth such
as I was then; first the town itself fenced in on two
sides by rushing streams and on the north side by
rocks scarcely to be scaled; also the stately buildings
and especially the library; and as I had the charge of
Philemon's books I took pleasure in learning here the
art of preparing parchments and smoothing and adorning them; for the place is very full of transcribers of
books and the banks of the river (which is called
Selinus) are covered with the shops of those who tan
skins and prepare them for the use of booksellers.
Thus passed seven days, pleasantly enough; and all
this time I saw not Philemon, for he spent almost
every hour apart from his friends in the temple,
engaged in processions and purifications and the like.

But on the eighth day he came to me with a cheerful
countenance saying that after he had thrice gone in
the sacred processions, and had daily heard solemn
music and been present at the thanksgivings of those
who each day had departed whole from the temple,
a sweet sleep had fallen upon him wherein he had
seen a vision, namely, a chasm round and not very
large, about five or six cubits in diameter, and himself
on the point of going down into it, and behold, one
prevented him and went down in his stead. When he
recounted the vision to the priests, they bade him be of
good cheer, saying that the interpretation of the dream
was this, that he himself should not die nor go down
to Hades (which was signified by the round pit) but
that he should recover and some other should die in his
place; and for the rest they bade him bathe daily in

cold water, and walk often and hear cheerful music and
abstain from overmuch study.   So we returned to
Colossæ with lightened hearts ; and already Philemon
began to shake off his melancholy and to recover apace.
But in the second month after we were come back,
Apphia fell sick and was nigh unto death.   And hereupon Philemon's distemper returned on him worse than
before ; and as his wife became better, he became worse,
insomuch that he began to despair of his life.   Then
Oneirocritus of Ephesus came a second time to visit
him ; and he, when he had heard the account of
Philemon's vision, how he had seen a round chasm
and one descending into it, affirmed that the meaning
of the god was that Philemon should go to the cave
of Trophonius in Lebadea in Greece, where there is
even such a chasm, the same in shape and dimensions
also, and men go down to it to learn things to come,
and this, he said, was without doubt the intention of
the vision ; but the ministers of the temple had interpreted it amiss.   Now therefore nothing would serve
but we must needs go to Lebadea.

§ 6. HOW I WENT DOWN INTO THE CAVE OF TROPHONIUS.

As soon as the season of the year came round for a
sea voyage, we sailed across to Athens, and thence to
Lebadea, where we were to make ready for descending beneath the earth.   When the day approached,
Philemon was advised by some of his friends (and also
by the ministers of the god) not himself to go down,

because of his age and infirmities, lest the suddenness
of some voice or apparition in the darkness beneath
the earth, should affright him and drive him out of
his wits or even slay him outright.   For although no
one that had at any time consulted the oracle had ever
suffered anything fatal (save only one Macedonian of
the body-guard of Antigonus who had descended for
sacrilegious purpose, and in despite of the sacred ministers, with intent to seek for hid treasure, and he had
been cast forth dead by some other passage and not
by the way he went down) yet did all, whether strangers
or natives, look upon the descent as a matter of some
peril not to be lightly taken in hand.   So when I
perceived that Philemon desired me to go down in his
place but would not urge nor so much as ask me, lest
I should think myself enforced to consent, I willingly
adventured to descend.

But I found it was no such short and simple matter as
I had supposed.   For on presenting my petition to the
priests I was caused to wait many days, first of all in a
kind of House of Purification, which was dedicated to
Good Fortune, and during all these days I offered up
several sacrifices, not only to Trophonius, and to his
children, but also to Apollo and to Cronus, and to Zeus
the King, and to Hera the Driver of Chariots, and to
Demeter called Europa; and even when all these sacrifices had been inspected by the priests and pronounced
propitious, yet my good fortune must needs still depend
upon one last sacrifice of all.   This was to be a ram
offered on the last night, whose blood was caused to
flow into a trench while invocation was made to
Agamedes; which, if it had been unpropitious, would

have made all the other sacrifices of no effect, and all my master's money and my pains would have been spent for naught. Although I was in no humour for scoffing at that time, yet on that last evening, while I awaited the report concerning the entrails, I could not but marvel that any god should desire mortals to approach him by paths so costly and so tedious. For had I been a poor man, I had long ago spent all and more than all my substance in the sacrifices which I had offered, and the purifications I had undergone, and the fees I had paid to the ministers of the god. During the period of purification I had abstained from warm baths, and had bathed only in the cold waters of the stream called Hercyna; but on the last night of all, I was bathed with a special solemnity in the same stream by two priests called Hermæ. Then I was made to drink of two fountains flowing forth, one on either hand, whereof the former was called the fountain of Forgetfulness, the other the fountain of Remembrance. All this was done, they told me, that I might forget the past and remember the future and in particular the response of the god. Last of all they took out of a veil a certain very ancient image of the god, said to have been wrought by Dædalus; and on this they bade me look very reverently and intently even till my eyes were weary. This done, I was clad in a white linen tunic, curiously girt round with garlands, and led towards the cavern.

This was a pit, round at the top, but inside in shape not so much like a cylinder as rather a cone whereof the summit has been cut off; for the base was somewhat larger than the opening, the circumference at the top being about a score of cubits, and the depth, as I should judge, fifteen cubits; but of the circumference at the bottom I cannot speak exactly. The way to go down into the pit was by a ladder. Before I went down the priest told me that when I had touched the bottom I was to feel about for two small round holes in the side, a handsbreadth or so from the bottom and near the foot of the ladder, each large enough to hold the foot and the lower part of the leg. Laying myself on my back I was to place my feet in these two holes, "and thereon," said the priest, "though the openings be never so small, yet through these will the god draw inwards the whole of your body, as with the irresistible force of some whirlpool, and then in an inner recess, if he be so pleased, he will hold converse with you either by voice or by apparition, or perchance by both. But be of good cheer, bearing in mind that, except that sacrilegious Macedonian of whom I spoke to you, there was never any one yet that was harmed by the god."

When I lay down, and the lights above had been taken away, my mind was all astir, not dizzy nor faint, nor disposed to torpor, but more active than my wont, tossing a multitude of thoughts to this side and that, neither believing nor disbelieving in the god. Then it came into my thoughts that Artemidorus had explained the wondrous pool of Cybele, fatal to cattle, by saying that some kind of creeping vapours adhered to the surface of the water, and he bade me take note at Lebadea, whether any kind of vapour could be seen or felt in the pit. So I drew a long breath or two but could neither feel aught nor taste aught, save only that my mind seemed still busier than before, tossing and

E

retossing thoughts without end. Next, falling on a different course of thinking, I considered with myself whether perchance I was playing a sacrilegious part in thus coming into the midst of the god's mysteries in order to spy them out and reveal them to Artemidorus; and I resolved that I would submit myself to the god and think only of the image of Dædalus, even as the priest had bidden me. Now all this takes indeed some time to set down, but to think the thoughts needed scarce a moment, and countless other fancies and imaginations and resolutions passed through my mind; but the last determination of all was that I would rebel against the god and not suffer myself to be drawn through the crevices; and scarce had I conceived this rebellious fancy, when lo, my chest began to heave and my heart to beat more and more violently, and I felt the throbbing of the veins in my temples; and then whether my body was indeed carried into an inner recess, or whether my spirit alone was carried, being separated from the body, or whatever else happened, I know not for certain; but there was as it were the clapping-to of a great door shut with a loud jar, parting me off from all things, and then a singing in mine ears, and a bright light that grew brighter, and then methought I lay as it were living, and yet beyond life, and not able to move hand or foot, yet able to think and hear; and there was a voice from the depths of the cave in the Bœotian dialect "Philemon must go first"; and presently I felt myself drawn upwards and heard the voices of the priests saying that "the man will soon come to himself," and behold I was being carried to a throne called the throne of Recollection; whereon they placed me and straightway questioned me concerning the things that I had seen or heard while I was still staring and groping about me like one distraught. When I had made reply according to my ability, they wrote down my words on a tablet and gave me back to my friends who led me away, being still unable to guide myself and ignorant both of myself and them. But not many minutes had passed before I recovered my mind; and then a spirit of lightness and mirth possessed me, insomuch that I laughed loud and long and this without cause, and could not restrain myself from laughing; but when I was ashamed thereat and even Philemon was fain to rebuke me, one of the priests that stood by, said that there was no cause either for my shame or for his rebuke, for laughter after this fashion was ever wont to seize those with whom Trophonius had held converse.

§ 7. HOW ARTEMIDORUS SPOKE AGAINST THE BELIEF IN GODS.

That I had received a vision none doubted; but concerning the meaning of the vision there was much dispute. For the priests of Trophonius (though it was not their special duty to interpret the visions vouchsafed by the god, but only to prepare the way for them by introducing those that desired to consult the god) interpreted the words of the voice and the shutting of the gates as meaning evil for my master, namely, that he should enter Hades first, and that the gates should then be shut, so that I should not follow him till afterwards. But I thought, and so did some others, friends of my master that were with us, that the meaning rather was, that Philemon should enter into happiness first, but that I should be shut out; and even now methinks that was the truer interpretation; for Philemon indeed entered first into the Kingdom of Light, and I followed after. Notwithstanding at this time, between these two interpretations, we knew not what to think; and my master returned to Colossæ even more melancholy than before. Artemidorus said, scoffing, that we had a goodly time with the gods, only that they were slow of speech or fond of circuits; for Oneirocritus had sent us to Asclepius, and behold, that god had given us a dream but not the interpretation of the dream; and afterwards we had gone to Trophonius, and he had given us a vision, and an oracle in broad Bœotian to be the interpretation of the dream; and now nothing remained but we should go to Delphi to obtain some oracle that might serve as the interpretation of the dream; or last of all, if the son of Zeus should answer, like the rest, doubtfully and darkly, then must we go to Zeus himself in Dodona that the Father might enlighten for us whatever the Son might have left too obscure. I was not greatly moved by the gibes of Artemidorus; for the vision that I had seen, or seemed to have seen, weighed with me more than his mockery; nor did I then believe the word of the Epicurean, who constantly affirmed that the fit which had befallen me had arisen from the vapour of the cave, aided by the trickery of the priests and the force of imagination. But another scruple (so the Lord willed it) troubled me much more, coming into my mind again and again; I mean that all these rites and ceremonies, purifications, sacrifices, and the like were only possible for the rich, not for the poor; wherefore the religion that required these things was for the few and for the free-born and not for the many, and the miserable and the oppressed.

Yet can I not deny that Artemidorus also had a great share in loosening me by degrees from the worship of false gods. For as Philemon grew more and more melancholy, and I may almost say morose, he shunned all company and mine with the rest, and so left Artemidorus and myself to hold discourse together. At such times, when our speech naturally fell on the metamorphosis (for we could not call it otherwise) of my master, Artemidorus would speak at great length concerning the miseries of religion, and how great evils it had wrought on mankind, leading them to wicked sacrifices, and orgies, and to self-torturings and agonies of soul, and all to no purpose ; and how much more beautiful it was to believe that all the universe is bound together by one fixed and unchangeable order which gives life and decay to all things according to law. And oftentimes he quoted to me the verses of the Latin poet Lucretius, praising those who with a discerning eye can look upon all apparent wonders in heaven and earth, perceiving that there is a cause of each. When I alleged on the other side such wonders as Philemon had spoken of, as being abundant in our own land—the burning mountains, hot wells, fatal vapours, and rivers and cataracts that changed into stone,—concerning all these he had causes and explanations to set forth, as also concerning the thunder and the lightning and many other supernatural things ; and when he perceived that some of his

explanations convinced me, then he would always add
that there was no place left for the gods in the Universe,
but that when men had learnt entirely to give up all
thought of gods and Elysium and Tartarus, and had
attained to seek and expect happiness in naught save a life
of virtue upon earth, then all things would go well
with us on earth, or at least much better than at present.

Now as for the immortality of the soul and the life
beyond the grave, to these things I adhered, mainly
because I loved to think of Chrestus as still existing;
and as touching the existence of a god also, Artemidorus himself could not make it clear to me how the
beginnings of the world came to pass without some
Mind; so that as to these matters, though I was somewhat moved by him, I was not greatly shaken. But as
for the myths and fables of the wondrous deeds and
transformations of the gods he quite overthrew all my
faith in any such things; urging that the order of the
world testified against them, and that our often experience of the invention and refutation of like marvels
showed that they were necessary for the vacant truth-
contemning minds of the multitude, but none the less
false and to be discarded by seekers after truth.

Even to this day do I call to mind the time and
place of that particular discourse of Artemidorus which
most moved me. We were walking near the city of
Hierapolis (which lies close upon Colossæ) amid the
hills covered with the snow-like marble made out of
water, whereof I wrote above, and I had taken him to
see some of the vaporous springs which Philemon had
shown me, inferring from such wonders the existence of
the gods. Then Artemidorus spoke his mind to me

freely, after his cynical manner, concerning these and
other so called metamorphoses and miracles. For after
he had with very great clearness and not a little cogency
of words and reasons set forth his theory concerning
the marble cataracts, finding me obstinate against his
conclusion that all things are according to order and
that all the stories of the metamorphoses are false, he
suddenly changed his humour and said mirthfully,
" But come now, most devout of mankind, lest perchance I should seem to you unfair, pressing unduly the
argument on the one side but neglecting what might be
said on the other side, see, I will take the part of
Socrates and will maintain the truth of the ancient
stories. At Philemon's supper last night, you heard
how stoutly the pious Nicostratus supported our most
excellent host in affirming that it was possible that the
loving Halcyone was translated into the sea-bird of that
name, which is said ever to mourn for her husband.
Now mark how far inferior is the devout Nicostratus to
the more devout Artemidorus." Then, adjusting his
cloak and speaking in a pompous fashion with a
sonorous voice after the manner of some philosophers
of our acquaintance, " Alas," he said, " blind creatures
that we mortals are ! Alas, purblind judges of the
possible and impossible ! For we, deluded ones, pro-
nounce according to the ignorant and dull abilities of
faithless men. And therefore many things, in themselves easy, seem to us difficult, and many things in
themselves attainable seem to us not to be attained.
And this befalls us sometimes through our inexperience,
sometimes through the infancy of our minds. For, as
compared with the First Cause of all, every man, be he

never so old, is but a child ; and human life, when compared with eternity, is but a childhood's span. Who
therefore shall decide what is likely ? For which, think
you is the harder or the more unlikely ? To raise a
stillness out of a blustering tempest, and to spread a
cloudless sky over the whole of Europe and of Asia, or
to change the shape of one woman into the form of a
bird ? We see even children every day shape distinct
forms and figures from wax and clay. Then certainly
God, who is too excellent in greatness and wisdom to be
brought into comparison with the wisest of human beings,
can effect more wonderful actions than these which are
easy and familiar. Nature, we see, finding in a comb
of wax a shapeless worm without legs or feathers,
bestows on it wings and feet, and enamelling it with
great diversity of fair colours produceth a bee, the wise
artificer of divine honey ! Seeing therefore this marvellous transformation, why doubt we of thy lesser
wonder, O Halcyone, most dutiful of birds ? Nay, but
from henceforth I will not cease to scoff at the folly of
poor puny mortals, who can neither comprehend great
matters nor small, but doubt of most things, even of
those which concern ourselves, and yet dare to deny the
power of the immortal gods to transform halcyons or
aught else. And for my part, even as the fame of the
fable hath been conveyed to me from my ancestors, so
will I extol the praise of thy songs, O thou bird of
mourning, conveying it to my children and to their
posterity after them ; nor will I cease to repeat the story
of thy virtuous love for thy husband, thy constancy
and thy patience, to my wives Xanthippe and Myrto."

Then, putting aside all mirth, " Do you not see, my

dear Onesimus," said he, " that, upon such reasoning as
this, any impostor can palm off any portent upon the credulity of mankind.   Nay, so eagerly does the multitude
seek after portents that they will oftentimes refuse to
pay homage even to the truth, unless it come accompanied with portents : and indeed such is the nature of
our Phrygians in this region (and the Paphlagonians
are no better) that if a juggler will but play his tricks
before them, taking with him a player on the flute
or tambourine or cymbals, straightway they will gape
upon him as on a messenger from heaven, and believe
as he instructs and do as he commands.   But it is not
the part of a philosopher, my dear friend, to accept
falsehoods through laziness, or credulity, or enthusiasm,
but rather to esteem sobriety and incredulity to be the
very sinews of the soul, remembering the words of him
who said, ' I love Socrates well and Plato well, but
Truth best of all.'   And surely, if there be a god indeed, as you and your philosophers will have it, and
this god a good god, then to such a god that man
must be most pleasing who most honours truth ; but the
man who serves falsehood must be unpleasing, whether
folly or knavery be the cause of such a servitude."

His words moved me not a little ; for I seemed forced
at least to this conclusion that whether there were an
Elysium or not, whether gods or no gods, in any case
truth must needs be better than falsehood ; and when
he spoke of falsehood as a " servitude " his words galled
me all the more because I was a slave ; and I confessed
in my heart that I had been acting slavishly in resolving
to believe what was pleasant, merely because it was pleasant,
and without much regard to the truth of it.

So I vowed within myself that howsoever Philemon
might enforce my limbs to his service, he should not
constrain my mind to this or that opinion contrary to
what I believed to be the truth ; for though my body
might be the body of a slave, in my mind and thoughts
I would be free.

§ 8. HOW I JOURNEYED WITH PHILEMON TO ANTIOCH IN SYRIA.

Now began my old fit of doubt and trouble and
moroseness to return upon me. I had long misliked
the excessive and, as it seemed to me, pusillanimous
superstition of Philemon ; and the more because,
although he spared no pains nor cost in resorting to
oracles and practising new superstitions, he had not yet
bethought himself of his promise that he would emancipate me.   Lately also he had built for himself a tomb
at a very great expense, saying that it was unreasonable
to prepare for oneself a sumptuous house wherein we
should spend threescore years at the most, and yet to
take no thought of that other abode wherein a man
needs spend all his time hereafter for many years.   But
while he made this so costly and careful provision for
his bones, he made none for his family nor for his
slaves ; for it was known that he had some months
since destroyed his former will and he had not as yet
made another ; so that both I and all the rest of the
household were now in danger to be sold to we knew
not what master, if anything evil should suddenly befall
Philemon.   Yet when Artemidorus urged him to the
making of a will, he resented it as if it were done upon

some expectation of his death. For at times, in his melancholy, he came to such a point of suspicion as to imagine that all men, even his household, were set against him and wished to murder him. So I began to rebel once more against the worship of the gods, partly (as before) because it seemed to be a religion for the rich and not for the poor, but partly also because it seemed possible to be religious and yet to be swallowed up with thoughts of self, having no regard unto others. Notwithstanding I gave not up as yet all belief in divine things ; but I became a seeker after some religion which should afford redemption not for the few but for the many.

Now it chanced that one Eriopolus, a wool-merchant of Antioch in Syria, coming to Colossæ about this time to buy wool, and finding Philemon well-nigh despaired of, spoke to him concerning a certain sect of the Jews who, said he, were marvellously skilled in exorcising evil spirits and in the healing of certain diseases, adding, however, that not all the Jews possessed this power, but only those who worshipped a certain Chrestus or Christus, in whose name they adjured the demons. Then another, a dyer from Ephesus, confirmed his report, saying that the Jews which worship not this Christus, persecute the others, calling them " magicians ; " and said he, " not many weeks ago, at Ephesus, when some of the Jews which worship not Christus, had'assayed to drive out evil spirits in this name, the man that was possessed leaped upon them, and overcame them, and drove them away grievously wounded." " By what name then," asked my master, " are these Jewish magicians known ? " " At first," replied Eriopolus, " they were called Nazarenes or Galileans, but, of late, they go

by the name of Christians (so at least the common
people call them), and there are certain of them scattered up and down in several cities of Asia, and one of
more than common note among them, Paulus by name,
is at this time tarrying at Ephesus. But for the most
part they congregate now in Antioch, although, as I
have heard, the root and origin of the sect is at
Jerusalem, the chief city of Judaea."

Hearing this my master determined to journey to
Antioch to make inquiry of this new sect; and Artemidorus also himself now encouraged him in his purpose,
judging that anything was better than thus to remain at
home brooding over his ill health and imagining evil.
Apphia also assented. So in the spring of that year (it
was the second year of the emperor Nero, and I was at
that time in the twenty-first year of my age) we made
ready for our journey. Though I loved to see new
sights and faces, after the manner of youth, I was
nevertheless loth to go on so superstitious an errand;
and besides, I despised the Jews, so far as I knew them,
as being a gain-loving people, full of pernicious superstitions, and so inhospitable as not even to eat with
strangers. However, I would not willingly have suffered
Philemon in his melancholy to go alone, even had I been
his friend and not his slave. When we were to set
forth, Artemidorus bade me write to him, as often as
I had occasion, concerning the Jews at Antioch, and
especially concerning this new sect; "for," said he,
" to those who have taken their stand upon the hill of
Truth, it is sweet to look down upon the wanderings of
them that stray in error, wherefore I ever take pleasure
in the hearing of some new superstition or error among

men." So I promised that I would send him letters as often as messengers went to Asia from Philemon.

Our journey was first by land to Ephesus through a very fertile country; and thence by sea to Seleucia, a city which lies at the mouth of the river Orontes, and it is as it were the harbour of Antioch; which lies higher up the river, about forty miles by reason of the wanderings of the stream, but by the road distant no more than a score of miles or less. If I admired the country between Colossæ and Ephesus, the fruitfulness of the soil, the greatness of the mountains, and the beauty of Ephesus itself and the far-famed temple of Ephesian Artemis, much more did I admire the city of Antioch, which is the third city of the empire for greatness, coming next after Rome and Alexandria; and it lies along the river Orontes, for the space of four or five miles, stretching between the clear waters of the river and the high mountain called Silpius, surrounded by a wall not less than five and thirty cubits high and ten cubits in thickness. Being very spacious and indeed equal to three or four large cities in amplitude, it is divided into four wards or demes; and it has royal streets, built by kings desiring to do favour to the citizens of so goodly a city, and called after the names of the sovereigns that built them, namely, the street of Herod, the street of Seleucus, and others. Through the midst there runs a broad street adorned with four ranks of columns forming two covered colonnades with a wide road between, and along the whole street (which is more than thirty-six furlongs in length) there are statues and busts beautifully wrought of white marble. Greek names have been given to all the region round about,

such as Pieria, Peneus, Tempe, Castalia, insomuch that
to hear the names of the villages one might fancy oneself in the haunts of the Muses ; and not two hours
distant from the city there lies a fair large garden or
paradise (as the people in these parts call it) Daphne by
name, which the citizens of Antioch often frequent, and
it is full of all manner of flowers and goodly trees and
watered with a great abundance of streams, and noted
for the worship of Adonis. Such and so full of all
manner of delight was the place in which I now found
myself, a city no less populous than spacious (for it
numbered as many as five hundred thousand souls) and
no less full of mirth than of beauty ; for the people of
Antioch are known throughout the world for their gaiety.
Here therefore I laid aside the austerity of my recent
thoughts, and forgetting questions of religion and philosophy I disposed myself to be merry with the multitude
of those who were making merry around me, so far at
least as I could be permitted to do so by the duty of
constant attendance on Philemon ; and, if I had had
my own desire, I should never have set foot in any
synagogue of Jews or Christians.

But blessed be thou, O Guide of the misguided, who
didst not suffer me for ever to stray in the paths of
false pleasure and in the ways which lead to delusion,
but in due course thou didst bring me to the door of
thy fold ; and though I stumbled at the threshold, yet
didst thou not suffer me to fall for ever, but didst still
uphold me and step by step didst turn me back again
to the pastures of eternal peace.

THE END OF THE SECOND BOOK

THE THIRD BOOK

§ 1. OF MY FIRST THOUGHTS CONCERNING THE CHRISTIANS.

I AM now to describe how I first came to the knowledge of the brethren in Antioch, though I attained not yet to the truth. For I stumbled at questions of philosophy and of tradition, and therefore I entered not into the fold of Christ. But the main reason for my failure was (as I now think), first, that I came not in faith, and secondly that I came not to Christ and the teaching of Christ himself, but rather to a sort of doubtful disputations about Christ, which, whether a man believe or disbelieve in them, do not contain the revelation of the Lord Jesus.

Concerning this part of my life I am in a strait what to set down and what to pass over. For if I should endeavour to call to mind and repeat all the evil things that, in the days of my ignorance, I said and thought about the Saints, then I fear lest I should seem profane and almost blasphemous, thus a second time reviling the Lord Jesus in speaking evil of his church. But if on the other hand I gloss over the truth, blanching and

extenuating my error and presumptuousness, then I
seem to be dealing falsely and hypocritically, making
myself to be better than I was, instead of magnifying
the mercies of the Lord shewn forth upon one that was
perverse and obstinate in error. In this perplexity
having chanced to light upon certain letters which I
sent at this time to Artemidorus by his request (but he,
long afterwards, not many days before his death, delivered them to me and bade me keep them), these same
letters (which till of late I had altogether forgotten) it
now seems good to me to set down faithfully word for
word, neither altering nor extenuating anything. The
first letter shews how I was unwilling at the beginning
to go into the synagogue, and what slanders the common people falsely reported about the brethren; which I
in my folly supposed at that time to be true. The next
(after the reply of Artemidorus, rebuking me for my
proneness to believe the rumours of the common people)
shews how I went for the first time into the congregation of the faithful, and how the Lord began even at
that time to draw me towards himself.

"ONESIMUS TO ARTEMIDORUS, HEALTH.

"Concerning Antioch and all the pleasures of this
delightful city I wrote to you in my former letter; but
whereas you marvel because I have as yet written
nothing touching the Jews; you must know that up to
this time we have found no occasion to be present at
their worship. For we find that there is a greater discord than we had supposed between this new sect of the

Jews and the rest, insomuch that the latter will scarce own the new sect to be Jews, nor do they frequent the same temples nor practise the same kind of worship. Hence it happens that these new Jews, out of fear to be persecuted, do all things in secret, having no public processions nor sacrifices, and allowing none to see the statue of their god (if indeed any of the Jews have any god at all) and celebrating their mysteries in great privacy. However, all the philosophers with whom I have spoken, as well as the men of rank in the city (such as are among Philemon's acquaintance), agree that it is a vile and execrable superstition, which would fain subvert all laws and all the dignity and peace of the empire. It is also commonly reported that none are admitted to their sacred rites until they have committed some monstrous crime ; so that, whereas in other religions the priests of the several mysteries say, ' Let none approach but the pure,' the priests of this sect on the other hand say, ' Whosoever is a murderer, whoso a thief, whoso an adulterer, let him draw near that he may be initiated ; for all such does our god invite.' Likewise the common folk say that at their sacred rites a most shameful sacrifice is made of a little child, on whose flesh and blood these wretches feast as if they were the choicest dainties, and also that brothers and sisters among them commonly practise incest. But all this I write, not of my own knowledge, but from the general report, which notwithstanding comes from so many different witnesses, that I cannot doubt but it is mainly true. However, I will write no more concerning these people till I have somewhat to say of my own seeing or hearing. But for my part I could be well

F

pleased if the good Philemon would be persuaded not to seek further into this superstition.

" In my last letter I omitted, in so great a multitude of new things, to make mention of a garden belonging to one Onias, a citizen here, which contains not only many goodly flowers, but also runlets and fountains of water quaintly devised, and many apes and peacocks for show and for amusement, and above all several parrots, of which one has been so excellently trained to speak, that it surpasses by far any starling or any other talking bird that I have ever heard before ; and the common people say it is possessed. But even you would marvel to see with what aptness and semblance of understanding it collects and most seasonably utters the sayings of those around it, reminding me not a little of the saying which I have often heard from your lips that the reason of some inferior animals borders upon the reason of man himself. Farewell."

" ARTEMIDORUS TO ONESIMUS, HEALTH.

" Whereas you write that you have resolved to make no further mention of these innovating Jews until you find out something of your own knowledge concerning them, more weighty than such old wives' fables as are reported by the common rabble, by lazy philosophers, and by pompous town-councillors, all of them indifferent to truth and accuracy, so I beseech you for the future to carry out this resolution ; for, believe me, knowledge is not to be thus cheaply and painlessly acquired without judgment and labour. But I hope that before very long you may have discovered something certain of this sect, no less worthy of reporting than your experiences of the parrot of Onias.   Farewell."

§ 2. OF THE DOCTRINE OF THE CHRISTIANS.

"ONESIMUS TO ARTEMIDORUS, HEALTH.

" Having been now twice present in their temple or synagogue I have much to say of these Christians.

" It happened that, about ten days ago, the friend with whom my master lodges, introduced to us a certain merchant of Cyrene who had some slight acquaintance with one Lucius, a man of Cyrene, and a notable teacher among this sect.   So by his means we were .invited to be present at their synagogue on a day when the un-initiated are called together, as many as desire to make a trial of the new religion or to learn the truth about it.   When we were all assembled to the number of four or five hundred, there stood up one Simeon, surnamed Niger, who delivered a speech by no means so foolish as I had thought likely, and it was to this effect: There was but one God, he said, who had made no distinctions of nations, as Greeks, barbarians, Scythians and the rest, but all men of one blood, intending them to be one brotherhood.   This God sent unto mankind signs and testimonies of his good will, giving unto all nations the sun and moon and stars to be for signs and seasons; moreover to the Jews he sent special messengers, or prophets, to proclaim his will.   But when, notwith-standing all these testimonies, mankind still disobeyed the divine will, it seemed good to the superior god to

send down to them no longer a prophet or common
messenger, but a son, as if the time had arrived when
they should no longer grope after God, but apprehend
the divine nature.

"Then this Simeon went on to affirm that this son of
god had verily come into the world about threescore
years ago, during the reign of the Emperor Augustus,
in the shape of a man, one Jesus (called also the Naza-
rene, because he was of the city of Nazareth in the
north of Palestine), who had proclaimed a Gospel or
Good News, namely, that God is the Father of men,
not merely their Maker, but their Father, loving all men
as parents love their children. Moreover the Son had
manifested the Father's nature by many works, especially by healing the souls of men, not only taking away
sins, but also giving unto his disciples the power to take
away sins. In a word the Son had done for the Father,
if one might trust Simeon, much the same deeds as
Apollo is said to have done in early times for Zeus, introducing into the world purifications of the soul. Then
also (quoting, as I was told, from some of the ancient
books of the Jews) Simeon declared that this Jesus of
Nazareth was the Redeemer of whom those books had
prophesied ; for, said he, 'to them that sat in darkness
Jesus hath shewn forth the light of truth, he hath
opened the eyes of them that were blinded by sin and
ignorance and caused those whose souls were maimed and
were crippled with vice to walk straight in the paths
of virtue, and he hath raised up them that were dead
in sin.'

"Now followed a marvellous paradox, or rather what
our friend Evagoras the rhetorician would call a *bathos*.

For it was actually confessed before us all by this same Simeon that this son of god, who had wrought all these marvellous works, was slain in the sixteenth year of the Emperor Tiberius, and this, not in battle nor in a tumult, but by command of the governor Pontius Pilatus, dying the death of the vilest criminal, being actually crucified! And, not content with this ignominy, they confess also that he was most shamefully insulted and scourged before his death, and that he was rescued neither from insult nor from death by the superior god whom they call the Father. But to compensate for all these disgraces, the speaker affirmed in the first place that this death constituted some kind of sacrifice or expiation, wherein this Christus played at once the part of priest and victim, offering himself up for the sins of the whole world (he having been no unwilling sacrifice but having surrendered himself to death and having indeed predicted his own death as a prophet); and in the second place, as the crowning marvel of all, he affirmed that the superior god had raised up the inferior, that is the Son, after the latter had lain for several days in the tomb, insomuch that, long after his death, he appeared to many of his disciples, of whom some are still living as witnesses.

" ' Nursery tales '—replies my wise preceptor, nor do I say otherwise. But what filled me with astonishment, almost more than was fitting, was to note the gravity, earnestness and sobriety and yet at the same time the enthusiasm wherewith Simeon delivered himself, especially when he bore witness to the rising again of Christus (for by this name Jesus is commonly known among them); speaking as if at that very moment he were

standing in the presence of him that was risen from
the dead, and yet enjoining chastity, truthfulness,
honesty, and all other virtue, with such a calmness
that not a few of those present, and Philemon among
the rest, were well-nigh carried away with the force of
the man's belief, and themselves persuaded to believe
the like. Nor could I altogether marvel; for it was
not possible to suppose that the man was a knave or
cheat; yet neither did he appear to be a madman, and
certainly he spake not as a fool.

"But I omit too long the main matter for which
Philemon came hither, the healing of diseases. Concerning this, Simeon said little; rather taking it for
granted, as I judged, than arguing of it or dwelling
upon it at any length. But he said that signs had
been wrought both by Christus and by his disciples,
in the casting out of devils and in the healing of
sickness; and he appealed to some of those present,
as if they knew this of their own knowledge. Afterwards I spoke with many of them on this matter.
Almost all told me that they knew others who had
been healed of divers diseases, and some few (not more
than three) affirmed that they themselves had been
healed of palsy, two of them by one Paulus, of whom
I made mention above, and the other by this same
Simeon. Of the rest whom they averred to have
been healed, some were said to have been healed by
Paulus, others by one Petrus, a man of great repute
among them, others by this Simeon and not a few by
one Philippus, who is even now (as they tell me)
sojourning in Hierapolis. Of these sick folk some
have been wholly healed and immediately; others

partly and only by degrees; but for the most part
more completely and suddenly than any cures wrought
by Asclepius. The diseases are mostly palsies (which
abound here) and also fevers, and partial dumbness or
lameness, and the more severe kind of ophthalmia; but
the most common is that kind of insanity which by the
common people is termed 'possession.'

"Of this latter kind one instance I myself witnessed
on the very day on which I heard Simeon thus discourse; and it was wrought by Simeon himself in the
synagogue. For after he had made an end of the first
part of his discourse, he began to call upon all the
people to repent, saying that the superior god whom he
named the Father, would speedily judge all the world in
righteousness, punishing the bad and rewarding the
good, and in that day the Son,—namely, that very
Christus whom Pontius had crucified,— should come
again with great glory. Hereon one cried out in the
assembly after the manner of demented people, saying
'Avaunt! Away! Away from me!' adding loud ex-
clamations against the name of Jesus. Simeon forthwith ceased from speaking, and looking very intently on
the man's countenance caused him to be brought near,
and stretching out his hand as with authority in a loud
voice adjured I know not what evil spirit to go forth
from the man. The demented man immediately fell to
the ground as one dead; but Simeon took him by the
hand, and raised him up and restored him to his
friends; and he went forth from the building delivered
from his disease.

"The man happened to be the brother of our host's
door-keeper; and his madness was confirmed to me by

many witnesses, as being of long continuance, yea, and
I myself had seen him in a pitiable plight, gibbering and
gaping as one mad in our courtyard a full month
before ; and our host himself (who is no friend to the
Christians) constantly affirmed that he had been mad
for the space of at least fourteen years. Wherefore
thus much is certain and not to be denied, that a man
who was demented for fourteen years, up till the seventh
day of this month, is now on the fourteenth day of this
month in his sound mind and to all appearance likely to
remain therein ; and this has been wrought by certain
words uttered by this Simeon Niger. Now if this effect
proceeds from natural causes, as the great Epicurus
would doubtless assert, the causes (none the less) seem
worthy to be sought out and examined.

"When the madman was led forth delivered from
his disease, I had much ado to prevent the worthy
Philemon from standing up publicly and praying that
he also might be initiated into the sacred rites of this
new religion by means of purification with water ; which
they practise not many times, as with us, but once for
all, and with more than usual solemnity ; and I suppose
that Christus himself instituted this purification ; at all
events no one is admitted without it. But I besought
the excellent man not to do so rash a thing with such
precipitate haste, and at least to wait till he should
have discovered whether those who are initiated into
the Christian rites, are also to submit themselves to the
whole of the law which the more ancient religion of the
Jews enjoins upon that nation. For the time I suc-
ceeded and kept him from his purpose. But I could
wish that Archippus or Apphia were here present with

him, and not I alone. For I greatly fear that, if he be so violently moved a second time, I may no longer be able to restrain him. Concerning the second visit to the synagogue, having many things to write, and the messenger of Philemon being already on the point to depart, I must defer what I would further say to another occasion.

"One matter had almost slipped my memory; and it is perhaps hardly worth setting down. Going this day to the garden of Adonis I saw the youths and maidens passing in procession through the golden gate of Daphne; and there calling to my mind other processions such as I had seen in my youth (but this far surpassed them all) I remembered how I was wont as a child to make comparisons between a certain Diosdotus, a priest of Zeus of a goodly presence and lofty stature, and a certain unknown wandering priest or juggler, mean of aspect, bald-headed and hook-nosed, who in my presence had healed one that was lame and known to have been lame for thirty years. This happened when I was a mere child scarcely (as I think) past my tenth year; but to-day it came into my mind that both that wandering priest and this Simeon — albeit differing greatly in countenance and appearance, Simeon being tall and the other short or inclining to shortness — nevertheless agreed in this one point, that they spoke of things invisible not only as if they saw them, but also in such wise as to make others fancy that they saw them. And, if I err not, that prophet also spoke, as did Simeon, concerning a certain son of god whom the superior god had sent into the world. Wherefore I now conjecture that that same wandering prophet belonged to no gods of the Greeks, but was, even as this Simeon, a Jew, and one of this sect that believes in Christus.

"One other matter also I omitted to mention, that this new religion makes no distinction between those of different nations, nor between rich and poor, slaves and free ; for all that belong to the sect are esteemed citizens of one nation, or rather brothers of one family ; and certainly I noted in the synagogue that there were observed no distinctions of wealth or rank ; for whether a man were a town-councillor or a water-carrier, it was all one ; we all sat together.   Farewell."

§ 3. HOW ARTEMIDORUS QUESTIONED ME FURTHER CONCERNING THE CHRISTIANS.

"ARTEMIDORUS TO ONESIMUS, HEALTH.

"Your letter was acceptable to me, my dear Onesimus, because it contained no longer mere hearsay concerning these Jews, but the things that you yourself had seen and heard.   Now you will do well to make inquiry more particularly on the following points : 1st, Does this sect of Jews, (or Christians if they are to be so called) possess any sacred books ? 2nd, As touching this son of the Divine Being, of whom you speak, was he (according to their saying) begotten by the superior god from some human mother ; or came he into the world as the child of some divine mother ? or in what other way ?   For I assume, of course, that his followers do not believe him to have been born of a human father. But if he was also not born of a human mother, then what certainty is there that he had human flesh and

blood ; and in that case, how could he be subject to
death ? But perhaps they say that he did not really
die ? In that case, however, he did not really rise from
the dead ; so that both his death and life would seem to
have been a make-believe, the death a not dying, and
the life a not existing ; yet it is not easy to see why
even an inferior god should come into the world for the
purpose of not existing ; 3rd, Touching the wonderful
works said to have been wrought by this Christus, were
they all acts of healing such as you describe ? Or were
there not also some such tricks and portents as wizards
and enchanters and jugglers profess to perform, such as
the breathing of fire from the nostrils, and the changing
of earth into bread, and of water into blood, and the
producing of sudden banquets and then causing them
to vanish again, and the summoning up of apparitions,
and drawing down of the moon from the sky, and other
such vulgar marvels ? 4th, This rising again of Christus
from the grave, was it seen and attested by enemies as
well as by friends ? And, if so, did the enemies turn to
his side, being convinced by the marvel ? Or, if not by
enemies, was it at least seen (according to what the
Christians themselves affirm) by impartial witnesses ?
And did these, by reason of what they saw, believe in
him and follow him ? And after his rising from the
grave, did he eat and drink and bathe and lecture and
sleep as before ? Or, if not, in what respects was his
manner of life changed, and in what guise did he
appear, and moving with what motion ? Also if he
was, as you say, executed like a slave upon the cross,
did his limbs manifest, to all that saw him, the marks
of his execution ? Or did these scars appear to some,

but not to others ?   Lastly, forget not to inquire (for
this is of the greatest importance) whether any touched
him, and also how he came among his followers, after
his rising again ; whether by opening the doors in the
usual way and ascending stairs, or whether the doors
being shut, he shewed himself in the midst of his
friends.   My fifth and last question is, what laws has
this leader laid down for his followers ? and on this
point I would have you inform me as fully and exactly
as you can.

" Because I have asked you so many questions, my
dear Onesimus, you will probably infer (and you will
not be wrong) that the subject attracts me and that
I set much value on your information : which indeed
comes to me all the more seasonably because here, in
this very neighbourhood, these Jews, or Christians,
have been of late making no small stir ; especially
at Ephesus, where that same Paulus of whom you
speak, has been these many months, openly teaching
the philosophy of your Christus, and his lectures, (or
as some say his portents) have drawn away many pupils
to hear him, who also have accepted that purification by
water which gives admission to this sect.   And from
what I have heard I gather that their philosophy—for
religion it can scarce be called having no gods except
perchance one, nor scarce any rites or sacrifices, nor any
processions, nor feasts, nor holidays—after the manner
of the doctrine which is ever in the mouth of our young
friend Epictetus, deals mainly with the practice and not
much with the theories and speculations of life.   For
many that were before noted for thieves or drunkards
or loose livers are reported to have been turned from

their swinish living by Paulus, so as to live lives well-nigh worthy of philosophers. Moreover, strange to relate, this magician, for so they call him, sets himself against all magic in others; and many of his followers, turning from their so-called magic arts, have brought their Ephesian charms and their books of magic, yea, and even their lawful silver shrines of Ephesian Artemis herself, to·be burned or melted down. So great indeed is the diminution of the purchase of the shrines that by this time the silversmiths begin to cry out; and I heard but yesterday that complaints are coming in from the graziers who fatten the victims for the temples, that their business is diminished and like to slip away from them altogether if this new superstition be not checked.

" As to exorcism, you did not amiss to remind me that attested cases of sudden healing are not to be put aside merely because the illiterate multitude calls them by absurd names and explains them by absurd causes; but perhaps I also shall not do amiss to remind you (surrounded as you are by all manner of superstitious and credulous people) that every such case is assuredly to be explained, if not by deceit and fraud, then by some moving of the imagination (for imagination is a powerful causer of many undreamed effects), or else by some other cause or causes of which we may for the time be ignorant.

"Take for example the following instance of one reported to have been raised from the dead; which I myself have with great expense of time and labour but recently searched out and for the truth of which I can vouch. About a month ago our friend Nicostratus came to me—in that state of frenzy which, as you know, is customary with him when he has anything to relate which he cannot himself explain—saying that a nobleman in some part of Phrygia or Cilicia had been raised from the dead after being a month or more entombed, and that he had spoken with a Laodicean, one who had either seen it done or at least knew all the facts, and could attest their truth ; but Nicostratus himself knew no more about the matter, and, as I found on questioning him, he proposed to inquire no further about it, but to spread the rumour throughout all Colossæ, just as he had imparted it to me. With much ado I obtained from him the name of the Laodicean (for the futile creature had well-nigh forgotten even that), and on the first occasion that offered itself I went to Laodicea to see him. The story of the Laodicean was to this effect, that the dead man had died of a fever, and had been buried so long that the body must needs have become corrupt ; and behold, a magician came to the door of the sepulchre and pronounced charms and incantations, and straightway the door flew open and the dead man came forth alive, wrapped in his grave-clothes ; but what was the name of the deceased, and who it was that raised him up, and when and where it was done—concerning all these points he neither knew anything, nor had he himself seen it, nor heard anything from any eye-witness. Tracing the matter backward I learned at last the name of the man supposed to have been raised from the dead, no nobleman at all, but an honest dyer of Hierapolis, Tatias by name, and my informant told me that the said Tatias, though he had indeed died from a fever, had not yet been buried at the time when he

was restored to life ; he added the name of the physician
who had seen Tatias laid out for burial ; but who had
raised him from the dead he did not know. So to the
physician I went ; and here at last I gained some
glimpse of the truth. For I understood from him that
Tatias had not died of fever, but of a sudden flux of
blood to the head, such as is commonly called syncope.
Notwithstanding, the physician stoutly affirmed that
Tatias was really dead ; not unnaturally, because his own
credit was else like to have been diminished, if he had
suffered one that was still living to be laid out for burial.
Thence going to Tatias himself—a man of sense and
understanding and, in spite of his superstition, able to
discern truth from falsehood—I heard the whole story
according to the exact truth, and here it is, set down
exactly from his lips.

"It seems that he had been a pupil or hearer of
one Philippus, a Christian (who, as I take it, is the
same Philippus as he of whom you made mention in
your last letter to me), and having embraced this new
religion, he had been desirous for some days of receiving
the purification customary for the initiated ; but some
accident still delaying it, he grew perturbed, lest it
should be more than accident, and lest the gods were
against his being purified. At last, on the appointed
day, purposing to go with others of the uninitiated to the
pool where the rite was to take place, he was suddenly
called away to see his mother, who being seized with a
violent fever was said by the messenger to be on the
point of death. But finding her sickness to be only
slight, and no danger at all of death, he determined to
hasten with all speed to the mysteries, hoping that he

might after all not be too late, for the day was not yet
far spent.   So coming at last into the place of assembly
in great heat and fatigue of body and still greater
trepidation of mind lest it should be all in vain, and he
a second time 'disappointed of salvation'—for these
were his very words—in this condition of mind and
body he was called upon in the midst of a great multitude already assembled to stand up on some kind of
platform and there to make profession of his new
religion.   So mounting up he adventured to speak in
due form; but behold some demon (to use the man's
own words, for he spoke as one of the ignorant) had
wholly possessed him, depriving him of the power of
speech and causing all things to appear to turn round
before him; and anon he fell to the ground, and was
taken up for dead, and brought back to his own house,
and being given over by the physician as dead, he was
washed, laid out, and all things made ready for his
entombment.

"But during all this time, though the man was
lying on his back not able to move hand or foot,
yet was he not wholly dead.   For though he could
not so much as stir an eyelid, yet was he aware, he
says, of the presence and words of the physician,
and of the wailing of the women and the mourners,
and able to understand the speech of those who stood
around him; and a deep horror fell upon him lest he
should be carried out and entombed alive, and die
miserably before he had attained to salvation; · 'but,'
continued he, 'the more my horror grew upon me, the
less seemed my power to move, being bound fast by
the fetters of Satan.'   However he took some comfort

because he heard his friends say that they had sent for Philippus (who was at that time absent from Hierapolis) to come and offer up prayers. What followed I will now recount in the words of Tatias himself. "When," said he, "the man of God entered the chamber, I was at once aware of his presence, all standing up to salute him, and I also desired to stand up but could not; then I was aware that he drew nigh to me, and I felt that he looked on my face though I saw him not; and he said aloud that it was not well that I should die till I had made confession of my faith and been washed in the living water; then the sound of the mourners ceased and there was a deep silence, and I knew that he was looking on me again, and a certainty began to possess me that I should be delivered; and he spoke a second time saying that he did not believe that I was dead, but that I slept, and that it was the Lord's will that I should be awakened; and at the word he took me by the hand, and I felt a thrill through my body, as if the bands of Satan began to be loosened; and then calling me by name he adjured me in the name of Jesus of Nazareth, who arose from the dead, to rise up and walk. And straightway strength seemed to flow into every part of my body, and my limbs no longer refused to obey me, and I sat up and spoke and magnified God."

"My reason, dear Onesimus, for describing to you thus fully this matter of Tatias, is two-fold; first, that you may perceive that no truth is to be rejected or passed over; secondly, that you may be encouraged to remember that many things which at first seem false or fabulous, or else contrary to nature, will, when sifted

and examined, appear to be neither false nor unnatural,
but true and in accordance with nature. Therefore I
beseech you, as long as you are in Syria, and in condition to find out anything new about these Jews,
search with all zeal; and trust not to hearsay but test
all things yourself as far as you may, seeking the
truth with a just sobriety and incredulity. Spare not
pains nor labour : for without doubt some great cause
must needs be at work to produce so great effects as
are wrought by these Christians; men for the most
part illiterate and inexperienced in philosophy; who
notwithstanding appear to have attained a remarkable
skill not only in the healing of certain diseases but also
in turning many of the viler sort towards courses of
honesty and virtue. Search therefore and with all
diligence ; but forget not the proverb :

> *Sober incredulity*
> *Is the wise man's security.*

§ 4. HOW THE CHRISTIANS HONOURED THE PROPHETS OF THE JEWS.

" ONESIMUS TO ARTEMIDORUS, HEALTH.

" To proceed with the answers to your questions.
These Christian Jews have no sacred books of their
own ; but they use in their worship the sacred books
of their countrymen. For although they (or at least
many of them) reject the sacrifices and festivals and
laws ordained by their ancient lawgiver Moses, yet do
they by no means reject the books of oracles or prophecies which they commonly call ' the Prophets.'

Now many of these prophecies predict that there shall come a great ruler of the nation of the Jews, who shall deliver them from all their enemies and make them to be conquerors of the world; and this their future Ruler or Redeemer they use to call 'Messiah' (which word means 'sent' because he is to be 'sent' from God). So far therefore both the older Jews and the new Jews agree; but the great difference is this; the former still look forward to the coming of their 'Messiah,' the latter say he is already come, and that he is no other than he whom they call Christus. Now because it is a great stumbling-block to the older Jews to suppose that their conquering Messiah was not only himself conquered but also slain with insults and with the death of a slave, for this cause the Christians spare no pains to shew that the oracles of the older Jews themselves predicted that he should be so slain; and they also labour to shew that the same books of prophecy foretold how the Messiah should be born, and the manner of his life; and that all these predictions are fulfilled in the birth and life of their Christus. Hence it comes that they think it of little account to say that Christus did this or that, or that he was born and died at such a place and at such a time, unless they can also add that 'all this was done that the words of this or that prophet might be fulfilled.' And more than this; as often as they have read one of the passages of the prophecies appointed to be read in their worship, first one arises and then another, water-carriers and tent-makers and leather-cutters and the like, all attempting to shew that this sentence and that sentence point to none other than Christus; and in this fashion not only do they strain the words of their prophets and enforce them to receive all manner of meanings which they could not naturally have, but also they unwittingly encourage and, as it were, vying with one another, provoke their own and one another's imaginations to remember some new things that Christus did, or said, that perchance fulfil the words of the prophecy.

" Hence proceeds already a manifest alteration of the doctrine of the Christians, and more is likely to proceed. For you may already perceive different shapes of teaching among them, and each later shape departs further from the truth in order to come nearer to the ancient prophecies. Thus, for example, there was read in our presence in the synagogue an ancient dirge which is commonly interpreted to predict the death of the Messiah, wherein it was said that his hands and feet were pierced, and that gall and vinegar were given him to drink, and that his enemies divided his raiment and cast lots for it, and that the passers-by wagged their heads at him and mocked him for his trust in God, saying, ' He trusted in God, let God therefore deliver him, if He will have him.' Now, after this had been read and after the principal speaker, who was a man of some discretion, had pointed out that this prophecy was fulfilled by Christus, I took occasion, when we left the synagogue, to question the man thus :

Onesimus. Say you then that in all points this prophecy was fulfilled by Christus ?

The Speaker. In these points—that his hands and feet were pierced, and that his enemies derided him, and that vinegar was given him to drink.

Onesimus. You say well, for a draught is wont to be given to those who are condemned to death ; but tell me further, did any cast lots for his raiment, and did the bystanders say these precise words ' He trusted in God,' and the like ? And is it so handed down in your Tradition ?

The Speaker. It is not indeed so handed down in our tradition ; but it may have been so.

When I had thanked him for his courtesy I hastened forwards to an honest and illiterate leather-cutter to whom I put precisely the same questions ; but now mark the different replies in this, which I call the second, shape of the Christian doctrine.

Onesimus. Tell me, good friend, was this prophecy, whereof we heard but now, fulfilled in all points by Christus ?

Leather-cutter. Assuredly.

Onesimus. And did his enemies cast lots for his raiment ?

Leather-cutter. Assuredly.

Onesimus. And did the bystanders say ' He trusted in God ' and use these exact words ?

Leather-cutter. Assuredly.

Onesimus. And are these things taught in the Tradition concerning the acts and deeds of Christus ?

Leather-cutter. Not that I remember.

Onesimus. Then did Simeon, or Lucius, or Petrus, or Paulus or any other ever teach thee these things in the synagogue ?

Leather-cutter. Not that I remember.

Onesimus. Then prithee, how knowest thou that these things are so ?

Leather-cutter. Because it must needs be that all things that are written in the Law and the Prophets should be fulfilled in Christus.

"Behold, my dear Artemidorus, the second shape of the Christian doctrine; which, if it be not speedily committed to writing, what third or fourth shapes it may assume, the wit of man cannot conjecture. But one thing is certain, that in every case the leather-cutter will carry the day against the learned man, and the man who believes everything against the man of discretion who believes some things and rejects others. Thus, although Christus died not a generation ago, and was born (as is thought) scarce more than two generations ago, yet already are there current many fables and stories which overshadow the things that he really did, and the doctrine that he really taught, and all this because of the ancient prophecies of his nation; so that, for my part, whensoever I hear one of their teachers say that Christus said or did this or that, and make no mention of any prophecy, then I incline to believe him; but when he adds that Christus said or did anything 'that a prophecy might be fulfilled,' then I shut my ears against the man's words, knowing that they are, in all likelihood, imaginations and fancies.

"A second noteworthy point is, that they make frequent use of figures of speech, and these sometimes so mixed up with facts and histories that it is hard to understand whether they are to be taken according to the letter or not. Thus, for example, whereas they assert that their ancient Lawgiver gave them bread called manna and water from the rock, this they mean

literally ; but whereas they say that Christus was in
no way inferior to him, for that he also gave them
' bread from heaven ' and ' living water,' yea, also and
(as some add) ' wine instead of water,' all these phrases
are to be taken, not according to the letter but (most
say) spiritually.　Yet even some of these relations my
friend the leather-cutter accepts as literally true, and
his opinion will soon prevail ; such confusion is there
between the figures of speech and facts of history in
the minds of the illiterate.　Again, when the teachers
speak of being ' delivered from death,' they mean (for
the most part) not that which we call death but rather
the decay and corruption of the soul ; and in the same
way, when they speak of the unclosing of the ears of the
deaf, and of the eyes of the blind, and of making the
lame to walk in the straight path, in all these cases
their meaning (and the meaning of the prophets) is
not to speak of the things of the body, but of the
things of the soul.　Yet even these the common sort
have begun to interpret not of the soul but of the
body, and hence have arisen already many perversions
of the history of the acts of Christus.

" From this cause have proceeded, I doubt not, many
of the false accusations which are commonly reported
against these Christians and which I myself once
ignorantly believed.　For example, whereas they are
commonly charged with slaying and eating a little
child (and many also add that the Christians cover
the child with meal, and then cause those who would
fain be initiated, to cut the meal with their knives so
that they may be unwittingly led to perpetrate murder),
the charge arises, as I am persuaded, from the misunder-

standing of certain words used by the Christians in their mysteries. For in these secret rites, offering up no sacrifice of their own, they commemorate (as I am informed) the sacrifice of Christus; calling by that name his miserable death, and affirming that it was voluntary and that he thereby offered up his life for the world ; and for this cause they not only call him the Son of God but also the Lamb of God, and just as those who offer up a victim partake of the flesh of a victim, even so do these Christians, partaking of bread and wine, profess solemnly that they eat the body and drink the blood of the Son or Child of God ; and hence has sprung the belief of the common people that the Christians slay and eat a little child. As touching the charge of incest commonly brought against them, I am persuaded that this also is groundless ; but it is possible that the Christians calling one another brethren and sisters (as being members of one brotherhood) have caused those who love them not, to suppose that brothers and sisters are permitted in their sect to unite in marriage. But another cause might be alleged, for they are wont to speak of their state or republic sometimes as the New Jerusalem, but sometimes as a living person, the Mother of the Faithful, and, speaking of the parentage of Christus, they say that this Mother gave birth to him, describing her (in poetic figures and with numbers that are customary in their sacred books) as a Woman clothed with the sun, and the moon under her feet, and upon her head a crown of twelve stars, and they say that she brought forth a man-child who should rule all nations with a rod of iron, which man-child is no other than the ' Messiah,' or Christus. But again, others

using a different figure describe the republic not as
a Mother, but as a Bride, chaste and spotless, being
betrothed to Christus, whom they praise as the Bridegroom ; and this manner of speech, strange as it may
seem to us Greeks, is familiar to them, being commonly
used in their books of prophecies, which often speak of
their nation as a Bride, and the superior god as the
Bridegroom. Now it is possible that some, hearing
that, among the Christians, the Son is betrothed to the
Mother, and not staying to consider whether this be-
trothal be a figure of speech or true according to the
letter, have affirmed that incest is allowed among them.
But whatever may be the cause of the error, an error it
is beyond all question. For these Christians, however
they may fall short in understanding, are not inferior
to philosophers in the purity of their lives. Much
more I have to write about the traditions of these
people, which I must defer till my next letter."

§ 5. OF THE ANCIENT HISTORIES OF THE JEWS.

" ONESIMUS TO ARTEMIDORUS, HEALTH.

"The further I proceed, my dear Artemidorus, search-
ing into the history of this strange sect, and always
bearing in mind your proverb that 'incredulity is the
philosopher's security,' the more I perceive the difficulty
of the task you have laid upon me. For I now find that
these very people who profess to worship Christus and
who recognise in him the fulfilment of ancient prophecies, nevertheless neglect, and I might almost say,
despise all modern writings and records, insomuch that

even at this present time no account of his words and deeds is committed to paper. Of this strange neglect there are several strange causes, and the first the strangest of all. You must know then that these people commonly believe (even the wisest or least foolish of them) that Christus will speedily return enthroned upon the clouds to make himself governor over the whole world; so that it is needless to write the words of one who himself will soon be speaking upon earth. The second cause is, that there is a tradition among the Jews, current now for many hundreds of years, not to write new sacred books, but to hand down by word of mouth from teacher to pupil, through many generations, such traditions as may be needful. A third cause is, that, Christus having given unto them no clear and definite law nor even many distinct precepts, his followers stand not upon his exact commandments; and indeed some fear not to say openly that they care little for the letter of his commandments, for that he himself promised to send them a certain good demon or Spirit (even such a one as Socrates had) which should prompt and warn them what to do and what to avoid, and teach them how to defend themselves against their persecutors and before their judges. I have omitted a fourth and last cause which is not the least important; namely, that most of the followers of Christus have been, from the first beginning of the sect, men of no education, but illiterate and scarce able to write at all, so that they naturally preferred speaking to writing.

"So much for the books or no books of the Christians. But there is yet another obstacle in the way of my search. You have been wont to hold up to me

Thucydides the historian as a pattern of the truth-loving disposition and as the model to all that desire to record that which has happened. But in this nation there neither are, nor ever were, any such historians; nor is it their nature to relate things according to the exact truth. Not that they love falsehood better than truth; but the minds of their writers seem ever on the poise between poetry and prose, between figures of speech and plain sense, between hyperbole and fact; and as in all their histories of their nation they discern evermore (as Homer has it) the 'accomplishment of the will of Zeus,' even so their pens lead them ever to speak of their God rather than men, and of things invisible rather than visible, and of the purpose and object of each event, rather than the how, and when, and where of it. Hence it has come to pass that all manner of poetic tales and legends having been embodied and as it were interlaced in their relations, it is impossible to tell where the poem ends and the history begins; and the constant reading of these ancient poems or histories, or history-poems (if you so please to call them) has made them careless of truth, and I might almost say contemptuous of it, unless it abound with marvel. Of which disposition, though I might set down many proofs, take these two only, as patterns of the rest. To this day it is commonly believed among them that, during a certain great victory wherein they gained possession of Palestine, the sun and the moon stood still at the bidding of one of their ancient generals; and that, about the same time, the whole of the wall of a fortified city fell to the ground at the sound of the trumpets of their army.

" Some of these relations of portents have come into
their histories from errors. For example, one of their
poets speaking, in all likelihood poetically, of a drought
which dried up the waters of the river Jordanus so that
the ancient Jews passed over easily to the conquest of
Palestine, and addressing himself in apostrophe to their
God who guided their nation across, uses these words,
' The waters saw thee, O God, the waters saw thee and
were afraid ' ; which words the historians straightway take
up and interpret literally, and behold, a relation, incredible
and portentous, how the waters of the river rose up like
a wall on this side and on that, so that the whole nation
might pass through dry-shod, as if through a defile.   I
deny not that, in this and some other cases, error may
excuse their exaggeration ; but my complaint is that all
this nation (and the older Jews much more than the
Christians) are so given up to hyperbole that there is no
trusting anything that they say, that is at all marvellous,
without a careful testing of it.   For example, among
the older Jews, I have heard a certain teacher say that
the city of Jerusalem is situate on a river of clear
water many furlongs in length, though there be, in
truth, no river at all nearer to the city than Jordan,
which is one hundred and eighty furlongs distant ; and
the same man said that the smell of the sacrifices and
the sound of the music in Jerusalem goes down to the
men of Jericho, which city is distant a full day's
journey ; and another affirmed that the twanging of
the bow-strings of the multitude of enemies caused the
walls of Apamea to fall ; and also that a certain Rabbi
(for by that title they honour their teachers) was so
pious that he emitted from his body flames of fire,

insomuch that the beholders marvelled at the splendour, and whatsoever insect approached him, was straightway consumed.

"Judge therefore what kind of history the unwritten traditions of the life of Christus are like to contain when I have sought them out for you. However I will do my best to collect them, and to send you such information as I can obtain about them, together with the answers to your former questions. Having taken brief notes of the discourse of one Lucius of Cyrene, the chief speaker in the synagogue, I purposed to send it to you; but not having yet written it out fully, I will send it at my first leisure; and when you read it, you will more easily understand how much the traditions concerning Christus are in danger to be conformed to the ancient prophecies of the Jews.[1]

"This letter I see deals with naught but 'obstacles' and 'difficulties and 'burdens'; yet I beg of you, my dear Artemidorus, not to suppose that I murmur at the task you have imposed on me or that I count the labour wasted. For indeed the more I muse on the matter, the more I judge that this Christus must have been endowed with a truly divine genius, or force of character (or whatever faculty else you may please to call it) to have produced so vast an influence on a nation so perverse and morose as these Jews, not to speak of many thousands of the viler sort of Greeks

---

[1] This discourse (which should have found place here) was missing from the collection of the papers of Artemidorus, at the time when I was transcribing them; but having chanced upon it some months afterwards, I purpose to set it down at the end of the book.

who after attaching themselves to his sect have turned
from vice to virtue. Philemon is well, but still unquiet
and hardly to be controlled. Farewell."

§ 6. HOW ARTEMIDORUS QUESTIONED ME FURTHER, AND OF HIS RELATION CONCERNING THE CASTING OUT OF THE SWINE.

" ARTEMIDORUS TO ONESIMUS, HEALTH.

" Although I could have wished, my dear Onesimus,
that you had been able to answer my first questions,
point by point, yet your account of the discourse spoken
by the Christian priest Lucius was not without interest
for me ; confirming, as it did, an opinion that I have
ever entertained, namely, that no portents how incredible soever, and no absurdities however palpable,
can ever deter the multitude from embracing a new
belief, if there be somewhat in it of a nature to fascinate the soul and feed the imagination. But still my
desire is that you should do your utmost to discover
what this superstition contains, of a nature thus to
fascinate the multitude ; for it is not apparent to me
from anything that you have hitherto written, since
you describe a religion that has no sacred books, no
feasts, no processions, no code of laws that might unite
and regulate a disorderly mass of men.

" In addition to this I would gladly receive answers
to these two further questions, on the first of which you
yourself touched in your first letter but so as to suggest
rather than explain : 1st, Does this sect require that all,
as many as join themselves to it, Greeks as well as

Jews (for I understand that Greeks also are admitted by them), shall observe the laws of the Jews? Or does it remit the laws for those who are not Jews? Or are they remitted for all, Jews as well as Greeks? 2nd, I cannot understand from the discourse of Lucius whether he supposes Christus to be born of man and woman in a natural way, or in a divine way born of woman only. This question I believe I asked before; but now I repeat it, partly lest you should suppose it to have been already answered by the priest's discourse, partly because (in conversation with certain Christians of Hierapolis) I have heard that there is some diversity of opinion concerning this matter among the Christians themselves.

"Here might I well make an end; but because I have especially charged you to report to me concerning any portents related of the life of Christus, I will briefly explain to you my meaning and purpose herein. A thousand times, as you know well, I have wearied you with repeating that no religion can ever commend itself to the multitude unless it be first clothed, as it were, in a vesture, whereby the eyes of the many may be drawn towards it. For it is not given to the multitude to love the naked truth; but they must needs clothe her in their purple and set on her brow diadems of their own giving. Well, my friend, even such a clothing, adorning and crowning of religion, are you methinks now witnessing. For it is beyond all question that in a few years, if not already, the believers in this new faith will have clothed or embellished the life of their Leader with all manner of wonders, which in itself it had not. And already I discern this process of

clothing, in the beginning and first endeavour. For
whereas your Lucius preaches about 'the Star of Judah'
shining, and the 'preparing of the table in the wilderness,' and the stilling of the storm by him whose 'path
is on the deep waters,' and the testimony of Moses and
Elias on the right hand and on the left of Christus, and
the giving of the 'Bread of Life' and the 'living Water,'
and 'the Wine of the Lord's Blood'—I doubt not but
both these and many other figures and metaphors either
are, or speedily will be, so interlaced with the tradition
of the life of Christus, that his followers will soon
believe (even though they believe not already) that he
did really and actually walk upon the waves and bestow
upon them miraculous water, and miraculous wine and
bread, yes, and that a special Star shone forth at his
birth, and that saints rose from their graves along with
him, and that Moses and Elias did really appear on his
right hand and on his left bearing testimony to him,
and a thousand other portents which it would be easier
for you to enumerate than for me, but equally tedious
for both of us. Wherefore, since you assure me that
these people have as yet no sacred books, but only an
unwritten tradition, I would have you inquire diligently
concerning this tradition whether it contain any such
wonders as these; and if not, then whether their common
talk (which must needs in the end insinuate itself into
their tradition, unless there come some let or unfore-
seen hindrance) have not already begun to imbue itself
with miracles and marvels of this sort.

'As touching the transmutation—so let us call it—
of things metaphorical into things literal I myself have
of late obtained one instance which I will contribute to

our common store.　Upon receipt of your first letter,
discoursing with a certain acquaintance of mine—one
Evander, a physician and an educated man, not I think
unknown to you—concerning the causes and symptoms
of 'possession,' he made this observation, that it is the
custom of the patient in such cases (his stomach, as well
as his mind, being altogether corrupted and diseased) to
suppose that he has within his belly all manner of filthy
and foul creatures, such as toads, serpents, dragons,
scorpions, adders, dogs, swine and the like, which
creatures, when the possessed man is suddenly healed,
he often sees (or rather imagines and fancies himself to
see) going forth from his mouth into banishment or
destruction.　And he added that among the Phrygians
the possessed were wont to suppose that hooded snakes
or scorpions were within them, but among the Jews
(who have a special abhorrence of certain animals considering them to be unclean) it was more common to
imagine the presence of swine ; and not unnaturally,
said he, because these animals (having no real existence
but being the mere offspring of the imagination) neces-
sarily vary with the imagination that gives them birth.
Then he went on to relate how a Jew being (as all Jews
are) a great hater of the Romans, and also considering
swine to be unclean, had imagined himself to be possessed by a Legion, not however of soldiers but of
swine ; which swine, when they were cast forth into the
deep or 'abyss' (for by this name they are wont to
call the void place wherein bodiless spirits or demons
are supposed to roam) were seen by the Jew, the possessed man, to go forth from his mouth and run
violently down to the said abyss.　This tradition, he

H

said, he had heard some years ago from another physician who lived at Tiberias, not far from the place where the man had been healed ; and he that had healed him was, according to the saying of the physician of Tiberias, no other than this very same Christus, who is now worshipped by your friends, the Christians, as a god.

" When I heard this, considering with myself that in all likelihood, if this were so, some story of it would even now be current among the followers of Christus, I went on the morrow to Hierapolis, to that same Tatias of whom I made mention in my previous letter, and questioning him about them that are possessed, whether he knew of many that had been healed by Christus, I recounted to him my story concerning the man possessed with a Legion and asked him whether that was the true account of the matter. To which he replied that in his youth he had heard that account, or somewhat like unto it, but it was not exact ; for how, said he, could a legion of creatures of the size of swine, be shut in within the compass of one human belly ? But, according to him, the true story was, that the Legion of evil spirits having been cast out of the man, assumed the shapes of swine, and were then cast into the abyss. Then another of the same sect who happened to be present, said that neither was that version of the story altogether exact ; for why should demons, having shapes already, perchance of gnats or flies or whatever else, assume fresh shapes of swine ? But the truth was, that the legion of demons being two thousand in number—for the latest narrator of all, mark you, is assured of the exact number, which was not known in the earliest tradition—

finding themselves on the point to be cast out of the
man's body, and fearing to be without bodies and so to
be cast into the abyss, besought Christus that it might be
permitted to them to pass into the bodies of two thousand
swine; which swine happened to be at that instant pasturing—conveniently indeed for the demons but contrary
to the laws of the Jews—near to the demoniac. 'Then,'
said he (for it is worth while to recount his exact words)
'when the Lord suffered them, behold, the whole legion
of demons rushed into the two thousand swine; but
they gained nothing thereby. For the swine rushed
violently down a steep place into the sea of Tiberias' (no
longer you will observe into the abyss) 'and were
there drowned.' To this account another companion of
Tatias assented, as being the latest and truest tradition;
but he added yet a new fact, namely, that those who
were feeding the swine being terrified (as how should
they not be?) by so great a destruction, fled away into
the city, and that the citizens coming together in much
fear, besought Jesus that he would depart out of their
coasts.

"Meditate much, my dear Onesimus, upon this story;
and may it be profitable to you in your search after the
truth. But why do I speak of truth in such a case as
this, where so few grains of truth are inclosed in so
great a mass of falsehood? Sometimes, indeed, I repent
of having imposed on you so barren a task; nevertheless persevere, for there must be some powerful cause
to produce so great an effect upon the lives of
these Christians, even though they be unlearned and
superstitious. Farewell."

§ 7. OF THE TRADITIONS OF THE CHRISTIANS AND
OF THE NATURE OF CHRISTUS.

"ONESIMUS TO ARTEMIDORUS, HEALTH.

"Having long delayed to answer your questions I
will now do my endeavour to explain more fully,
1st, What are the traditions of these Christians ; 2nd,
What is their belief about Christus, whether born
according to nature or otherwise ; 3rd, What portents
are reported to have been wrought by Christus.

"1st. The tradition about the words and deeds of
Christus begins from the time when he first took upon
himself to profess teaching publicly and ends with the
record of a certain vision of angels, after his death,
wherein it was declared to some that had followed him
to the last, that he was not in the tomb but was risen
from the dead. There is also another tradition as I am
informed, of the longer discourses and prophecies of
Christus ; but this not having as yet been translated
into Greek, is not circulated in all the churches ; but
the shorter sayings and the acts of Christus are already
known in Rome and Ephesus and Alexandria, as well as
in Jerusalem and Antioch ; and there are two or three
versions of this Tradition already, and like to be more,
unless these are shortly committed to writing, for in
different churches different forms of the tradition spring
up. Also besides these versions of the Tradition (which
are for the most part the same among all their churches)
there are many additions or supplements concerning
the birth and childhood and death of Christus, and

concerning his manifestations to his disciples after his death ; but these have not yet attained to be considered parts of the Tradition itself.

"Some of these relations many of the Christians now desire to have set down in books and to cause to be read in the synagogues. But the Jewish part of the brethren are against it, saying that it is not the custom thus to commit doctrine to writing ; however the Greeks are mainly for it, and within a few years I doubt not but that it will be done. But for the present (as I told you before) the Christians use no sacred books save the ancient books of the Jews.

"2nd. As to the nature of Christus, and what he is supposed to be by his followers, I conversed with Simeon himself, and I found that there was diversity of opinion. 'There are,' said he, 'some of our sect who, while they admit that he is the Christ'—for that is their manner of speech, meaning by 'Christ' the 'Anointed,' that is, the future Ruler, as I think I wrote to you before—'yet hold him to be a man and born of men. With whom I do not agree, nor would I, even though most of those who believe as I believe, were to say so ; since we are enjoined by our Master to put no trust in human doctrines but only in such things as are proclaimed by the blessed prophets and taught by himself.' Further he added that some, on the other hand, believing Christus to be a god, would not admit that he was born of woman, but supposed him to be begotten of the Supreme God without aid of humanity at all, and so to have come into the world, a man in appearance, but in reality a spirit or angel. 'And seems it not to you,' said I, 'that such a belief does more honour to your leader than to suppose him to be born of woman ?' But he replied 'No, for under appearance of doing him honour, this heresy makes the life of our Master to be feigned and false ; for we believe that for our sakes he hungered and thirsted, and felt pain and sorrow, and that for our sakes also he died ; none of which sufferings could he have veritably endured, if he had not been really a man born of woman, but had only appeared to be a man, being in truth a spirit.' Then I said to him, 'But what hinders that your leader should have been born both of man and woman and yet be a god ? Might not the superior god, if he chose to send his son into the world as a man, send him thus into the world ; conforming him in all things, and in his birth no less than in his death, to the nature of mankind ?' Hereat he mused, and for some while made no answer ; but afterwards he said that it was not so believed in any of the churches, and that it did not seem to him possible that the common people should believe any man to be god, unless he were begotten of some god, as the story went even about the inferior gods of the Greeks, such as Heracles, Asclepius, Amphiaraus, Romulus, and the like.

"3rd. Your third question is concerning the wonders said to have been wrought by Christus, whether they are portents, or such as may be explained according to nature. To this I reply that, in the Tradition, almost all the works are works of healing, and all to be explained according to nature, saving some four or five ; and these four or five relations seem to me to have arisen from figures of speech, or prophecies or hyperbole even as I wrote to you before. For example, the Tradition contains already that story of the casting out of the swine from the demoniac, whereof you wrote to me ; but diversely reported, some saying that the matter happened at a place called Gerasa, but others at Gadara, and some affirming that one demoniac was thus healed, but others two.

" The other portents in the Tradition may be briefly mentioned, and some of them you yourself have already mentioned, by anticipation, in your letter; 1st. A certain testimony of Moses and Elias to Christus which is now said to have been delivered upon a 'holy mountain,' and it is added also that Christus conversing with them was suffused with a celestial splendour, and that there was a voice from heaven proclaiming Christus to be the Son of God. But as for this, and another case of a voice from above and a vision of the heavens opened and a dove descending, I know not whether it is not fitter to set it down as a vision or waking dream, rather than an error springing from a figure of speech ; 2nd. The second is some story of a storm stilled by Christus wherein he walked upon the waves ; as to which again I know not whether it has sprung from metaphor misunderstood, or may not also in part have sprung from some phantasm apparent to the first followers of Christus (for they were fishermen) while fishing in the lake in Galilee either before or after the death of Christus ; 3rd. The third is, a relation how Christus fed many thousands of his followers with bread in the wilderness, and this on two occasions. Now this, as I judge, springs altogether from error of metaphor. For as I wrote before, Christus himself

taught his followers to call him the Bread of Life,
meaning that his doctrine must be the sustenance of
their souls, and this manner of speech appears to be
common with the Jewish Rabbis also, who say that in
a certain ancient book all 'feasting' is to be understood
of the feeding upon the Law, yea, and one even speaks
of 'eating' the Messiah ; and to this day the disciples
of Christus use such language as this, which I myself
heard but of late spoken by the priest of the Christians;
'O thou who didst come down from heaven to be the
Eternal Bread, and didst refresh the race of men,
sojourning in the wilderness of the world, with the
Bread from heaven, even with thine own body.'

"Now it might have been supposed that such figures
as these would bear upon themselves clear token that
they are but figures ; but that which has persuaded
men most of all to interpret them according to the
letter, is that all the Jews alike, both those who observe
the Law and also the Christians, believe that Moses
gave real bread from heaven unto the ancient nation of
the Jews, when wandering in a barren wilderness. And
to increase the wonder they add that on every seventh
day (which, as you know, is to them a day of rest
whereon no work is done) no bread came down, but a
double supply on the sixth day ; and they say also that
each was to gather no more than a prescribed measure
according to the number of his household, and if any
gathered more, it stank and became corrupt. Nay, and
among these Christians (who are firmly persuaded of
the exact truth of all this ancient fable) I have heard
it said that this bread of Moses—or manna, as they call
it—had this marvellous virtue, that to several people it

had several tastes, according to that which each desired, so that to one it became as it were flesh of kids, to another of sheep, to another grapes, to others figs, and so on. Now believing that Moses wrought so great a portent, these Christians are well nigh constrained to believe also that Christus wrought no less; else were their Christus inferior to Moses.

"And indeed having of late turned over the histories of the Jews—for they have been translated into Greek, though of a very barbarous and corrupt dialect—and having there read of innumerable portents; the sun and the moon stayed by human voice; asses made to speak with the voices of men; rivers dried up by being smitten with a rod; city walls cast down by the sound of trumpets; iron made to float; water brought out from a rock; chasms caused to open in the earth; chariots of fire wherein prophets ride aloft; pillars of fire to give light to the faithful by night if there were no moon; flames of fire called down from heaven by the word of a prophet to light his sacrificial fire or to consume his enemies; I have been filled with amazement that there are so few marvellous relations in the Tradition about Christus. For example, the ancient books of the Jews contain two accounts how prophets raised up them that were dead; but the Tradition has no such relation except one concerning a little child who had but a few minutes been pronounced dead, and in whom (doubtless) the life was not extinct. Concerning this matter I myself heard a dispute between a Jewish Rabbi and certain Christians; to whom the Rabbi affirmed that Christus must needs be inferior to the prophet Elisha because Christus had only raised up a little child whose

breath had scarce departed from her body, whereas
Elisha, even when dead, by the mere holiness of his
tomb had given life unto a man that had been many
hours dead, when he was now being carried out for
burial. Hereat the Christian was manifestly at a stand.
However, he made shift to reply that it was reported
in the church at Ephesus, that Christus had raised up
a man that was dead, and carried out to burial. But
the Rabbi rejoined that, 'even if that were true, it
would but prove that Christus was equal to Elisha, not
that he was superior; for if he had been superior he
would have gone beyond Elisha and have raised up
some one that had been dead and buried three or four
days; for during three days the angel of life is still
present with a man, but on the fourth day he fleeth
away.' To this the Christian had naught to reply, but
growing angry he declared that Moses and the Prophets
testified concerning Christus that he was indeed the
Messiah; and 'if the Jews would not believe Moses
and the Prophets, neither would they believe though
one were raised from the dead.' Thus the conference
broke up, but methinks the Christians were somewhat
perturbed in their inmost hearts that they had no
relation to bring forward of some dead man who had
been raised from the tomb by Christus, after he had
been some days buried; and methinks, before many
years, some such relation as this is like to find a place
in the traditions of the sect, and I marvel that it has
been delayed so long.

"Many other relations of portents (especially concerning the birth and the manifestation of Christus) are
current in the supplement—if I may so term it—which

is made by the talk and common speech of the Christians, and diversely in diverse churches ; but I know not
if any other portent be contained in the Tradition,
except it be one, which is as it were half way between
the Tradition and the Supplement, not of equal weight
with the former, but more commonly reported than the
latter ; and it is clearly a misunderstanding of an
allegory. You must know then that in the sacred
books of the Jews it is customary to speak of both
men and nations as trees, either a vine, or a cedar,
or an oak, or an olive, or bramble, as the intent may be,
to represent severally fruitfulness, or protection, or
strength, or prosperity, or peace, or a malign disposition. It seems therefore that Christus was wont to
compare his own nation to a barren fruit-tree, and
especially to a fig-tree making a great show of leaves
but bearing no fruit ; and on this theme he was wont to
utter divers allegories ; one, how the gardener prayed
the Lord of the orchard to spare the tree for three
years, but after the third year, if it were still
barren, then to cut it down ; and a second allegory
in a higher strain, how the Lord looked down from
heaven upon the tree which he had planted, and
behold, it had abundance of leaves, and he came to it
seeking fruit and there was none ; and then he sent a
spirit of destruction on the tree, commanding that no
fruit should henceforth grow on it, and the tree withered
beneath the breath of the Lord, and on the morrow it
was dead even to the roots. This allegory therefore, as
it seems to me, the Christians, mis-construing and supposing the Lord to be Christus himself (for they
commonly call him 'Master,' 'Lord'), have imagined

to be no allegory, but fact, wrought by Christus himself upon an actual fig-tree; and some even add the place where the deed was done, and other minute matters, after the manner of the growth of such relations.

"I would gladly have added some words concerning the rising of Christus from the dead, but the merchant by whom you will receive this, being now about to set forth, and the messenger no longer able to wait, I must defer what more I have to say to a second letter. Farewell."

§ 8. OF THE RISING OF CHRISTUS FROM THE DEAD.

"ONESIMUS TO ARTEMIDORUS, HEALTH.

"The Tradition, as I have said before, is silent concerning the rising of Christus from the dead; but in divers churches divers manifestations are reported; concerning which I questioned Simeon, asking him whether he himself had spoken with any that had seen Christus risen from the dead. He said, 'Yes, assuredly, with at least ten persons, of whom one was Paulus, to whom Christus appeared ten years after his death.' Then I questioned him whether these men had touched Christus, or only seen him. He made reply that they had seen him but not touched him. Then I asked him how they that saw him knew that it was he indeed, and no phantom, or perchance some evil spirit deceiving them. He made reply that Christus had showed unto them his hands and feet, bearing the wounds of the cross; and further, that phantoms appear not to many

assembled in one place, but only to solitary persons,
whereas Christus had appeared oftentimes to large
numbers of his disciples. He said also that it was
currently reported that Christus had suffered one of his
followers, who doubted, to touch his side ; and that he
had eaten in the presence of many ; and that he had said
'Handle me and see that I am not a bodiless demon';
but all these things, he confessed, were not in the
Tradition. Also, in answer to my further questioning,
he said that no enemy of Christus had seen him after
death, nor had any save those that loved him most
dearly ; nor had any been converted to the side of
Christus by thus seeing him, save only one, namely that
same Paulus, about whom I have more than once made
mention, who, about ten years after the death of
Christus, while grievously persecuting the church, and
after he had slain many of the Christians, had suddenly
been changed from an enemy to a friend, by seeing
Christus and hearing words from him.

"The sum of all seems to be that the body of Christus
was not indeed raised from the grave—for that were
against all course of nature ; and besides, if it had been
so, why was the Tradition silent on the proofs of so
great a wonder?—but that some kind of image or
phantasm of the mind represented him to his followers
after his decease. And musing often on the matter I
have called to mind how many relations are current of
the apparitions of the deceased, and how they may be
explained according to nature. For after looking
intently on the sun, the eye, being closed, sees an image
of the sun floating through the air ; and methinks in
somewhat the same fashion those followers of Christus

who best loved him, and to whom he was as the sun and
brightness of life, suddenly finding themselves bereft of
him and in the darkness of sorrow, might perchance—
even in the course of nature—receive an image of him
so imprinted on their minds that even the eye itself
might be enslaved to the mind's desire, and be impressed
with the same image. Still the marvel is that it appeared
not only to many at once—which, if the influence were
more than commonly powerful, might possibly come to
pass—but even to an enemy, namely Paulus, which
cannot be so easily explained.   However, I have no
other answer to this riddle ; and yet of late I have pondered for hours together on the answer, wandering as
it were in a labyrinth of questions and riddles and
problems, and sometimes catching a clue, and then losing
it, and as far as ever from the truth.

" But whatever be the answer, these Christians are of
a certainty rather deceived than deceiving others ; for no
one can have had to do with them, as I have, without
perceiving that they are altogether devoted to virtue.
And this indeed is the marvel of marvels, how this
Christus should have had the power to turn so many
thousands of souls to virtue, being many of them base
and vile and given to all vice, and most of them of the
common sort with no natural magnanimity or nobleness,
and all, with few exceptions, unlearned and illiterate.
Yet even this ill-ordered and confused rabble, Christus
hath been able so to transmute and temper and purify
that, out of so many thousands, there is scarce one that
would not be willing to lay down his life, I say not
merely for the name of Christus himself, but even for
his ' brethren,' as he calls them, that is to say, the

cobblers and water-carriers and camel-drivers who sit beside him in the synagogue.

"And this brings me to your last question, what it is in this religion of Christus which naturally draws the common people to it ? Now were I to reply that it is the hope of blessedness or the dread of punishment after death, you would reasonably rejoin that these hopes and fears are held out by other religions, yet have little strength to prevent evil doing. And were I to give as reason the great concord which binds all these Christians together, you would no less reasonably ask me whence comes this same concord ? Lastly, were I to add (for this is indeed one reason) that the common people are drawn by the power which these Christians possess (although it is but in the course of nature) to cure certain diseases suddenly by working on the imaginations of men, still Artemidorus would be dissatisfied and would inquire, whence came this power ?

"Wherefore, although sorely perplexed and more perturbed than might perhaps become a student of philosophy, I confess that I can allege no other cause for the power of this Christian religion than Christus himself, that is to say, some kind of influence arising from the memory of Christus which he seems to have transmitted to his first disciples, and they to others, and so on till at last a very great multitude is infected with it, and seems likely to infect many more. Now if you ask me what plan of philosophy I have discovered in the Tradition, or what sayings of Christ lead me to attribute so great a power to his influence, I must answer that as the Tradition is not written, I have not been able to write down more than a few sentences of it, nor indeed have I had leisure for this till now, for I gave all my mind at first to the inquiry concerning the general tenour of the doctrine of the Christians. Nevertheless some few sayings of Christus which I have set down, ring again and again in my ears like some spell or incantation not to be forgotten, as if they would almost persuade me contrary to sense and reason that he was indeed a purifier of the human race.

"How greatly is the mind perplexed when it compares Christus with other philosophers! Must we not suppose Socrates, must we not deem Pythagoras, superior by far to this Christus? And yet who would die for the name of Pythagoras or Socrates? Or perhaps the merit is not in the man himself, but in some secret art which he has discovered, or happened on, by chance, of uniting men together and implanting in them the love of well-doing. Of such an art I sometimes think I have discovered signs in those sayings of Christus which have come to my knowledge. But when I have studied them more fully I will write to you further on this matter. Farewell."

§ 9. HOW ARTEMIDORUS BADE ME CEASE FROM FURTHER INQUIRY.

Being somewhat alarmed by my last letter (so he confessed to me afterwards) lest I should not only permit Philemon to join himself to the Christians, but also become a Christian myself, Artemidorus wrote to me as follows, more vehemently than became a philosopher.

" ARTEMIDORUS TO ONESIMUS, HEALTH.

" If I bade you make further inquiry concerning the mad doctrines of this mad leader of madmen, I do so no longer. He who converses with lunatics more than is fit is in danger to become himself infected with their insane delusions.

" Besides, what possibility is there that you should attain to the truth ? What aids have you, what instruments ? There are none. No witnesses, no written documents, no regard for truth, no power of reasoning, no faculty of distinguishing things in the course of nature from things against nature. Amid such a chaos you are fighting against error with your hands tied. Cease then, I beseech you, from your vain attempt to build where there is no foundation. But do your utmost to induce the worthy Philemon to return home with all speed, lest he be entangled in the cobweb of this imbecile superstition ; and lest perchance even Onesimus at last, by frequent converse with these miracle-mongers and forgers, suffer his regard for truth to be so far blunted that he himself may be tempted to gloss over and excuse their impostures."

§ 10. HOW I STUMBLED AT THE THRESHOLD OF THE DOOR AND WENT NOT IN.

I take shame to myself that I was not in any such danger as Artemidorus supposed, of becoming a Christian at this time. Had I, indeed, been enabled

I

to pursue the study of the words of the Lord Jesus,
perchance having been thus led to know him I might
have entered into the fold at once and so have been
spared much misery. But it was not so to be. For,
on the very day that I wrote the last letter to Artemidorus, it pleased Philemon to set out suddenly for
Jerusalem, nothing contenting him but that we should
visit the Christians, as he said, in the place which was
the centre and source of the sect. Now those disciples
with whom we conversed in the Holy City were of the
straiter sect of the Jewish Christians, all of them maintaining that it was fit to come into the Church by first
accepting the Law of Moses, and that the uncircumcised,
albeit Christians of a certain sort, were inferior in righteousness to them that had received circumcision. And
they spoke against Paulus and all others that denied
the need of circumcision, saying that Paulus was no
safe guide but a teacher of heresy.

In part the narrowness of these brethren, in part the
newness of the sights which I saw in Jerusalem, and in
part also the fear that I had, lest by becoming superstitious I should fall below the rank of a philosopher
and lose the esteem of Artemidorus, caused me to
harden my heart against the promptings of the Holy
Spirit which would fain have led me to the Lord Jesus.
But, in spite of all my efforts, certain of the words of
the Lord (both then and for many months afterwards)
kept coming to my mind, and in particular these :
"There is more joy in heaven over one sinner that
repenteth than over ninety and nine persons that need
no repentance," and again, "Come unto me all ye that
are weary and heavy-laden and I will give you rest" :

and there were times when these last words so fascinated me, and I felt so weary of myself and such a longing for the peace which he could give me, that I went near to calling aloud unto him "Verily I am weary and heavy-laden, I will come unto thee, O Lord." But the cares and pleasures of this world choked the good seed so that I could hear no more of the sayings of the Lord, and strove to forget such as I had heard. Hence it came to pass that my next letter to Artemidorus (though I had not yet received his message of warning) breathed not a syllable of any desire to become a Christian.

"ONESIMUS TO ARTEMIDORUS, HEALTH.

"O for an hour of Antioch or Colossæ! Never before had I understood how much of the joy of life we owe to the Muses till I came hither, where the Muses are despised. Here are no temples (save one) no processions, no dances, no games, no chariot-races, no plays, no pictures, no statues, no libraries; the very air breathes dulness and superstition. If one brings a statue into these streets it is sacrilege; and they shrink from our poems and songs, our literature and our very language, as if it were a sin to be a Greek. And then the hideousness of their temple, which during their festivals so recks with the multitude of slaughtered sheep and oxen that it resembles a kind of shambles! Never may I again see a whole nation offering sacrifice as it were wholesale! Even now I cannot forget the shrieks of so many ten thousands of victims, and the reek of the burning fat and all the ill savour of so many worshippers thus pressed together—and all this in a barbaric building, with not so much as a single statue to adorn it, nothing but eternal grape-clusters and stars and the like, all bedaubed with gold in true eastern fashion for ostentation's sake. Ostentation everywhere, beauty nowhere! O for an hour of Colossæ or the pettiest Greek town in Asia, to relieve the staleness of this Jerusalem, surely the weariest and dullest of dull places!

"But I am like to forget the occasion which caused me to take up my pen, and which indeed (together with the suddenness of the journey hither) has for the time driven out of my mind all thought of the Christians. You must know then that, ten days ago, I beheld for the first time a battle, if battle it is to be called, where one side kills and the other is killed. It was after this manner. Coming to Jerusalem and having now accomplished about half of the journey between the city and Jericho, we, being mounted on dromedaries, overtook a great multitude of mixed folk journeying on foot, four or five thousand or more, as I should judge, some with swords, some with spears, some with bows, but not a few unarmed or bearing nothing save pruning-hooks and mattocks. Making our way with much ado through this motley multitude (who would not have suffered us to pass, being Greeks, had there not been with us certain priests that were going up to the Temple) we found that this rabble called itself an army, and that they were following a certain prophet, whom I saw, but I did not rightly understand his name; only thus much, that he was from Egypt, and that, being able to work all wonders, he had promised them that he would take Jerusalem and destroy the Romans in

one day. And what think you was the prophet's plan ?
There is a mountain called Olivet on the eastern side
of Jerusalem. Hither the multitude was to journey,
and here to take their stand. Thereupon the prophet
was to lift up his hands in prayer; the walls of Jerusalem (even as the walls of Jericho in old days were
cast down by the sound of trumpets) were in like
manner to fall to the ground ; and the faithful would
rush in and slay every Roman with the sword. Heard
you ever the like, for simple credulity and self-conceit ?
And then to listen to the babbling and boasting of
these illiterate peasants ! What great things they
would do when they had smitten the Romans ! How
the prophecies should be fulfilled, and how they would
rule over the Gentiles and break them in pieces like a
potter's vessel ! How they would cut the throats of
every Samaritan, and destroy the temple ·in Gerizim,
and be avenged on Edom ! Never, never before have
I felt better content that the whole world is under the
firm and just dominion of Rome !

"However you shall hear how the Romans de-
spatched this business without much delay. Having
gladly left these dangerous companions, and hastening
up the steep road, we had not gone twenty furlongs
before we met a squadron of Roman horse, blocking the
road ; but after questioning us, they suffered us to pass
up to a village named Bethany. We soon came to a
winding place in the road, which, being very high up,
commanded a view of all the road below. Thence
looking down we saw the helmets of the horsemen in
an ambush, in a valley on the northern side of the road,
and we could hear the multitude (though we saw them

not by reason of the winding of the road) with psalms
and shouts, and without any order or discipline, coming
up the hill; and soon their vanguard (if vanguard it
could be called where all was unguarded) would have
passed by the mouth of the valley so that the Romans
could cleave the rabble in two parts whenever it pleased
them. Soon afterwards the trumpet rang echoing through
the hills, and anon we saw the helmets and swords all
flash together, and then such a crying for mercy, such a
shrieking and clamour, as made me stop my ears for
horror; and we hastily turned away towards Bethany.
But we were still some furlongs distant from the
village when the Romans overtook us, their arms and
armour all dripping with blood, goading before them
many hundreds of captives fettered together; and on
the morrow, near the western gate as I went out of the
city I counted no less than a hundred crosses.

"Most gladly do I again open this letter to add that
we purpose with all speed to leave Jerusalem, and to come
to Ephesus. Hereto Philemon is moved, not so much
by the unquiet times here, as by a letter announcing
that Apphia is sick; for whose sake I am truly sorry,
and I beg you to join with the worthy Evagoras (whose
zeal is greater methinks than his knowledge in medicine)
that she may be restored to health; but for Philemon's
sake I rejoice, for assuredly a month's sojourning in
Jerusalem would no less draw him to the Jews than it
would drive me from them."

On the morrow we left Jerusalem and came to Cæsarea
Stratonis; and then to Sidon and so home, as I shall
recount hereafter. And all this while I remained still
an unbeliever, outside the fold of the faithful.

But even so must it needs have been, O Lord. For to thee none draweth nigh through weighing of probabilities, no, nor through belief in thy mighty works, nor through trust in traditions concerning thy birth and rising again ; but it is through Love of thee and Trust in thee alone that thou art embraced ; for thou art Love, and by thee alone is the heart of man made capable of thee. Wherefore it pleased thee in thy mercy that I, in seeking to find thee should not find thee, to the intent that afterwards in not finding thee I should find thee. For now, I reasoned, I examined, I sought ; yet I found not. But afterwards, I reasoned not, I examined not, I sought not ; yea, I fled from thee that I might wander in the wilderness of sin; but even there didst thou meet me and through thy love mine eyes were opened ; and I could not choose but know thee to be my true Shepherd, and when thou didst call me by name I could not choose but come.

THE END OF THE THIRD BOOK

THE FOURTH BOOK

§ 1. HOW WE CAME TO ATHENS.

LOOSING from Sidon we were driven by violent winds to the Chelidonian isles. There the Pamphylian sea divides itself from the Lycian; and the floods, meeting several ways and breaking against the promontory, swell into terrible billows rising higher than the cliffs. But when we were now in great peril of our lives, the Lord had mercy on us. For he sent a star which, seeming to settle upon our top-sail, by a left-hand course directed our vessel again into the sea, just when it was ready to be dashed upon the cliffs. I had often before heard speak of these marvellous stars, but never yet had seen them; and although Artemidorus had taught me that they were no gods but mere effects of causes according to nature, yet, in such extreme peril, being filled with thankfulness for our deliverance, I could not but join myself with the mariners and the rest of the crew in doing worship to the twin-gods. That very night— having often before of late had visions of a man seated on the clouds and encompassed with brightness—there came to me another such vision, but of more than usual

splendour, and he beckoned to me and said that the
stars had been sent by him, and not by these twin-gods
whom I had ignorantly worshipped. But I shook off
the dream as being a mere phantasm of the night, not
knowing that it was from the Lord.

Escaping from the peril of the seas, we sailed through
the Arches, and thence were driven onwards, not
however to Ephesus, whither we desired to have come,
but to Piræus. There, owing to the sickness of Philemon, we spent some days, during which I lodged in
the house of Molon the rhetorician; and when at last
my master returned to Colossæ, I persuaded him to
suffer me to remain at Athens for a while, that I
might study rhetoric and attain the true Attic pro-
nunciation and idiom, so that I might be the more
useful to him as amanuensis and secretary. But
I had other reasons for desiring to remain. For
besides the delights and novelties of the city—which
were all new to me because I had not been able to
persuade Philemon to spend more than two days there
when we last came to Greece to visit Lebadea—I had
already conceived a love for Eucharis, Molon's only
daughter. But, of this, more hereafter. Meantime it
chanced that Philemon, returning to Colossæ, much
infected with the superstition of the Christians (as
Artemidorus termed it), had caused the latter to suppose
that I also was in the same condition of mind; which
(to my shame be it spoken) was far from the truth.
However, Artemidorus taking it to be true, and being
sorely incensed against me, wrote the following letter
which I will here set down, being the last I received
from him on this matter.

§ 2. HOW ARTEMIDORUS REBUKED ME, SUPPOSING THAT I WAS IN DANGER OF BECOMING A CHRISTIAN.

" ARTEMIDORUS TO ONESIMUS, HEALTH.

" So Onesimus thinks it possible to reconcile philosophy with the vilest and falsest of superstitions. Come now and let me demonstrate to you, if your ears are not yet altogether stopped against the truth, 1st, the blasphemy and absurdity of your new religion, 2nd, the uselessness of it, 3rd, the self-conceit of it, 4th, the uncertainty of it, 5th, the folly and puerility and degradation of the man who stoops his neck to the yoke of it.

" To begin, then, it is blasphemous. For it teaches that the Supreme God has sent down his only son in the shape of a man to deliver men from sin. What! are we to suppose that the Son of the Supreme can be made like unto a mortal ? As if a convention of frogs around a puddle should croak among themselves debating which is the greater sin, and should say, ' Behold, the Supreme God has sent down his only son, in the shape of a frog, verily born of a frog, to deliver all the race of frogs from their iniquities ' ; or as if a number of worms should examine their souls and say, ' Alas, alas, we are fallen away from the divine image of the Supreme ; and therefore our Father in heaven hath sent unto us his son made in the image of a worm.' Away with this impiety of likening the Architect of the universe to sinful frogs and self-introspective worms ! For if there be a god—which I do not myself believe, but if there be one—doubtless he is as little like a man as like a frog or a worm ; but infinitely superior to all his creatures, and transcending all their knowledge.

" But sin forsooth is a terrible evil, and the usefulness of this new religion consists in this, that it is to ' take away *sins* '! Which of the Greek or Roman philosophers, of any note, has recognised this absurd fiction of *sin ?* It is a mere Jewish phantasy, unknown among other nations, except where it may have been insinuated by these vagrant proselytisers into the minds of a few women and children or imbecile dotards. Error there may be ; but sin cannot be, whether there be gods or not. For if there be no gods there can be no sin ; and if there be gods, who made all things, it is inconceivable that they should have made sin. Nor, if sin had any existence, could it be increased or diminished. For all rational people know that there neither were formerly, nor are there now, nor will there be again, more or fewer evils in the world than have always existed ; the nature of all things, and the generation of all things, being always one and the same. And whereas these Christians profess, ' We were sinners by nature, but the All-Merciful hath changed us '—they ought to be taught that no one even by chastisement, much less by merciful treatment, can effect a complete change in those who are sinners by nature as well as by custom. Hence this boast of removing sins is an imposture, and the religion that makes the boast is useless. Moreover what an insult is it to their superior god that these men should admit that he made them after a certain pattern and then changed his mind and desired to remake them ! Or else they are forced to introduce a certain Satan, who by his devices, perverted men forsooth from the divine image,

and so for a time overcame the superior god. But it is
clear, even to a blind man, that a superior god, overcome, though but for a time, by an inferior god, is for
that time, no longer superior, much less Supreme and
All-Powerful. Therefore your religion is proved to be
not only useless, but also blasphemous.

"In the third place, mark the impudence of it and
the self-conceit. For admitting that the superior god
could send his son as a man, can we possibly believe
that he would send him as a Jew, and not as a Greek,
or as a Roman, or as a man of no particular nation? I
have heard you laugh at Zeus in the comedy when he
wakes up after his day's debauch and despatches Hermes
to the Athenians and Lacedæmonians to complain that
they curtail his sacrifices and keep him on short
commons. But why do you not laugh at your own
superior god who, awakening after the slumber of many
thousands of years, despatches his son to one single
nation, and that the smallest and vilest and most contemptible upon earth? Moreover consider how exacting
and impudent is your religion beyond all others. Heracles, Asclepius, and Romulus, claim not to be the only
children of god, but leave room for others also. And
how many others! Worship, if you will, him who was
put to death upon the cross, but set not yourselves up
above the Getæ who worship Zamolxis, or the Cilicians
who worship Mopsus, or the Acarnanians who pay
divine honours to Amphilochus, or the Thebans who
do the same to Amphiaraus, or the Lebedians who (in
company with you yourself) pay reverence to Trophonius. For how is your Syrian saviour better than the
Theban, or the Cilician, or any other of the host of his

rival saviours? Nay, he is inferior, if we are to trust that which is reported concerning him and them by the followers of each. For Christus did but shew himself to men in times past, whereas these others, if you are to believe those who worship them, are still to be seen in human form in their temples, appearing with all distinctness.

"Next, as to the uncertainty of your new religion. Consider that just such another as your Christus, might come into the world to-morrow, and indeed such are continually coming forward in the market-place of every town in Asia, who are wont to say, ' I am God, or I am the Son of God, or I am the Divine Spirit. I am come to save you because ye, O men, are perishing for your iniquities ; ' and they persuade their dupes by promises or threats : ' Blessed is he who does me homage ; on all the rest I will send down eternal fire.' And then the followers of such an one in a confident voice call on us saying, ' Believe that he whom we preach is the Son of God, although indeed he died the death of a slave ; yea, believe it the more on this very account.' If these people bring forward a Christus every year, what is to be done by those who ' seek salvation ' ? Must they cast dice to decide to which of all these saviours they should pay homage ?

"But lest you should imagine that I am entirely dependent upon you for my knowledge of this sect, understand that both here, and in Hierapolis, and in Ephesus, I have made search concerning it ; and I am become an adept in their ridiculous jargon which speaks of ' the narrow way ' and ' the gates that open of

themselves'; and 'those who are being slaughtered
that they may live'; and about 'death made to cease
in the world'; and how 'the Lord doth reign from the
tree'; and of 'the tree of life' and 'the resurrection
of life by the tree.' All this talk of timber, forsooth,
because their ringleader was not only slain on the cross
of wood but also a maker of crosses, being a carpenter
by trade! And I suppose if, instead of being crucified,
he had been cast down a precipice, or into a pit, or
hanged by the neck, or if, instead of being a carpenter
by trade, he had been a leather-cutter, or a stonemason
or a worker in iron, then these absurd people would
have exalted to the skies a 'precipice of life,' or a 'pit
of resurrection,' or a 'cord of immortality,' or a 'stone
of blessing,' or a 'sacred leather.' What child would
not be ashamed of such babble as this!

"And this brings me to my last point, the shame and
disgrace that any philosopher must needs bring both
upon himself and upon philosophy, in stooping to so
puerile a superstition. If you know not this, at least your
new friends know it; for like the hyena, they seldom
attack a full-grown man, but for the most part children
or imbeciles; and to the best of their power they would
destroy reason saying (like so many Metragurtæ, or
Mithræ, or Sabbadii) 'Do not examine, but believe,'
'Your faith will save you,' 'The wisdom of the world
is evil, foolishness is good.' For this cause, because
they distrust the wise and sober, they prefer to decoy
the young, saying to them, 'If ye would attain to the
knowledge of the truth, ye must leave your fathers and
tutors and go with the women to the women's apartments, or to the leather shop, or to the fuller's shop,

that ye may there attain perfection.' And they retail
the sayings of these illiterate creatures as if they were
repeating the precepts of a Socrates: 'Simon the
fuller, or Eleazar the leather-cutter, or John the fisher-
man affirmed this, or that.' I say nothing also of the
immorality of a religion, which asserts that God will
receive the unrighteous, if he humble himself, because of
his unrighteousness, but he will not receive the righteous
man who approaches him adorned with righteousness
from the first. All these immoral theories, these lies,
and myths, and vile superstitions, are taught by the
Christians; and taught in the name of whom? Of one
who died as a slave after being deserted (according to
their own confession) by his most devoted followers.
And taught for what cause? Simply because a phantom
of him was seen after his death by a half frantic woman
and some dozen of his other companions who conspired
together for the purpose of deception. For my part, if
I must needs give a reason why this most absurd
religion attracts the multitude, I should say that it is
because the multitude in their inmost heart, prefer
falsehood to truth; and if I desired a new proof that
the world is governed by chance, or by fate, and not by
gods, I should discern it in the growth of this pernicious
superstition. Farewell and return speedily to thyself."

§ 3. OF MY REPLY TO ARTEMIDORUS.

I was astonished at the passion of his letter; and
though I was at this time neither a Christian nor likely
to become one, the injustice of my friend moved me

to say somewhat on the other side. My reply was to
this effect :

"ONESIMUS TO ARTEMIDORUS, HEALTH.

"Your vehemence surprises me. That I am not, and
shall not be, a Christian, must be clear from my previous
letters ; and that which I saw in Jerusalem has set me,
even more than before, against the Jews and all things
Jewish. Nevertheless, Artemidorus, I am far from
agreeing with you in all your condemnation of this
sect, which you seem to me, of set purpose to mis-
understand.

"And why do you vent dogmas on me ? How
know you that God is unknowable ? Were it not more
seemly for a philosopher to conjecture, and not to know,
where knowledge is impossible ? Why therefore should
a man be ashamed of conjecturing (in Plato's company,
I think) that the most perfect image of the Supreme
God is neither a frog, nor a worm, but a righteous man ?
And if man be at all like unto the Supreme Goodness,
then to be virtuous, I suppose is to be most like Him ;
and to be sinful is to be most unlike Him, a calamity
from which the Supreme Being Himself might naturally
desire to deliver mankind. However, I purpose not to
argue with you, for I cannot think that you yourself
believe in your own arguments, you who say that there
is no difference between sin and error ; or else I suppose
you will be consistent and blame your slaves equally if
Glaucus to-morrow commits theft or murder, and little
Chresimus says that five and six make ten.

"But one word concerning Christus himself. It is
but a few weeks ago that I heard you praise some

Roman or other for saying that we ought to choose out some noble life, to be as it were a carpenter's rule, by which we might straighten our own crooked life; why will you not praise me then, if upon finding this Christus to be a truly great and noble man, I make his life the rule of mine? But you reply, 'What do you know that is noble and heroic in him?' I will answer this question when we meet. Meantime let me say that though I know but little, it is more than enough to assure me (for your letter proves it) that you know nothing of him. Do not again suppose that I am likely to be a Christian. I am prevented from this by arguments, and by feelings still more powerful than arguments. Yet I have at least this advantage, Artemidorus, over you, that I have not yet allowed prejudice unphilosophically to blind my eyes to the truth, and that, after studying the life of Christus, the store of the examples of great men, which you yourself have exhorted me to treasure up in my heart, is now enriched by the example of one more man, both good and great, who has been able, according to your own avowal (perchance by the mere memory of his goodness), to convert fullers and leather-cutters and thieves and adulterers into decent citizens. Farewell and be thyself."

Although I spoke thus in defence of the Lord Jesus against the unjust reproaches of Artemidorus, yet was I very far from following the Lord, yea and perhaps all the farther that I had learned to talk admiringly of him as of a man on a level with Socrates and Pythagoras and others. For this kind of admiration took up that place in my heart which should have been filled by faith or trust, and left no room for them. Nor indeed was I

K

fit at that time to come to the Saviour because my eyes
were not yet opened to discern my own sins so as to
desire forgiveness; for the Saviour calls unto himself
the " weary and heavy-laden," but I was not yet weary
enough nor felt as yet the burden of my sinfulness.
And as for all those questionings of words, and traditions, and proofs, on which Artemidorus had set me,
they had taught me indeed many new things about the
Lord Jesus, and what other people believed concerning
him, but they had not taught me the Lord himself, so
that I might know him and love him and believe in him.
And when at last I began to draw nigh unto him and to
listen to his words and to meditate on them, behold, I
was called away from my instructors in Antioch, and
found afterwards no one like-minded who was willing to
set forth before me the very words of the Lord; but, on
the contrary, those of the brethren whom I met in
Jerusalem, cared not so much for the Lord as for the
Law of Moses, and drove me back from him when I
was desirous to draw near.

But why do I blame others when I was myself mainly
to blame? For I erred in the pride of my heart,
because I preferred the wisdom of the Greeks to the
wisdom of the Lord Jesus. Therefore didst thou, O
All-Wise, permit me to have my heart's desire, and
to serve the Greek Philosophy and to take that yoke
upon my neck, that I might prove it and know it,
whether that service were freedom indeed; and then
didst thou make me to pass through the dark valley of
affliction and didst suffer my wandering steps to stumble
and sink in the mire of wickedness, to the intent that
I might understand at last that the Wisdom of the

Greeks, for all the beauty of it and the pleasant sound of it, has no power to lift up a drowning soul from the deep waters of sin.

§ 4. OF EUCHARIS AND OF MY LIFE AT ATHENS.

Partly perhaps because Eucharis had lived with her father some years in Rome (where women lead not so sequestered a life as in Asia and at Athens) and partly for want of slaves, and because her mother had died when she was still in tender years, but also in great measure because of the ability of her mind and the depth and extent of her knowledge, Eucharis was rather as a pupil and companion to Molon than as a daughter and housewife. Her grace and beauty were more than equal to her learning; but that by which she drew my heart to herself was the gentleness of her disposition and the singular modesty with which she bore her many accomplishments. For though she was the flower of the house and the delight of her old father, yet did she never in any wise strain or try his affection by caprice or humours; yea rather, by reason of his poverty, and because he had scarce a slave whom he could call his own, she, to whom all should have ministered, was content and glad to minister both to the old man and to his friends, and this with all willingness and aptness, and yet so modestly and quietly that her coming was as noiseless as the sunshine, and we only knew that she had departed because the brightness seemed to have passed out of the chamber. When I became the old man's pupil, and in no long time the most intimate of

all his pupils, I obtained also a share in the pleasure of
her constant and familiar society; and, by degrees,
gaining the liking of my old tutor, I was helped to the
friendship of his daughter as well; and conceiving for
her an affection more intimate than friendship, I was
blessed at last, in return, with the certainty of her
undivided love.

The time had now come for me to put the kindness of
Philemon to the proof. From the first, he had treated
me rather as a son than as a slave; and, whithersoever
I had accompanied him, his carriage towards me had
always been such as to lead even those who knew that I
had once been a slave, to suppose that I had been long
ago emancipated. So I straightway wrote to him, telling him of my affection for Eucharis, and how I had
obtained the consent of Molon; and although I did not
venture to express the hope that he would make me free
at once, yet I besought him to make some promissory
emancipation (after the custom common in Asia) that I
might be free, on condition of serving him faithfully for
such period as he might please to name. This limited
request I made, rather for form's sake than as supposing
that he would stand upon conditions; for, remembering
his constant kindness, I looked for nothing less than
that he should wholly emancipate me at once. So
having sent off this letter I confidently waited for an
answer. Meanwhile I spent the time pleasantly in the
society of Eucharis, and Molon, and my companions in
learning; and I also took a great delight in the beauties
and antiquities of Athens.

The dreams and visions with which I had been visited
in Syria, and still more while I was tempest-tossed

sailing to Peiræus, soon ceased after I had been some few
days in the house of Molon. Each day brought with it
some new thing to see or hear. Though the streets of
Athens were not to be compared with those of Antioch,
being small and mean and narrow and not evenly built,
yet the public buildings and temples and theatres far
surpassed anything I had seen in any city of Asia ; and
as for the statues of the gods, they fairly ravished the
heart with their beauty. Moreover an edge was given
to every pleasure of sight by the hearing of some history
or legend ; how Demosthenes spoke in yonder place
of assembly, and in these groves and porches walked
Aristotle amid his disciples, or Plato taught, or Socrates
conversed, and here the tyrant was slain by Aristogeiton,
and there Pericles pronounced the funeral oration over
them that fell in the wars. Also, it so chanced that,
besides the daily sight of the palæstra and the attendance at the lectures, the Dionysian festival with its
customary plays came round while I was still at Athens.
I had seen plays before in Asia, yet these so enchanted
me with the beauty of the masks and choruses and the
marvellous skill of the actors that I was well-nigh
swallowed up with the glory of the drama ; and finding
occasion to be introduced to some of the actors, I frequented their society and heard them rehearse, and
sometimes myself practised recitations in their presence,
endeavouring to gain some knowledge of their art.
Amid all these engaging pursuits and delights, the time
passed as if upon wings ; and in the evening the greatest
delight of all, after the thousand pleasant distractions of
the day, was to talk with Eucharis and her father
concerning all that I had seen and heard.

We conversed together of all matters of art and letters and philosophy, and not seldom about my own life, the sorrows of the past, and what remained in the future ; and, as was natural, my travels in Syria were not forgotten. Yet about these I spoke seldom and sparingly, lest I should be forced to make mention of the Christians ; concerning whom at that time I was loth, I scarce know why, to say aught either for good or evil. But on the last day of our being together, some fate (as I then called it) decreed that I should no longer keep silence concerning them. It was after this manner. We had been conversing together, Molon and I, touching the Pythagoreans, by what bond of fellowship their society was in former times bound together, and by what cause that bond was broken. And thereupon I all unwittingly let fall some words (and repented as soon as they had been spoken) how a certain Christus, a Syrian, had founded a society, somewhat akin to the Pythagorean sect. Then Eucharis straightway would have me give some account of this Christus and his society ; and when I made as if I had not heard her, and afterwards would have put her off on some pretext —saying that the matter was not worth her hearing, or that I knew not much of it for certain, and the like— she looking steadfastly upon me and perceiving (I suppose) that I was in some confusion, besought me not to hide from her anything that I knew. So I, not finding any escape, began to describe to her the new Brotherhood or Commonwealth of Christus, as I conceived it ; and being carried onward I spoke more freely than I had intended, and summing up all that I had heard and some things that I had imagined, I described how

wealth and violence were to have no more power in the
world, and there was to be no more oppression, and sin
was to be taken away by forgiveness; and those that
the world counted great were to be cast down, and he
that was humblest and made himself least was to be
lifted up and, in a word, the most willing servant of all
was to be king of all; and all the nations of the earth
were to be as one Family, wherein Christus was to be
the Elder Brother, and the Father was none other than
the Supreme God; and how (as his followers averred)
he had foretold that he should be slain, yea, and declared that he would willingly die, but that, overcoming
death, he should manifest himself to his disciples after
death, and be constantly with them; and how his
disciples alleged that somewhat of this kind had indeed
come to pass, for that many of them had seen him in
apparitions by day or dreams by night; and lastly how
(whatever error else there might be among this sect)
this Christus of a truth appeared to have a marvellous
power to turn the vile and wicked to lives of virtue
and purity.

All this time Eucharis was rapt in thought; but I
was so intent on the matter of my discourse that I
noted not her countenance till I had well-nigh made an
end of speaking; but when I perceived it, I broke off,
saying that after all, it was but a Jewish superstition,
and that as for these apparitions of Christus, they were
but according to nature, if there were indeed any
apparitions at all. But Eucharis, still musing and
pondering, made no answer for a while, and at last
asked my opinion concerning all dreams and visions,
whether they came from the gods or no. I said, "No,

but from natural causes." Then replied Eucharis, "Yes, but if, as your Artemidorus says, the twin-stars that bring mariners help, come to us from natural causes, and yet you worship the gods that send them ; may it not also be that some dreams and some visions, though coming to us—like air and light and the fruits of the earth—in the common course of nature, may nevertheless be sent to us by the immortal gods ?" Then after a pause she added, "And you too, Onesimus, while studying the life of this Teacher, have you too been visited by him in your dreams ?"

Fearing to be engaged in any further discourse concerning this matter I rose up to bid Molon farewell, alleging the lateness of the hour ; but at that moment there came a knocking at the door, and presently appeared Chresimus, a slave of Philemon, bearing a letter for me, and with the letter this message by word of mouth, that the old man desired my most speedy return. I broke the seal at once, fearing that Philemon might be sick and nigh unto death. But the letter said not a word touching his health, nor did it give any answer to my request for freedom, neither 'yes' nor 'no,' only bidding me use all expedition to return because "something of great import" had taken place, concerning which he would gladly have speech with me before resolving further in the matter on which I had written to him. I wished to have tarried yet a few days in Athens, but Philemon's command was express that I should return on the next day, and that Molon should excuse me to my friends ; and, so saying, Chresimus went forth to make ready for our departure on the morrow. My

heart sank within me as I turned to bid farewell to
Eucharis, foreboding that I should henceforth live
without her, and that life without her would be death.
But she comforted me, saying that her memory must
always live with me, as mine with her ; and that we
must take hope as our common friend ; and clasping
round my neck a little amulet which, I was ever to
guard with the token of my brother Chrestus, " On
thy brother's gift," she said, " there is written TRUST,
and on mine there is HOPE ; and with trust and hope
we must needs do well ; for as to love we need no
assurance " : and with these words she bade me her
last farewell.

§ 5.   HOW I RETURNED TO COLOSSÆ, AND OF MY NEW LIFE WITH PHILEMON.

Even while Philemon embraced me on my return to
Colossæ, I perceived that he was marvellously changed.
Whereas he had been wont to wear on his countenance
an anxious and restless expression, now he was calm
and composed, with a cheerfulness that seemed to
spring (not as in the former days of his settled health
when I first knew him) from easiness and good temper,
but from some deep change in his nature. The suspicion that came into my mind on beholding him was
confirmed by the first words he uttered thanking the
Lord for my safe return ; and he immediately avowed
that he had become a Christian. Had he then, I asked,
submitted himself to the Jewish law ? No, he replied :
Paulus (the same of whom we had heard so much while

we were in Syria) who had admitted my master into
the sect of the Christians, had taught him that it was
neither needful nor fitting that he, being a Gentile,
should observe the laws of the Jews. When I asked
him what Artemidorus said, he bade me no more
mention the name of the Epicurean, whose society, said
he, I have for some time renounced. Of others of my
best friends he spoke in the same way, especially of
Epictetus, and Heracleas ; but he made mention of other
persons, mostly bearing Jewish names, and men either
not known to me or known to be illiterate and of the
common sort, with whom he hoped I should soon be
better acquainted ; "for they," said he, "belong to us
—as will you also, my dear Onesimus, in due time, I
hope and earnestly believe—and the brethren of Colossæ are wont to meet at worship at my house." My
thoughts being in a maze I thought to turn the
discourse by questioning him concerning friends and
kinsfolk, and I inadvertently asked whether his sister's
son—who was wont to come in from the country to
visit him each year—was intending to come to the
city at the forthcoming feast of Zeus ; but Philemon,
making some hasty sign to deprecate my speech about
the festival, added gravely and with authority that he
was assured I should no longer wish to take part in
the procession nor to go to any of the games or public
spectacles ; "for," said he, "it is not gods but demons
that preside over such shows." Much more he said on
this topic ; and I found that my last letter to Artemidorus (as the Epicurean had reported it, misconstruing
it, I suppose, in his passion) had caused Philemon
to think that I was already a Christian in heart.

But, concerning Eucharis and emancipation, not one word.

After waiting a long while to see whether he would be the first to speak, I reminded him of my request. He replied that he had a good will, yea and a sincere affection for me, and that he fully intended to emancipate me; but he did not think it fit that I should take to wife the daughter of a rhetorician and declaimer such as Molon, one who was by pursuit, as well as by disposition and nature, devoted to the worship of false gods. He had therefore arranged for me a marriage with the daughter of a very worthy citizen, Pheidippides the wool-seller, who, though not as yet one of the brethren, was most favourably inclined towards them, and who was quite willing to give me Prepousa to be my wife, if Philemon would emancipate me and give me a sufficient estate; and this, said he, I shall willingly do.

I was speechless with anger. But Philemon supposed my silence to be caused by excess of gratitude unable to find vent in speech. So looking affectionately on me he said there was no need of thanks, for that he was willing to do much more than this rather than suffer my soul to be ensnared at Athens. Then, in the same tone of authority in which he had spoken throughout (unusual in him and to me most unexpected and distasteful) he said that I was wearied with travel and had need of rest; wherefore he desired that I should consider myself excused from my attendance and retire to my chamber. When I went forth from his presence, a great gulf seemed to divide me from Eucharis, and from freedom, and from all hopes of a happy future.

As to the religion of the Christians I was no longer
drawn to it even so much as before. Had I not in
former time restrained Philemon from joining himself
to it? Had he not in those days acknowledged that
my understanding was superior to his, deferring readily
to my advice? And now was I to confess myself in
the wrong? Was I, slave-like, to bow to one inferior
to me in mind, because he chanced to be the master of
my body? How could I meet Artemidorus or Epictetus after so great a disgrace? On the morrow
therefore, when I attended Philemon in the library
and he asked me what I thought of his proposals,
adding that he trusted I should soon be willing to
receive baptism, I with difficulty restrained myself so
far as to answer merely that at present I was unwilling,
and that in any case I did not wish to marry Prepousa.
He was silent for a while and evidently displeased.
Then he exclaimed, "If only Paulus were in Asia at
this time, my hopes of thee would be speedily fulfilled."
But as I had been often present willingly at the
Christian meetings in Antioch, he said that I could
make no objection to be present at the meetings of
the brethren in his house where I should receive in-
struction which, he hoped, would soon induce me to be
baptized. About manumission as before, not a word;
but I perceived that it was hopeless to ask for it.

That some day I was summoned to attend one of
the meetings of the brethren, at which were present all
the slaves of Philemon, and not a few belonging to other
citizens, and many freedmen also, and some that were
free-born; but these, few, and for the most part Jews,
and not men of any breeding or education. And I,

being wilful at that time, and contemptuous of others, and given to think far too highly of myself, looked down upon these unlearned brethren, and stopped my ears against the truth and hardened my heart, scoffing within myself at their faults of speech and solecisms, and at the barbarous dialect of their Greek; and besides, to speak the truth, the discourses of Archippus, the son of Philemon, were too much upon the prophets and too little upon him to whom the prophets bear witness. So they moved me no more than the discourses of Lucius at Antioch, or even less. Yet once when Tatias—the man whom Philippus had raised from the dead—stood up and testified how all things had become new for him since he had believed in the Lord, and how darkness had passed away and all was full of light and joy and peace, and how the Lord Jesus was a friend that never failed in the hour of need; then for the time, spite of myself, my heart was touched and I seemed ready to stretch out my hands to the Saviour; but at that instant methought I saw Philemon watching me narrowly to see whether I was moved by the discourse, and thereon my heart rebelled again and I could think of nothing but the great gulf which my master placed between me and Eucharis. Thus was my heart still hardened against the truth.

Being in this condition of mind, I found my new life full of dulness and melancholy. Each day passed like the day before, and prepared for a morrow that should be still the same. The images of the gods had been removed from the hall and from the court-yard; no pictures, no songs, no garlands, no feasts, nor meetings of friends; our old acquaintance seemed to have

disowned us, and there were no longer any occasions for
discourse on arts, or letters, or philosophy. Even the
library had been despoiled of many of the best and
choicest books; the busts of most of the great poets and
authors had been removed; and Philemon employed
me during many hours of the day in transcribing, no
longer Euripides or Menander, but the Greek trans-
lations of the books of the Jewish prophets. The only
diversity in the circle of our daily life was that on
certain days the household met for worship; but if I
profited little from the first day of meeting, I gained
even less from those that followed; for then a certain
Pistus, a Paphlagonian slave, took a great part in the
prayers and discourses, especially when Archippus was
absent, and one might as well have hoped to gather
grapes from brambles as good from the words of Pistus.
If such was our life at home, it was vain to look for
change in life abroad. For I was no longer permitted
to go to any public spectacle; and the society of every
friend and acquaintance for whom I had any affection
was proscribed. In this solitude and dejection I looked
for counsel, but could find none. To Artemidorus,
being so near a neighbour, I durst not resort, for fear
lest Philemon should be informed that I had disobeyed
his prohibition, but I resolved that I would use the first
occasion to go to Hierapolis that I might there ask the
advice of the young Epictetus.

When I came to Hierapolis I found Epictetus keeping his bed and scarce able to move a limb. His master, he told me, had tortured him most cruelly, twisting his leg so as to force the bone from the socket; and the physician had declared that he would be lame for life. In answer to my execrations against all masters of slaves and Epaphroditus his master in particular, " Peace, my friend," said Epictetus, " our masters are becoming better and not worse ; and besides, ever since the sixth year of Claudius, we have a law in our favour. For before, if we were turned out to die in the streets, and then were impudent enough to recover, our masters could claim us back again ; but now the divine Claudius has decreed that if Death spare us, our masters shall spare us also. However my chief consolation lies not in the laws of Claudius, but in philosophy; for since you and I were last together, you must know I have become a philosopher. " Prithee," said I, " if slaves can indeed become philosophers, let me have some benefit of your philosophy ; for assuredly I have need of it. Did not your philosophy fail you when that cruel wretch so wantonly injured you ? " " Pardon me," replied Epictetus, " he did not injure me, as indeed I explained to him at the time." " Explain then to me," said I, " this most mysterious riddle." " I told him that he could not injure me though he would injure himself. Hereon he retorted that he would break my leg. I replied, ' In that case my leg would be broken, but what of that ?' At this he stared like a bull, and said that he would cut off my head. To that I rejoined, 'And when did I ever tell you that I had a head of such a kind that it could not be cut off?' Upon that he burst into a passion, threw me down, kicked me, and began to twist my leg. As he proceeded, I warned him and said, ' If you continue, you will certainly break it.' He continued ; and then I said to him, ' There, now my leg is broken ; but you have not injured me, but only my leg, and perhaps yourself.' "

All this seemed to me new and yet not new. Sitting down on the bench beside his pallet, I said, " Well, but, Epictetus, this differs not much from the philosophy of the Stoics or the Cynics." " I did not maintain," replied he, " that my philosophy was new. Nevertheless I do not perceive that it is very common in these parts." " You mistake," said I, " a great many in Hierapolis read Chrysippus, and not a few even in Colossæ." " Read Chrysippus," exclaimed my friend with a laugh. " Yes, read Chrysippus, but how many act Chrysippus ? Much as if we were to go to a wrestler, and say to him, ' Come, Milo, shew us how you can give your adversary a fall,' and Milo should reply, ' Nay, rather step into the next room, and feel the weight of my dumb bells.' " Then he turned affectionately to me and said, " It is not the object of life, my dearest Onesimus, to have read the hundred and forty volumes of Chrysippus, but to put the precepts of Chrysippus in use, and to set them before men in a brief form fit for use ; and this is what I am endeavouring to do." " Set them before me then," said I, " for Zeus knows that if you have any philosophy fit for use, I can find use for it.   What therefore is the foundation of your philosophy ? "

" The foundation," replied my friend, " consists in the distinguishing of things in our power from things not in our power.   The things that are needful are in our power, viz. justice, temperance, truthfulness, courage and the like ; but the things that are not in our power are not needful, such as wealth, beauty, reputation, health, pleasure, life, and the rest.   Many philosophers admit this in word, but do not carry it out in deed, partly because they talk much and do little, and being immersed in speculations are not ready for actions, when the hour for action is at hand.   But if a man have this foundation once solidly built within his heart so as to be able to base all his actions on it, from that time he will be perfectly free and do all things according to his own will.   Therefore make up your mind once for all what is your object in life ; what it is you want.   A dinner ? or to escape a whipping ?   Well, then, you will do your master's bidding to gain your dinner, or to escape a whipping.   But a philosopher will not do this, because he does not fear hunger, nor a whipping, nor any master.   ' What,' you say, ' must not a philosopher fear Cæsar ? '   No, for he does not fear the things that Cæsar can bring.   For, mark you, no one fears Cæsar in himself, but only the things that Cæsar brings with him, such as the sword, banishment, poverty, torture, disgrace.   But fetch me Cæsar here without his thunders and lightnings, and see how bold the veriest coward will be.   Why then should a philosopher fear Cæsar, since he has no fear of Cæsar's thunder and lightning ?

L

"Distinguish therefore between what you can and
what you cannot do, and in that knowledge you will
find freedom. If you are thoroughly persuaded in your
inmost mind that those things only are yours which are
really yours and which are needful to you, then you will
aim at nothing which you will not attain; you will
never attempt anything with any kind of violence to
yourself; you will blame no one, you will accuse no
one; nobody will ever hinder you from the accomplishment of your desires; in fine, you will never be subject
to the least regret. Take an instance. My leg, you
will observe, is inflamed, and it has certain sensations
which are called painful. Good: that is the popular
manner of speaking. But it is a mere imagination. My
inflamed leg does not hinder me from being honest, just,
and courageous; in other words from attaining the
objects of existence and the aim of all my desires.
Consequently I have accustomed myself to bear always
in mind that pain of this kind does not concern me and
is no real evil. For it is of the nature of things that
have no dependence on me. 'But you will be lame for
life,' say you. That is very probable, and indeed our
physician tells me it is certain. But what then? When
I am lame, my lameness will be an obstruction to my
feet in walking, but not to my will in doing what it is
inclined to do. It follows that sorrow and the signs of
sorrow such as weeping and groaning, are all the mere results of false conceptions and imaginations. What is mis-
fortune? Prejudice. What is weeping? Prejudice. What
are complaints, discontents, repining, fretfulness, restless-
ness? All so many forms of prejudice, and prejudice
moreover concerning things uncontrollable by the will.

He paused. " You have defined sorrow," said I, " and
how do you define death ? " " A mere mask," he replied.
" It has no teeth. Turn it on the other side and you
will find it does not bite you. It is a mere going away.
Life is as it were a feast. At birth God opens the door
to you, and says, ' Enter.' At death, the feast being
now ended, God opens the door to you once again and
says ' Depart.' Whither ? To nothing terrible. Only
to the source whence you came forth. To that which is
friendly and congenial : to the elements. What in you was
fire, goes away to the fire ; what earth, to earth ; what
air, to air, what water, to water. There is no Hades,
nor Acheron, nor Cocytus, nor Pyriphlegethon ; but all
is full of gods and divine beings. He who can think of
the whole universe as his home, and can look upon
the sun, moon and stars as his friends, and enjoy the
companionship of the earth and sea, he is no more
solitary nor helpless exile. Let death come to you
when he will. Can death banish you from the Universe ?
You know he cannot. Go where you may, there will
be still a sun, moon, and stars, dreams and auguries
and communications with the Gods."

I interrupted him. " You say there is no Hades ;
are there then no Elysian fields ? " " I do not know,"
replied he ; " but why seek any greater reward for a good
man than the doing of what is good ? After being
thought worthy by God to be introduced into His great
City, the Universe, so that you may discharge for Him
the duties of a man, do you still cry for something more,
like a baby for its food ? Do you need coaxing and
sweetmeats to induce you to do what is right ? Be not
like a bad actor that forgets the part assigned to him,

when he steps upon the stage. ' I was sent into this
world to play a part.' Well said, Mr. Actor; and what
part ? ' The part of a witness for God.' Good : repeat
your part. ' I am miserable, O Lord ; I am undone ; no
mortal cares for me ; no mortal gives me what I want.'
What babble is this ! Away with the fool. He has
forgotten his part ; hiss him off the stage.

" Or take another of my metaphors. God is your
general, and you must be to him a loyal, obedient
soldier, having sworn an oath of obedience, which you
will sooner die than break. Dost Thou wish me to live ?
I live. To die ? Then farewell. How wouldst Thou
have me serve Thee ? As a soldier ? Then I go cheerfully to the wars. As a slave ? I obey. Whatever
post Thou shalt assign to me, I will die a thousand
times rather than desert it. Where wouldst Thou that
I should serve Thee ? In Rome, or in Athens, or in
Thebes ? Thou art not absent from populous cities.
Or on the rock of Gyarus ? Thou wilt be with me even
there. Only if Thou shouldst send me to live where it
is no longer possible to live conformably with nature,
then, but not till then, should I depart, accepting as it
were Thy signal of recall."

Here he made an end, and I sat for some time silent.
His words were to me as a trumpet-blast arousing
within me a host of virtuous resolutions, which I at that
time mistook for virtuous acts, and thought myself
already an athlete or a hero ; even as a drunken man
supposes himself Heracles, or as the reader of the hundred and forty-three volumes of Chrysippus believes
himself to be a man of virtue. Presently I arose and
thanked him, saying that I went forth as it were to the

Olympian contest, to put in use the precepts of Epictetus my trainer.　He smiled, and as I went forth from
his chamber, he called after me, " Yes, but Onesimus,
for this contest you need not wait four years."

§ 7. HOW I TRIED THE PHILOSOPHY OF EPICTETUS.

Epictetus was right ; I had not long to wait for the
contest of which he spoke.　It began on the morrow,
and continued without intermission ; for day by day I
was constrained to be present at the meetings of the
Christians, and day by day Philemon questioned me
whether I had not now at last been persuaded, and
whether I was not willing now to be baptized.　However, I followed the advice of Epictetus, and said to
myself, " Truthfulness is in my power, but the goodwill
of Philemon is not in my power, therefore it does not
concern me, and I will not trouble myself about it."
But, in the evening of each day, when I perceived that
the breach was widening between me and my master,
and when I called to mind that it depended on him
whether I should be free or a slave, and united to
Eucharis or parted from her for ever, then my mind
misgave me that I could not honestly say, " His good-
will concerns me not."　Oftentimes I checked myself,
saying that I was placed in the Universe as a sentinel
by God, and that I must not neglect my post wherever
it might be ; but as often as these words came to my
memory, there came others also, namely that "if we
were placed by him where we could not live conformably
to nature, then we might accept this as the voice of a

trumpet, sounding recall and bidding us quit this life for another." And said I to myself, can it be considered living according to nature, that I should live in subjection to such a servitude as this? Or is it living according to nature, to be removed from all learning, just when I have been trained to use and enjoy it? and to live apart from all friends, consorting with none but slavish dispositions? and, in a word, having many faculties trained to noble uses, to be placed in a position where all those faculties must needs rust unused?

Meanwhile the conduct of Pistus widened the breach between my master and me and altogether envenomed my very soul against the faith. This man had been Philemon's secretary during my absence at Athens; and now, finding himself like to be supplanted, he began to alienate Philemon from me by sly insinuations, hints, letters unsigned in a strange hand, and sometimes also by open questions cunningly asked of me in Philemon's presence. As, for example, on the day when I had visited Epictetus, he asked me, in my master's hearing, whether Epaphroditus was in good health, he being the master of Epictetus, and a very dissolute man. When I said "Yes, as far as I knew," I could see from Philemon's countenance that he greatly disliked my going thither; and I at once explained that I had not gone to see, nor had I seen, Epaphroditus himself, but only his slave Epictetus, who was sick. Yet the cloud on my master's brow did not altogether vanish; and he did not forget it. For that same evening he took me aside, saying that it was time to have done with youthful passions and caprices, and had I considered his proposal—not about baptism, for he would not at that season make mention of higher matters—but concerning marriage, and was I willing to marry Prepousa? I said "No." Hereat he became very grave, saying that it was a very suitable match for me, and well fitted to keep me from evil courses, such as young men were liable to ; and he bade me think further of it and meantime to be more discreet what company I kept, for he disliked that I should so much as enter the house of such a one as Epaphroditus, though it were but to visit a sick slave. It was all in vain that I attempted (perhaps too obscurely, for I could not now speak freely with Philemon as in old days) to explain that I stood in need of counsel and that I had gone to Epictetus for it. "That is settled"—was all he had to say, before he dismissed me to my chamber. Only, as I was departing, he called me back, and asked me whether I had at least given up the thought of Eucharis. I said "No." To which he replied that he was very sorry for that, for he could not consent that my soul should be ensnared by such a marriage, and so long as I entertained that foolish passion it was not possible for him to entertain the project of emancipating me. So saying, he dismissed me to my chamber, speechless with passion. In this mood I took up my pen and wrote thus to Epictetus :—

"ONESIMUS TO EPICTETUS, HEALTH.

" I leaned on your philosophy, and it has proved a broken reed. No longer can I live under the insupportable yoke of my slavery here. Yet what am I to do ? I cannot live conformably to nature. ' Then die,' say you. And what then becomes of Eucharis, who would break her heart for my departure ? Your philosophy takes no account of wife, or children, or those dear friends who are second selves. Their happiness is not in your control ; and yet how can you be tranquil in their unhappiness ? Answer me that.

" One question more. A fellow here, a Paphlagonian, one Pistus, is poisoning Philemon's mind against me, drops notes, in a strange hand and nameless, accusing me of deceit, theft, frequenting brothels and all manner of impurity. His last stroke has been to persuade Philemon to forbid me from visiting you. I hate him, and intend to hate him. Does your philosophy allow of hate ?

" A third question. You say, We are soldiers and must die sooner than desert our post. But who shall go bail for our General, that he is not a fool or a knave, or anything but a name ? Looking on the battle-field of the Universe I see a conflict but the issue doubtful ; no signs of generalship, or at least of victory ; in one place joy, in three places sorrow ; pleasure here, pain there ; virtue sometimes prevailing, more often vice ; one master, twenty slaves ; animals preying (by necessity) on other animals ; men (by necessity or choice ?) oppressing other men ; everywhere conflict, the General nowhere. Read me these riddles, or be no Œdipus for me.

" Pardon me, dearest friend and guide, but I am beside myself with passion, anxious, not for myself but for one beyond the seas, who sits awaiting tidings from me and feels her life to be bound up with mine. Strong in your presence, absent from you I am most weak. Impart, I beseech you, some of your strength to one who sorely needs it."

§ 8. HOW I WAS ACCUSED OF THEFT BY THE DEVICES OF PISTUS.

At this time, and before I had heard from Epictetus, I received a letter from Eucharis. After some delay, vainly hoping to be able to impart more joyful tidings, I had written to her putting as bright a colour on the future as I could, but not concealing Philemon's strong objections and present refusal; and now I received her answer. It was inclosed in a letter from Molon, in which he spoke of his class and his pupils, and hoped that I was continuing my studies at Colossæ, entering also into details about his recent lectures; at the close of his letter he added that Eucharis was not in good health, and that he feared she was troubled in her mind, being infected with superstition. Her old nurse Thallousa affirmed that she had been fascinated by the evil eye; but he thought the mischief had been in part caused by certain women of her acquaintance, Christians from Corinth, who had brought to Athens some strange rites and doctrines of one Paulus, and who seemed to have disturbed her mind. However he trusted that her trouble would pass away when better tidings came from Colossæ. The letter of Eucharis was to this effect.

"Do not cease to hope, dearest Onesimus. If I grieve, it is because I seem to see thee grieving. Could I but know that thou wert hopeful, I also could be both hopeful and happy. Thallousa would fain console me, when I weep, by telling me sad stories of others who have loved and have been made sad by separation, but I am not so cruel as to be made happy because others are sad; so I seek comfort elsewhere. Dearest, when we were last together, some doubtful words fell from thy lips, questioning, methought, whether there be any Elysian fields such as the poets sing of. Yet does it not seem (this present world being so very full of sadness) that there must needs be some Isles of the Blessed, called by whatever name, where those whom hard fate has divided here, but whom the good gods must surely destine to be some day united, shall meet again never to be parted? Dearest Onesimus, dearer to me than my own life, what if we meet not again on this earth? May it not be that we shall meet elsewhere? Yet, even for this life, I still trust and hope; and do thou the like for my sake. To think of thee hopeless kills me. O dearest friend, sweet cause of my heart's most bitter sorrow, think not that I reproach thee because thy love is cruel. Sweeter, far sweeter, to mourn as I mourn for thy absence, than never to have known and loved thee. Farewell and hope on; and believe me faithful to thy love, whether I live or die."

At the end of the letter were added these words:

"I see I have ended my letter with a word of evil omen. Onesimus laughs at omens; but for my own pleasure I will avert the evil by repeating a former question. The visions concerning Christus that thou didst speak of, have they ever appeared to thee too in thy dreams? Because thou didst forget to answer this same question when I first asked it of thee, let this violet, which I now kiss, be my ambassador that thou forget not a second time."

While I sat with the withered flower in my hand, musing on Athens, seeing, as if before mine eyes, the little chamber in which even at that instant perchance Eucharis sat spinning, and Molon reading by her side, a message was brought to me by Pistus that Philemon desired to see me in the library; "and," said the Paphlagonian in a malicious tone, "you were best think of some subtle defence, for the old man knows what you have done.   But you will probably prefer to appease him by confessing."   The man's malice angered me, and I entered the room in some heat.   It soon appeared that a copy of the plays of Aristophanes was missing from the library.   Philemon was at that time reviewing his books with great exactness, destroying such as seemed unfit for a Christian household; and he had expressly enjoined on me not to take any of the works of the poets of the Old Comedy out of the library, and I had obeyed him.   But when this book was missed, Pistus had affirmed that he had seen me reading it in my chamber.   Understanding this I replied roundly that the Paphlagonian lied.   But Philemon bade me bethink myself whether unwittingly I might not have taken it from the library, being always fond of the works of that poet, and having in former times been accustomed to take freely from any part of the library such books as I desired; and he added that, of the rest of the household, very few could understand the book, being illiterate, and those who could have read it would not do so, because they had received the seal in Christ and belonged to the saints.   I could but repeat that I had not taken the book.   On this Pistus said, with a sneer, that, if that were so, the worthy Onesimus would probably be quite willing that his room should be searched. I at once assented; but scarcely had two slaves quitted the room on their quest, when the villainy of Pistus was revealed to me; and I turned and took him by the throat saying that, if the books were found in my chamber, the Paphlagonian had hidden them there. Hereat Pistus fell on his knees, making as if he were terror-stricken by my violence, and calling the Lord to witness his innocence. Philemon indignantly bade me desist; but his indignation became still greater when the two slaves returned bearing the missing volumes, which they had found it seemed, hidden under my couch. In the presence of all the slaves he ordered me to return to my chamber, saying that at first he had never thought to accuse me of stealing the books, but only of thoughtlessly or wilfully borrowing them, but now he knew not what to think. So I went back to my chamber under suspicion of being a thief; and entering I found on my table this letter from Epictetus.

§ 9. HOW EPICTETUS FURTHER EXPLAINED HIS PHILOSOPHY.

"EPICTETUS TO ONESIMUS, HEALTH.

"A bad performer cannot sing alone but only in a chorus. In the same way some weak-kneed folk cannot walk the path of life alone, but must needs hold somebody's hand. But if you intend to be ever anything better than an infant, you must learn to walk alone. It angers me to hear a young man say to his tutor, 'I

wish to have *you* with me.' Has not the fellow God
with him ? But, Onesimus, you are not willing to take
God as your guide in practice, though you profess to do
so in theory. For with your lips you say, ' O Lord,
suffer me to go straight on for twenty-five furlongs and
a half, and then to take the first turning to the left.'
However, let me attempt to answer your questions; but
not in order, for first I must shew you that whether
there be a good God or no, you must needs act as
though there were a good God or else you must die.
First then, that there is Demeter, is it not clear to all
those who eat of bread ? And that there is a Helios or
Apollo, is not that also clear to all who enjoy the sunlight ? Call the former Bread, and the latter Sunlight,
if you will; still there they are, and you must partake
of them and acknowledge them, as long as you partake
of the Feast of Life.

"But you complain that the Host of the Feast is
unkind or foolish, not making proper provision for his
guests. Foolish man ! Then why remain a guest ? Do
not be more foolish than children. When the game
ceases to please them, they say ' I will play no more.'
So do you, if the feast please you not, say ' I will feast
no more ;' and go. For remember the door is always
open. But if you remain at the Feast, do not complain
of the Host; for that is silly. Remember therefore
that if the Host intends you to remain as His guest, in
that case He has made all needful provision for you ;
but if He has not, that is a token that your way lies
towards the door.

"Apply this rule to yourself and her whom you
love. As it is better that you should die of hunger and

preserve your tranquillity of mind to the last gasp, than
that you should live in abundance with a soul full of all
disturbance and torment, so is it better that Eucharis
should die and you be in peace, rather than that your betrothed (or any else the nearest and dearest to you) should
live and you be in perturbation of mind. Nay, a father
ought rather to suffer his son to become undutiful and
wicked rather than himself to become unhappy. You
are not to say, ' If I chastise not my son, he will prove
undutiful ; ' but you are to prefer your own serenity of
mind to the dutifulness of a son and to all other objects ;
and the same rule holds as regards Eucharis. Thus and
thus only will you be always at peace, and able to
despise the worst of omens."

After this Epictetus fell to speaking in a more general
way about philosophy and philosophers, and of their duty
to the multitude ; of which some part I omit, but the
rest was to this effect :—

" But perhaps you say, ' The multitude has not this
knowledge of the folly of sorrow ; and if we bewail not
with them when they bewail, we shall seem to them
brutish, and be hated. Or how shall we explain our
theory to the multitude ?' For what purpose should
you desire to explain it to them ? Is it not enough that
you are convinced yourself ? When I was a boy at
Rome, as I remember, and when my master's children
came to me clapping their hands and saying, ' To-morrow
is the good feast of Saturn, did I tell them (think you ?)
that good does not consist in sweetmeats nor such things
as they desired ? Nay, but I clapped my hands too. In
the same way, when you are unable to convince any one,
treat him as a child, and clap your hands with him ; or

if you will not do that, at least hold your tongue.
When therefore you see a man groaning because he,
or his betrothed, is likely to be given in marriage to
another, first do your best to recover him from his evil
and mistaken opinion.   But if he will not be persuaded,
nothing hinders but you may pretend some sadness and
a certain fellow-feeling of his affliction.   Only have a
care that grief do not effectually seize your heart while
you think only to personate it.

"You see then that I forbid you sorrow either for
yourself or for others.   No less do I forbid you hate.
For why should you hate, or even be angry, with a
wicked man, a thief, say, or an adulterer ?   ' Because,'
reply you, ' they take from me that which I most dearly
value, my wealth or my reputation or the affection of
my wife.'   In other words they take from you those
objects which you love, and desire to excess, though
they do not depend on you.   But the remedy is to
abstain from loving these things to excess.   Always
remember also when any one injures you, as it is called,
that the cause of the injury is ignorance or erroneous
opinion.   For no one would commit a crime if he knew
that he was thereby destroying his own soul.   Through
erroneous opinions Medea slew her children and Clytem-
nestra her husband.   Why therefore hate a man merely
because the poor wretch is terrribly ignorant and is
doing himself the greatest of all injuries, while he
falsely supposes he is injuring you ?

"Bear in mind further that everything has two faces,
whereof one is endurable the other unendurable.   For
example, when your brother is injuring you, look not
upon him as an injurer but rather as a brother.   Even

if you cannot do this for your brother's sake, you must
do it for your own. For in all things you must consider
not your brother nor your brother's interests first, but yourself and your own serenity of mind. ' My brother '—perhaps you say—' ought not to have treated me so shamefully.' Very true ; so much the worse for him. But that is
his business, not yours, and you are not to injure yourself
on his account.   However he treats you, you must treat
him rightly.   For your treatment of him is in your
power, and therefore is your concern ; but how he treats
you, is not in your power, and therefore concerns you
not.   If therefore your enemy reviles you, try to think
well of him for not having struck you. ' But he has
struck me.' Then think well of him for not having
wounded you. ' But he has wounded me.' Then think
well of him for not having slain you. ' But I am dying
of the wound he gave me.' Then think well of him for
having opened unto you that door which the Master of
the Feast has appointed as your exit from His banquet.
Apply this rule to Pistus, and if he has poisoned
Philemon's mind against you, think well of him that he
has not yet poisoned your body itself.

   " But the former rule is the more important, that you
are not to set a value on the things that are beyond
your own control.   Does Fortune take things away ?
Laugh at her then.   When Philemon and his friends
deprive you of your wonted freedom, and take away
your books, your reputation, your prospect of marriage,
you must consider yourself before a tribunal of boys who
are mulcting you of knuckle-bones and nuts.   ' So
Epictetus makes light of love and marriage and the
bands of family affection.'   Not so ; he recognizes

them for the common people but not for Onesimus and Epictetus, nor for other philosophers in the present war of good against evil. For as the state of things now is, the philosopher should hear the trumpet sounding for all good men to make ready, like an army drawn up for battle in the face of an enemy ; and he should be without all distraction, entirely attending to the service of God.

"Finally, whatever betide, be not a slave. 'I must go to the ergastulum' says Onesimus. And must you go groaning too ? 'I must be fettered like a slave.' Must you lament like a slave too ? 'Marry Prepousa,' says Philemon, 'and become a Christian.' 'I will not.' 'Then I will slay you.' 'Did I ever assert that I could not be slain ?' That is the language that befits my Onesimus ; not to look at the spectacle of life like a runaway slave in the theatre, who shivers whenever any one touches him on the shoulder or mentions his master's name. Instead of swearing allegiance to Christus to conciliate Philemon, swear rather never to dishonour God who loves truth, nor to murmur at anything that betides ; for all things betide according to His will. At all times endeavour to listen to His voice ; for He accosts you and speaks to you thus : 'Onesimus, when you were at your lectures in Athens, what did you call death and imprisonment and all other such external things ?' 'I ? Things indifferent.' 'And what do you call them now ?' 'The same.' 'What is the aim and object of thy life ?' 'To follow Thee.' 'Go on then, boldly.'"

M

§ 10. OF METRODORUS AND HIS ADVICE.

I read and re-read the letter of Epictetus; but it
could no longer settle my doubts nor quiet my mind.
What was true in it seemed to be stale and useless,
namely, that each man was able to do whatsoever he
wished, provided that he wished only for those things that
he was able to do.   And again, what might have been
useful, if true, seemed not true, or at all events not
certain, I mean that the Master of the Feast was good.
For all that Epictetus had said came to this, that if we
remained as a guest at the Feast, each one was bound to
act as if the Master was good, or else to depart from the
Feast.   But why was a philosopher bound to suppose
something that might be false, or else to slay himself?
For, all the while, there might be no Master of the
Feast at all, but only a talk about Masters, and in
reality neither Master nor Feast, but only a kind of
scramble for sweetmeats.   Or else there might be not
one Master, but many, some good and kind, others bad
and unkind.   Or what if the Master were Himself good
but thwarted by His wicked servants so that the guests
were starved and not fed?   In that case might not the
guests fairly complain?   And to make believe that the
Master was perfectly good and wise (and all for the purpose of attaining for oneself calmness and tranquillity of
mind)—this seemed a kind of flattering of the Master
and deceiving of oneself, that was scarcely worthy of a
philosopher.

This peace and tranquillity of Epictetus, the more I
thought of it, the less I admired it.   For, in spite of

his denial, it seemed to loosen all love and friendship, as well as hate. How could I "preserve my serenity of mind" while I was reading the letter of Eucharis? Ought I to say to myself, "Whatever may betide Eucharis, I at all events shall be completely happy"? That seemed to me not possible; no, nor desirable. If Eucharis sorrowed, I felt that it would be sweeter for me too to sorrow than rejoice. Then again, as to hating, Epictetus would have me not hate Pistus for being bad, but speak well of him because he was not worse. Now this perchance might tend to tranquillity, but how could it be consistent with truth? For if a man steal from me one mina, am I to thank him for not stealing two? As well, when a man gives me one mina, abuse him for not giving me two! It is the duty of a philosopher neither to speak better of a man, nor to speak worse of a man than he deserves. Besides, Epictetus seemed to err in speaking of all wickedness and crime as merely caused by erroneous opinions, for to me such faults as slander, cruelty, and baseness, seemed altogether different, and fit to be differently regarded, from such a fault as an unskilful reckoner might commit in saying that six and seven make twelve. In all these matters Epictetus seemed to me (and indeed still seems) to go astray because he had wholly set his mind upon the attainment of an object which perchance the Master of the Feast does not intend His guests to attain in this world, I mean perfect and unchangeable serenity of mind.

Being in a great perturbation with all this conflict of thoughts, and inclining now more than ever to believe that there were no gods, I determined to disobey

M 2

the command of Philemon and to resort to my friend
Artemidorus that I might ask counsel of him. So I
went to him on the morrow, when both Philemon and
Pistus chanced to be absent from the city. But he had
gone on some business of law to Laodicea. However I
found in the courtyard of his house a certain friend of
Artemidorus, known also to me, one Metrodorus, whom
I believed (but did not for certain know) to hold the
same opinions as Artemidorus. I saluted him gladly ;
and, because the sight of a friendly face was now rare
for me, I took pleasure in conversing with him (although
I had not been greatly inclined towards him in former
days) walking up and down in the portico and discoursing about divers matters and in the end about matters
of philosophy and religion. And to be brief, not
having any other counsellor to go to, I imparted to this
man (although I knew but little of him) some of my
troubles and perplexities, asking what would philosophy
advise me to do in my sore strait ?

When I had made an end of speaking, Metrodorus
ceased walking and stood still, near a broken slab of
pavement in the portico, where some ants had built a
nest and were passing busily to and from the crevice. So
here Metrodorus coming to a stand, and looking down
upon the ants and then up at me, said, " If there be
gods indeed, as perchance there are, I will now shew you
what it is likely that they think of us mortals. Certain
people say that the gods being infinitely wiser and
nobler, as well as stronger, than we are, must needs
have a care for us, and rule our actions aright. Now,
my young friend, here stand we two upon this pavement, two human beings as much (I suppose) superior

to these myriads of little busy insects at our feet, as the gods are superior to us. Well, my friend, do we have a care for these ants ? Surely not. Do we sorrow for their sins and compassionate their errors ? I think not. Do we rule their actions aright ? Do we stir a finger to help them in the storing of their food or to avert the destruction of the whole republic of them ? Nay, but we take not a single thought for all their doings and misdoings, their virtues and their vices (for doubtless these creatures have their virtues and their vices even as we have) except it may be to amuse ourselves withal, or to rid ourselves of them if they become inconvenient. But you say, men are so vastly superior to ants. Not more, I take it, than the gods (if any) are superior to men. But in men, you urge, there is so much more of diversity in character and in action. Who knows ? Only stoop down and look at these diminutive beings more closely. Mark what a bustle they are in ; all working, but not all doing the same work ; some, look you, are the scavengers, carrying out the ordure, others the marketers carrying in vast fragments of bean-shell or hastening onwards along with pieces of barleycorn in their mouths ; some also, as it seems to me, standing still and ruling or instructing the rest. And who knows also but, besides their architects and masons, they have their demagogues and counsellors, cooks also and musicians, yes and philosophers too after their manner, philosophising perhaps about us two at this very moment, and very prettily demonstrating the truth of the theories of the priest-ants, saying that ' Man being a noble Being, infinitely powerful, and wise, and good, must needs take thought for us, poor mortal ants, and rule our

actions aright, and in the end conform us to Himself'
—whereas, my dear Onesimus, so far is this from being
the case that on the contrary "—and here he stamped
heavily upon the ant-hill—" I thus with one little
movement of my foot, subvert the whole ant-universe,
for no other cause but my own particular pleasure.

"O my dear Onesimus, is not belief in the gods by
this time almost too antiquated ? If there were some
new fashion of it, I might recommend you to try it ;
but every fashion has been tried and has become stale.
Your young friend Epictetus shows a preference for one
god ; but to the true philosophers his theories are like
the rest, quite musty and past discussing. However, if
you are resolved to deal in such wares, it is good to
have a choice ; and the choice is large. Perhaps you
prefer a legion of gods and demons ? Or, aiming at the
golden mean, what say you to choosing a moderate few,
an oligarchy of gods ? Then there are in the market
for you some gods that speak, and others that are
mutes ; some that are still active and vigorous, such
as Isis, Serapis, and Sabazius ; others that are past
work and cashiered, such as old Ares, Enuo, and
Hephæstus ; or if you are curious about rank and
precedence, you can have gods of different ranks, first
class, second class, third class ; some with bodies, some,
if you prefer it, bodiless. Last of all in the market
come the atheists, who will sell you a vacuum, if you
will give them many years of your life for it. But is
not the best course after all to keep your time and pains
and money and avoid the market altogether : neither
believing nor disbelieving, but never giving a thought
to the matter ?"

"And does Artemidorus hold these opinions?" said I, after a pause. "I think so," he replied, "At least he never mentions the gods to me; and you best know whether he has often spoken of them to you; but from what you say yourself, I infer that he has not. However, even Artemidorus is not so consistent as I am. For he is ever fretting himself about the sun, and the moon, and the planets, and their motions, and about the tides and their courses, and sometimes he busies himself with noting the diverse superstitions of men; whereas to my mind the best kind of life is to vex oneself with none of these trifles, but to be content with myself and with all things around me, believing that they cannot be better, and so to eat and drink like Sardanapalus and to—

> *Sleep soundly stretched at ease—*

as Homer sings of Ulysses sailing sweetly homeward. Therefore my advice to you is to take the goods which the gods (if there be gods) at this instant clearly destine for you. Make friends with Philemon. Become a rich man and obtain your freedom. Marry Prepousa and be happy with her, and, if need be, with others. And as for this Jewish purification, if, to obtain Philemon's good will and a fortune to boot, it be necessary to endure a washing, why not wash? You can be as dirty as you like when you are rich and free. However time presses, and I must go. But in fine, I would have you take as your Mentor my sepulchre, for you cannot have a better precept than that inscription." "What inscription?" said I. "You must surely have seen it," answered he; "it was the talk of all Colossæ three

months ago, and they cannot have quite forgotten it so
soon. However, you have not been much out of doors
of late. You must know then, that some months ago,
when my poor wife departed this life, she ordered these
words to be engraved upon her tombstone :—

> *Though my soul dwelleth in earth*
> *My soul dwelleth in heaven.*

Now I could not gainsay the poor woman's last wish,
and therefore I permitted the inscription. Yet I felt,
as a philosopher, that it was due to my philosophy that
my epitaph should be of a very different character,
consistent with my life. So considering with myself
that my executors might possibly not carry out my
instructions if I gave orders for an inscription over my
body, in opposition to that of my lamented wife, I
therefore caused these words to be cut in my lifetime,
beneath my wife's inscription, over the place where my
body will in due time be laid :

> *Enjoy the present,*
> *For when the spirit has left the body,*
> *Descending to Lethe,*
> *It will never again look on the world above.*

"And you have not seen it ? You will find it on the
Laodicean road, on the right-hand side, about three
furlongs from the gate. But I must be going. Farewell, my young friend, and take my advice. As for the
wise people who profess to know everything and to
teach everybody, no two of them agreeing together,
pay no attention to them. Snap your fingers at all

their philosophics and controversies. Take in a sub-
stantial cargo of good things. Trim your sails for a
pleasant voyage through life, making up your mind to
be often merry, seldom serious, and never sad." So
saying, he departed, and I returned to the house of
Philemon.

§ 11. OF THE DEATH OF EUCHARIS AND HOW I WAS AGAIN ACCUSED OF THEFT.

The words of Metrodorus himself had not much
weight with me. But the image of that ant-hill came
again and again into my mind, making me ask, "Is it
so indeed that men are but as insects in the eyes of the
immortal gods?" And as day after day went on, and
still no letter nor message from Molon, my nights being
sleepless and my days given up to expectation and
suspense, I resolved (even as a weak mariner yielding
to wind and tide) that I would suffer myself to drift
with the event: if the gods led me to good then I
would believe in them, but if to ill, then I would not.
So for the space of ten days my mind swayed this way
and that, tossed with a very tempest of increasing
troubles, and still no tidings from Athens, although
nearly a month had passed since Molon's former letter.
At last I began to suspect that Pistus might have
intercepted some letters from Eucharis; and if this
suspicion had rankled long in my mind, it would have
gone nigh to make me mad.

But toward the end of the month one of the slaves
who was well affected to me brought me a letter bearing
the familiar seal of Molon, which, when I had in all

haste opened it, contained no letter from Eucharis, no, not so much as a little piece of paper, nor any words written in her hand, nor even a flower or aught else by way of token ; and I shook it again, but still nothing fell out.   So I sat down holding the letter in my hand, unread, foreboding the worst ; and how long I sat I know not, but in those minutes (if they were minutes) there seemed to have passed over me years, yea ages of misery ; and I had reckoned over my life even to the grave, and beyond the grave, into a darkness that was without end.

" Eucharis is dead "—so the letter began.   The rest was very long and full of lamentations, telling how the Christians had caused her death, or else perchance her sorrow for my sake ; how the followers of one Paulus had persuaded her to be baptized ; how her father, though he had foreseen and noted the mischief, could not stay the progress of the disease, and how, for the rest of his life he must live alone in the world.   But my eyes travelled idly over this to return again and again to the first words: " Eucharis is dead."   So suddenly had she passed away that at the last she could not so much as write me one word of farewell, nor do more than bid her father send me this message, that Onesimus must always keep the token she had given him and not forget her last words.

During my torpor, while I sat in a kind of trance of misery, the letter had fallen to the ground.   Stooping to pick it up I unwittingly took in its stead the letter of Epictetus, and began to read it.   " A bad performer cannot sing alone, but only in a chorus : in the same way some people cannot walk the path of life alone."

Most true ! And I was one of those " bad performers,"
one of those who " cannot walk the path of life alone."
But what then ? Were there not " bad performers " as
well as perfect actors, and was there no place for them
in the world ? I was not meant nor made to walk
alone. But why had the gods made me of a nature to
walk in dependence on some guide, and then, after
mocking me with the semblance of the gift of so
precious a guide as my beloved one, snatched her away
that they might see me stumble and fall ? Even so
they had given me Chrestus, and snatched him away.
So it had been with all their gifts to me. They had
given me a love of learning ; but now they forbade me
to learn ; they had given me a thirst for truth, but had
driven the truth far away ; they had given me the
breeding and habits of a free man, but had condemned
me to be a slave. Each gift had been a curse in
disguise.

Now came back into my mind the image of the
ant-hill of Metrodorus, and then there rose up from
the depths of darkness the lessons I had learned in the
ergastulum, which I had thought I had forgotten, but
now they seemed as fresh as yesterday, and more real
than any other memory of my life. And now once
more I inclined to believe that some bad demon or
demons possessed and governed the world, exulting
in our miseries and mocking at our foolish prayers and
silly gratitude. Either they, or chance, ruled over the
Universe. In either case, no good God ; no one to
love, no one to trust, no one to whom in some invisible
world I could intrust my darling Eucharis and my
brother Chrestus, feeling confident that all was well

with them. Eucharis and Chrestus ! Say rather Dust
and Ashes. Then Satan filled my heart and I lifted
up my voice in blasphemy and cursed the Master of
the Feast who had given command that I should depart,
yet would open no door for my departure, and I looked
about me for means to destroy myself. But the hand of
the Lord delivered me. For when I had made a noose
with the thongs of my sandals, and having fixed the
end to a beam was now in the act of placing it round
my neck, behold, Philemon entered the chamber with
a stern countenance, and two or three slaves behind
him. He at once accused me of taking many precious
volumes from the library with intent to steal them.
I denied it, but he affirmed that it must needs be so,
for they had been found yonder, pointing to a hole
beneath the floor in my apartment, and, said he, " your
attempt to slay yourself convicts you ; for having
perceived that the books have been recovered, you
desire to prevent the punishment of your theft."

Perceiving that I was speechless—as indeed I was,
marvelling at the iniquity of Pistus, or whoever else was
my enemy—Philemon bade all the slaves depart the
chamber, and then taking me by the hand, with tears
in his eyes, he besought me to confess the truth,
saying that he had noted, now these many days, how
Satan had taken advantage of me because I had
hardened my heart against the word of the Lord ;
and he implored me to repent and to wash away my
sins. Now if I had shewn him the letter of Molon
describing the death of Eucharis, I might perhaps have
persuaded him that I was not guilty of theft, and that
other causes drove me to attempt my life. But I

could not do it; for in my madness I regarded him
as her murderer. Therefore I in no way endeavoured
to persuade him, but merely answered with much
vehemence that in truth I was not guilty, and that
either Pistus or some enemy had devised this plot
against me. Upon this, Philemon clapped his hands
and called in the slaves, saying, in their presence, that
it was useless to argue with me or to beseech me,
and that I was fascinated by some woman who had
ensnared my soul, adding withal some words not indeed
gross nor unseemly, but very bitter to me at that
season, knowing poor Eucharis to be but lately dead.
So in that instant I leaped upon him and seizing the
stilus which he held in his hand I attacked him with
it, and assuredly, had not the slaves run together and
stayed me, I should have slain him outright; but as
it was, the Lord had mercy on me, and I did but
wound him very slightly. But I foamed at the mouth
as one mad; yea, and indeed I thank the Lord that
I was verily mad at that time, and that I spoke not,
but Satan spoke within me. For I seemed to see
Christus as an evil demon pursuing me without ceasing,
setting Philemon against me and inspiring Pistus with
malice, and now last of all slaying my beloved Eucharis;
wherefore I uttered such terrible execrations against
the Lord Jesus, as even now fill me with horror so
much as to think of; and write them down I durst
not. But Philemon, stopping his ears, rushed in haste
from the room, wringing his hands as if all hope
were now lost, and leaving me struggling in the hands
of Pistus and the rest of the household who were
binding me.

That evening I heard what had been resolved concerning me. Philemon's brother, a decurion of Smyrna, who had not yet been converted to the faith was very earnest that I should be crucified according to the custom; but Philemon was constant against it, partly out of his affection for me, even then not wholly destroyed; but partly because the brethren have been from the first always unwilling that any should be punished with that death whereby the Lord Jesus was slain. So it was determined that I should be sent into the country to an ergastulum about one hundred and twenty furlongs north of Laodicea.

But here must I needs pause. For now begins my pen to describe the deepest of the depths of my most sinful life; whereof, whensoever my mind unwillingly goes back to that black darkness, I can say no more than this: "All things are possible with thee; thy blood, O Lord Jesus, can cleanse from every sin."

THE END OF THE FOURTH BOOK

THE FIFTH BOOK

§ 1. HOW I ESCAPED FROM THE HOUSE OF PHILEMON.

REMEMBERING the ergastulum of Nicander I determined not to endure that manner of life a second time. My bonds had not been very firmly fastened, and the same good friend who had brought me word what was resolved concerning me, had loosened them still more. So when it was past midnight, as near as I could judge, creeping out from my chamber I found the porter sleeping, and without difficulty obtained possession of the key. I was opening the door to depart, when I suddenly bethought myself that I was going forth into the world without an obol in my purse, so that I must needs beg my food ; in doing which I should surely be discovered and at once apprehended. So I went into a small chamber next to the library, wherein Philemon was wont to keep money, and I took out a purse. I extenuate nothing, I excuse nothing. Yet the truth may fairly be set down ; and it is true that I purposed not to take so much, but as I opened it, I heard, or thought I heard, a noise from Philemon's study, and straightway fled as I was, having the purse in my hand ; and so in great haste and trepidation, being now thief as well as fugitive, I opened the house-door and ran for my life. For an hour or more I wandered about the street avoiding the watch, and as soon as the gates were opened, I went forth on the Ephesian road.

Then for the first time taking thought whither I should go, I determined to break all ties of friendship and acquaintance and to betake myself to some large city such as Corinth or Alexandria where I might be easily unknown. Meantime I must needs hide somewhere in the upland country; for in the port of Ephesus constant watch was kept for runaway slaves, and the crier was soon likely to make my escape known in the streets of Laodicea and Hierapolis. So, leaving the Ephesian road, I made my way as best I could straight towards the mountain called Cadmus, which rises up in these parts very high and precipitous and containing many spacious caverns fit for fugitives to hide in. As I went, I found myself amid several tombs cut in the sides of the hill a little away from the road, and the sun now shining from the east lit up the inscription on the face of one of the tombs nearest to me so that I could read each word of it plainly, and it was the very inscription which Metrodorous had mentioned. "Enjoy the present, for when the spirit has left the body, descending to Lethe, it will never again look on the world above." Then began I to mock bitterly at that philosophy which could bid me, a slave and an outcast and one of the most wretched upon earth, to "enjoy the present." But at that very moment methought I heard the sound of pursuers, and putting my ear to the ground (which is all of pumice-stone in that region, very porous and hollow, and resonant almost after the manner of a drum) I plainly heard the hoofs of horses approaching. So I pressed on over rough and smooth making for the mountain. As the sun rose higher, I came to one of the spurs of Cadmus. High up in the sides of that mountain are many holes wherein eagles build their nests; and many of them were even now soaring in the air with choughs and crows screaming below them, but all so high that the eye could scarce discern them. The sounds of these birds together with the bleating of the flocks pasturing on the mountains, the scent of the flowers, the freshness of the morning air, and the beauty and the brightness of all things around, seeming to rejoice in the sunrise, constrained me in despite of myself to feel some pleasure in them, and I rested there for a while. But anon fear (and by this time hunger) forced me to hasten away.

Coming now to a building I desired to ask food ; but I found that it was a temple, as could be perceived from the notice set up at the entrance to the precincts ; which, even after the lapse of so many years, I am not able to forget, because at that time it seemed to me a type and pattern of all the religion and worship of the gods. For there were written up these words : "Let no man enter these sacred precincts who shall have tasted goat's flesh nor lentils for these three days, or fresh cheese for one day. But whoso shall have touched a dead body let him delay entrance for forty days. Likewise, whoever will enter, let him bring with him the highest purity, namely, a healthy mind in a healthy body, free from a guilty conscience." Then there came into my mind once again. only with much more force, the

thoughts that I had had at Lebedea, namely, that the
gods are helpful only to those who need no help, being
happy and virtuous ; or else only to the rich who can
pay for many sacrifices and purifications ; but as for the
poor man who cannot give them fat bullocks and lambs,
they have never a word to say for him ; and if a poor
man be a sinner and an outcast to boot, then a temple
is no place for him. With such thoughts as these, sorely
dejected in mind and beginning to be very weary in
body as well as hungry, and the heat of the sun
becoming now more than I could well endure, I betook
myself to some kind of shepherd's cot which I found
open and empty ; and there I lay down and slept.

I was awakened by the sound of music, ill played, as
though by a beginner ; and for a time, betwixt asleep
and awake, I lay still without moving, not knowing
what had become of me, or where I was. But presently
the music came to a sudden stand, and a voice cried,
"May the all-powerful Syrian Goddess, Parent of all
things, and the holy Sabazius and the Idæan mother
strike thee dead, thou dolt whom a week's labour has
not sufficed to teach thy notes. A pretty flute-player
art thou. I am a ruined man with thee." With that, I
started up and beheld an old man, very fat and with a
smooth face and having a cast in his eye ; and by his
side a youth, whom he was attempting to teach to play
on the flute ; but neither could the pupil learn, nor had
the teacher skill to teach. I soon perceived from his
attire and language, as well as from the ass bearing the
image of the goddess, and the company of dancing girls
who were with him, that he was one of the begging
priests of Cybele ; and it seemed that his flute-player

had deserted him so that he could gain no money from
the people by his sacred dances, for want of the music.
After watching them for a short time (unknown to them,
for the corner wherein I had been lying was very dark)
I lost patience to see how ill the old priest taught and
the youth learned; and coming forward I took the flute
from the hands of the youth and shewed him how he
was to use it. At first the old man stood speechless
with astonishment at the suddenness of my coming in
upon them; but when he perceived that I had some
skill in music, he asked whether I could make shift to
play for him. I told him that I knew not that kind of
music, and would have gone forth from the cot without
more words; but he stayed me and begged me to give
some proof of my skill; saying I must at least eat and
drink with him and his company, for the village people
had given them two kids and a cask of wine. So I was
overpersuaded by my hunger, and after we had eaten
our fill, he gave me to drink of unmixed wine, because,
said he, there was no water nigh; and my thirst constrained me to drink. Then he began again to ply me
with importunities to go with him at least as far as
Pergamus, adding that if I wished to escape notice (and
here he looked at me as if he knew that I had some
secret) I could take no better course than this, but if I
left him, who knew but questions might be asked, and I
might be noticed more than I desired? And hereon,
when he saw me wavering, and inflamed with wine, he
put the flute once more into my hands, and called out
that the dance should begin; and thus saying he led the
ass into the midst of the chamber, bearing the image of
the goddess which was covered with a silver veil. Then

I began to play and the women to dance, and the priest
applauded and cried that the music should go faster.
At first I played against my will and my heart was not
in it ; but as I looked upon the women dancing in their
many-coloured tunics with their eyebrows darkened,
and their Phrygian caps on their heads, and their
saffron shawls streaming 'in the air, all dancing, at first
slowly and then more quickly round the image, by
degrees it was given to Satan to have power over me
because I had not resisted him. So I began to take a
pleasure in it, and I said, Surely now is the time to
cast aside all virtue and to forget the name of goodness
and to begin a new life, wallowing in all sin. And even
as Satan thus moved me, I began to play the music
more furiously, as if possessed by some demon, and the
women, after their manner, brandishing their swords
and battle-axes, began to leap more furiously to the
sound of cymbal and tambourine, and they bared their
arms and shoulders scourging themselves with whips
wrought of pieces of bone till the blood flowed out ;
and because it flowed not fast enough, they scourged
themselves harder, yea, and in their leaping they bit
their own flesh and screamed like wild beasts ; and
then the old priest stopped the music and clapping me
on the shoulder bade me pledge him in another cup of
wine, for I must needs go with him to Pergamus and
be his flute-player ; and I like a dumb beast could not
say No, but drank of his wine and so consented.

§ 2. OF MY LIFE AT PERGAMUS.

Let it be permitted me to pass over the story of my wanderings until I came to Pergamus. Not that I would conceal or gloss over any of the sins I committed at this time. Yet although thou, O Lord, hast forgiven all things, methinks I could not set down those deeds of darkness, without seeming to pass through a second course of sin. Suffice it that in all the acts of my companions, in all their thieving and lying, their blasphemings, revellings and impurities, I was not behind any, the vilest of the vile. But it pleased the Lord, after three months of thus wallowing in the mire, to hold out the hand to me, though it were but for a season ; and it was after this manner. When we came to Pergamus, going on a certain day to visit a priest of Asclepius I chanced to speak of the children that were daily exposed upon the Temple steps, and I shewed him (but not as from myself) the token of my brother Chrestus, saying that it had been given to me by one of my acquaintance to whom it had belonged, who was now dead. When the priest read the inscription TRUST, he started and changed colour, and very earnestly questioned me whether my acquaintance had ever spoken to me touching a brother exposed at the same time, and wearing a token with another inscription, mentioning at the same time the words of it, I LOVE THEE. Then it was my turn to start, and I confessed that I had heard mention of it, but that this brother also was long since dead. "Truly then," said the priest, "I sorrow greatly for their poor mother's sake, who came to the Temple

not more than six or seven months ago, to make inquiry
concerning two children who had been exposed in the
first year of the emperor Claudius, twins, and wearing
two such tokens as you have described." So then, com-
paring the date, as well as the other circumstances, I
knew that the children could be no other than myself
and my brother Chrestus.

Now all my dissimulation was swallowed up in the
eagerness of my desires, and I gave the priest no peace,
questioning him again and again about the lady of whom
he spoke ; insomuch that I doubt not he suspected the
truth. But all my questioning was vain ; for he said
that the lady would tell neither him nor his fellow-priests
whence she came nor whither she was going ; but she
had declared in parting that she should come again to
the Temple before long, if she lived. She was of tall
stature, with brown hair and grey eyes, of fair complexion and somewhat pale, with a slight scar on the
left cheek, and of a sad expression, and she spoke Greek
with the Attic accent ;. moreover she informed the
priests that she had sought in vain for her children for
many years. Straightway from his words I conceived
the image of one who could not have been guilty of any
cruel or unnatural deed, and I became assured in my
mind that some foul play or irresistible constraint, but
not her own will, must have separated us from our
mother. And a new feeling possessed me that, if I could
find her, I might still have some one who would love
me. But when I seemed to see her coming again to the
Temple, and myself meeting her and telling her all my
story, and the story of Chrestus, and shewing her my
token, and falling on her neck and embracing my

mother, and how she also would embrace me as a son, then it came into my mind, "And how could such a mother own such a son as Onesimus is now?"

In that moment, thou, O Lord, didst shew me unto myself that I might hate myself; and on that same day I left the priest of Cybele and cast off my old companions, and having found a lodging with one who prepared skins for the covering of books, I determined to earn my living if possible as a transcriber. For the space of three or four months I lived after this manner, forswearing my former dissolute life and letting no day pass but I visited the Temple; for the sun never rose but I said to myself 'this day perchance she may come'; and I ruled all my life by the thought of her, and the hope of her, if perchance I might yet find one that would love me. But the Lord had ordained otherwise. For on a certain day (about the beginning of the fifth month after I had first come to Pergamus) taking my work to the shop of a bookseller with whom I had dealings, I found there two or three men of learning standing together, conversing of books and parchments and the like; and taking up a parchment, one said to a companion that he had seen even such a book as this, so transcribed and adorned, in the library of Philemon of Colossæ. Then a terror fell upon me lest I should be discovered, and without so much as waiting to be paid for my labour, I made shift to leave the shop, upon some slight pretext, and returning to my lodging for a few minutes I went forth thence to the city gates, and ceased not travelling till I came to Ephesus, where I went on board a ship bound for the city of Corinth.

§ 3. HOW I CAME TO CORINTH AND SAW THE TOMB OF EUCHARIS.

At Corinth I found no man to employ me as a transcriber. But because of the number of rich people in that city (some living there but many more resorting thither for pleasure) and many spending their whole lives in continual revelling, there was a great demand for such buffoons, and mimes, and inferior actors, as attend at great men's feasts to make them merry ; and to this occupation I was now forced to stoop. And so being cut off from all hope of finding my mother, I fell again into my old ways of reprobate living. Besides the baseness of my mode of life, I was weighed down by a perpetual slavish dread. Whithersoever I went, or whatever company I frequented, I was never secure, fearing always lest some one should take me by the throat and claim me as Philemon's slave, a thief, and a would-be murderer ; and whenever I saw a slave's body hanging on the cross, with the crows fluttering round it, or a gang of branded wretches with shaven heads dragged in manacles through the streets, at such a time I would say, " Sooner or later this will be thy fate, Onesimus." This took all the heart and spirit out of my resolve to lead a virtuous life. Sometimes I determined at all hazards to go back to Pergamus ; for it made my heart sick to think of her who had been seeking me there many years, perhaps even at that instant standing on those steps of the Temple which I had been wont day by day to frequent in the hope of seeing her. But at first I durst not, and after some

days when I had at last determined and made ready to
depart, I remembered how I had told the priest of
Asclepius that both Chrestus and Onesimus were dead ;
which he belike had by this time conveyed to my
mother, so that she would now give over seeking in
despair, and come to Pergamus no more. The thought of
her new sorrow was heavier than I could bear, and thus
that image of her which had been but of late so precious
and helpful, became unto me now so full of sadness that
I sought to flee from it in revellings and drunkenness.

The end of all was that the hand which seemed to
have raised me for a breathing-space out of the deep
gulf of destruction now plunged me down again ; and
I fell once more to a life not worse perhaps, but assuredly not much better, than that which I had led
with the priest of Cybele. Yea, such a wretch was I
now become that I began to be content with wretched-
ness, preferring darkness and fearing any glimpse of
light lest it should make my darkness more visible ;
insomuch that once or twice at this season, as I
remember, I took off the little tokens from my neck,
the gifts of Eucharis and Chrestus, and thought to cast
them away, because when I felt them upon my breast
they troubled me at nights, suggesting visions of the
past and hopes not possible. But, base and vile though
I was, my courage failed me, and I could not do it.

One day, after late revelling, when thoughts like
these had been disquieting my soul, I found myself
wandering through the streets near the quays where the
ferry takes passengers across to Peiræus ; and scarce
knowing what I did I stepped with the rest into the
boat, and presently I had disembarked and was walking

up toward the city of Athens, yet all the while cursing
my folly in coming whither I should not have come.
For I feared lest I might be recognised, and still more
lest I should rouse up memories that were best forgotten. Yet on I went, for all my self-reproaches, as if
I were a lifeless engine impelled by some power outside
me, till I came to a little garden hard by the wall,
wherein was a tomb of Charidemus, a brother of
Eucharis, who had died these many years ; and entering in I read the words over the grave, which
oftentimes I had read with my beloved by my side :

Golden youth, read here thine end :
I sprang from dust, to dust descend.

Eucharis had always been wont to find fault with
this inscription as being too sad, and she would protest
that, when she died, she would have somewhat more
hopeful inscribed upon her tomb. This saying of hers
coming to my memory reminded me of that which
in my lethargy had all this while escaped me, that her
tomb also would in all likelihood be in this same
garden ; and as I turned round my eye fell at once
on a new-made sepulchre and on it this inscription :

Twenty years of fleeting breath
Then Eucharis went down to death
Whom I fondly called my own,
Not knowing she was but a loan
Lent by Death, who from below
Sends short delights to make long woe.
Too short a loan, poor twenty years,
For such vast interest of tears
Which he must weep, who now remains
To feel a lonely father's pains.
Dear dream, sweet bubble, painted air,
Break, leave poor Molon to despair.

When I read these words I could not but feel some
touch of pity for the poor old man mourning alone in
his chamber where we three had been wont to sit so
happily together; and looking on the wreaths and
garlands that were on the sepulchre and perceiving that
they were all very old and faded, I remembered that
Eucharis was born as on that very day, and I marvelled
that the old man had not come forth to do honour to
the tomb and to deck it with fresh flowers, and methought some strong cause must have hindered him;
for it was now nigh upon sun-down. So though I
durst not have looked him in the face, I arose and went
into the city again, even to the street where he lived, in
case I might see him coming forth from his door; and
up and down I walked till sunset, my head muffled in
my cloak, and all that time I saw him not. Nor was I
like to see him. For when I inquired of one that
came forth from a neighbouring house whether Molon
yet lived in that street, he looked on me as if pitying
me for my ignorance and said that the old man had died
but two days ago and was to be buried on the morrow.

Now I would fain have persuaded myself that it was
well with me, because not a single friend remained to
reproach me, nor any one whose love or good opinion
might deter me from leading a life according to my own
desires, or the drift of fortune: yet at night when I
lay down in Corinth, the thought of Eucharis would
force its way into my soul, and when I shut my eyes I
could see nothing and think of nothing but the inscription on her tomb; and at the last the memory of my
beloved one prevailed, and tears fell from my eyes for
the first time since I had read her last farewell. But

on the morrow all was forgotten. I went forth to my
task of buffoonery as usual ; and the day and the night
passed according to custom, in jesting, and drinking,
and revelling, and sin.

What shall I say unto thee, O Lord, concerning these
things ? Shall I say, Blessed be Thou, O Lord, who
didst suffer Thy servant to sin much, that he might be
forgiven much, and that he might love much ? Nay,
but Thou art a righteous Lord and hatest unrighteousness. Lord, this only can I say, Thou knowest all, and
yet Thou hast forgiven.

§ 4. HOW I SAW THE HOLY APOSTLE PAULUS, BUT
           KNEW HIM NOT.

Though I had at this time no lack of employment,
yet I began to be in debt as well as in want. For by
continual revelling and gaming and drinking, I had
spent all the money that I had brought with me from
Pergamus, I mean the money of Philemon. Therefore
about this time (it was the ninth year of the Emperor
Nero) certain of my companions, who were in the same
case as myself, persuaded me to accompany them to
Rome, where they would obtain no less employment,
they said, and better pay. At any other time I should
have been not a little moved, coming thus for the first
time to the chief city of the world ; but such a lethargy
had fallen on me that I took little or no note of all the
greatness and splendour of the place, save only that I
well remember the day when I first saw the Emperor
presiding at the games in the Circus Maximus. For

on that day seeing one that was a matricide, and a murderer, and an abuser of nature, thus enthroned in the chief seat of empire, and worshipped as God with the applause of such a concourse as would have gone nigh to make up a great city, and beholding also what vile sights were there exhibited—things detestable and not to be mentioned, with which the deaths of thousands of gladiators cannot be compared for horror—then it was borne in upon my mind that there need be no more dispute as to whether Good or Evil reigned over the world; for here before mine eyes was Evil visibly reigning, and called God by all. Wherefore, though I went to no greater excesses than before at Corinth, yet was I hardened and confirmed in evil, drowning my shame in wine and striving to banish all distinction between evil and good.

Yet even at Rome there were seasons when, in my heart of hearts, I was weary of my sinful and desolate condition, and longed for the touch of a friend's hand ; and at times I yearned to be a fool and to believe in something, cursing the wranglings and disputations of the philosophers who had taken from me all faith in the gods, so that I could no longer put trust in anything; yea, at such moments I would fain have been a peasant in the poorest village of Asia (such a one as poor old Hermas or lame Xanthias whom I remembered in my childhood), worshipping Zeus, or Pan, or aught else, so that I might only be not myself. Life wearied me, yet I feared death, yea, I feared even sleep ; for the darkness was full of terrors, and my couch brought me no rest, but only horrible phantasms of dread abysses, and visions of falling

down for ever, and of hands stretched out to stay
me and then drawn back, and of sad faces veiled or
turned away. The daylight which chased away the
terrors of sleep, brought ever back with it shame and
remorse. Thus all things, both by night and by day,
seemed set in array against me. But indeed (albeit
I knew it not) my miseries were of the Lord; for by
these means, didst thou, O Judge that judgest rightly,
even by these righteous torments and just retributions,
prepare me to be delivered from unrighteousness and
to be made free in the Lord Jesus.

After I had been in Rome a few weeks, I was admitted into a club or collegium of actors; where I
made acquaintance with the actor Aliturius, a Jew by
birth, one that was in great favour with Poppea who
had that same year been married to the Emperor.
Now the lady Poppea, like many others of rank and
quality at that time, was given to the observance of
the Jewish law; at least so far as concerned Sabbaths
and abstinence from meats and the use of certain purifications; and she had with her a certain Ishmael, who
had been high priest among the Jews. Hence it came
to pass that, by help of Aliturius and through favour
of Poppea, I was admitted to perform and recite at
several feasts and drinking parties in the palace, and
sometimes even in the presence of the Emperor himself,
but more especially before the officers of the Pretorian
guard.

One evening, as I came from a feast where I had
been making mirth for some of the officers, returning
through that part of the palace which looks towards
the Circus Maximus, there passed by me a guard of

soldiers having a prisoner in chains, whom they led
into an adjoining chamber, and I understood from
them that the man was to lie there for that night,
that he might be ready on the morrow ; when the
Emperor himself proposed to hear his cause in the
temple of Apollo, which was near at hand. "And who,"
said I, "is this prisoner whom the divine Emperor
thus deigns to honour ?" The man, they said, was
one of the Christian superstition. Now at that time,
being in favour with Poppea and the Jew Aliturius,
and it being my occupation to be a jester for the
officers and soldiers, I was wont to make the Christians
matter for jest and scoffing, not sparing sometimes
(may the Lord forgive me) to assail even the Crucified
One in my jesting. So being inflamed with wine,
I thrust myself unbidden into the chamber, telling
the guard that we would examine the prisoner at
once, "Wherefore," said I, "be ye *judices* or jury,
and I, for the nonce, will be the divine Emperor
himself."

Having therefore made for myself a kind of tribunal,
I sat down on it, taking a centurion to be my assessor,
and the rest of the soldiers, joining in the jest, sat
down upon the floor ; and when I bade the soldiers
"produce the prisoner," he sat up, but not so that I
could see his face clearly, the lamp being behind him.
Then I accosted the man in derision, saying that from
his aspect I discerned him to be Heraclitus the crying
philosopher, and I asked him whether he also, like
Heraclitus, taught that "men are mortal gods, and
gods immortal men." To this he replied, as if willing
to enter into the jest, that he was a teacher of joy and

not of sorrow, but that indeed he taught that God and
men were at one.   After this, mocking at his baldness,
I asked him whether he were Pythagoras risen from
the dead, or whether he could teach us to be something
more than men and to be in harmony with the Universe.
He laughed gently at this, replying that, though indeed
he could teach these things, yet was he no philosopher
but rather a soldier; and saying this, he raised his
head and looked at me very intently as if he were
weak of sight; and at this moment the light of the
lamp, just then falling on his face, perplexed me,
because I felt sure that I had seen this man before;
but where or when I could not tell.   However,
recovering myself, I asked him in what legion he had
served and under what Imperator, and he replied, still
preserving a calm temper and smiling, that he served
in the Legio Victrix and under the auspices of the
Imperator Soter, or Salvator.   Hereat the soldiers
applauded, and I perceived that I was being beaten
on my own ground.   So thinking to catch the old
man by some slip, or to drive him into an inability to
answer, I asked him what were his weapons.   But
he replied that he used the shield of faith, and the
breastplate of righteousness, and the belt of truthfulness,
and the sword of the word of God; and, said he, I fight
the good fight of righteousness against unrighteousness,
wherein the victory must needs be in the end upon·
my side, as your own hearts also testify; for which
cause is our legion rightly called Victrix.   He added
some words which I cannot now recall, about the
nobleness of such a battle, and the glory of it, which
moved even the drowsy soldiers; insomuch that they

said with one consent that the man had reason on his side and that they wished him well. "Then," said I, making one last adventure to have the laugh on my side, "where then is thy Imperator that he does not bear witness unto thee?" At once he replied, "He will bear witness for me, and he is with me at this instant"; and these words he uttered with such a force of confidence and with a look so fixed and steady, gazing methought on some one whom he discerned behind me, that I leaped up and looked over my shoulder, trembling and quaking lest there were some phantom in the room. The soldiers also were, for the moment, somewhat moved, howbeit less than I was; and thinking perchance to shift the shame of their fear from themselves, they called out that I was not worthy to sit on a tribunal, nor to represent the divine Emperor. So, to put the best face I could upon my discomfiture, I concluded briefly with a mock-oration, saying that the prisoner appeared to be a valiant soldier, and that he seemed worthy to be allowed the privilege of abstaining from swine's flesh, and of worshipping an ass's head, if it so pleased him, and with that, I proclaimed the meeting dissolved.

§ 5. HOW I LEARNED THAT PAULUS WAS THE PROPHET THAT I HAD SEEN IN MY CHILDHOOD, THE SAME THAT HAD CURED LAME XANTHIAS.

As I was going forth from the chamber with the rest, he that was guarding the prisoner stayed me, questioning me concerning the Emperor's health, and asking me

whether it was likely that the Emperor would hear his
case in person to-morrow.   I said that it was not
unlikely ; for though he had not been in good health,
yet now that he was wedded to Poppæa, she made him
give heed to all Jewish matters.   " Yea but," said the
guard, " this fellow is no Jew, such as the other Jews,
but of a different faction, which they call seditious ;
and the rest of his people hate him."   " I understand
that," said I, " but whether the Jews love him or hate
him, in either case Poppæa will be for him or against
him ; and of that he is like to have experience
to-morrow."   Then the soldier began to explain to
me the nature of this sect; but I interrupted him,
saying that I knew everything concerning them,
" having learned their customs at Antioch " ; and
whereas I was always wont to preserve silence about
my life in Asia and about everything and every one
that had to do therewith, now on the other hand, something I know not what, made me add the words—" and
at Colossæ ; " and as soon as I had said it I repented of
it and hastened to go forth from the chamber.   But the
prisoner rose up from his couch and, catching me by the
cloak, asked whether I had been lately at Colossæ and
whether I knew one Philemon, who was a citizen of
that place.   I said " no ; " and he sat down with a sigh,
keeping his eyes fixed upon me ; and then, as I was
going forth, the expression of his features came back to
my mind on a sudden and I remembered the hook-nosed
prophet who had healed lame Xanthias in years gone by
at Lystra, and I could not forbear asking him whether
he had ever been in the region of Pamphylia ; and
he answered " yes," and when I mentioned Lystra, he

said he knew that city and had been there. Then I
asked in what year, and he answered in the fourth year,
or thereabouts, of the Emperor Claudius. So perceiving
that the times agreed, I questioned him further whether
he had healed a sick man there, and to make sure,
I said one sick of the palsy; but he replied " No, but a
lame man, that had been lame many years," and with
that he leaned forward to me as if still desirous to
answer and ask further questions.

But at this point the soldier, he I mean to whom the
prisoner was chained (for the rest were gone forth)
having now laid himself down upon the pallet to sleep,
smote the prisoner upon the face with the palm of his
hand, saying that it was bad enough that he should lose
his seat for the games in the Circus Maximus to-morrow,
where the people were even now gathering (and indeed
we could hear the noise and shouting of the multitude
outside) and that he would not further be cheated of
his slumbers by a miserly Jew, who refused to give
a single denarius to the soldier that was at the pains
of guarding him. Hereat the prisoner began with a
cheerful countenance to compose himself to lie down
by the side of his keeper, only saying that his friends
had been very willing to fee the keeper; but the guard
having been that day changed, and he himself being (as
it chanced) without money, it was not possible for him
to give any fee at that time. But the soldier, nothing
moved, struck him twice, yet harder than before, with
his fist, bidding him hold his peace and saying, with
a curse, that excuses were not denarii.

I know not whether it was the patience and constancy
of the prisoner that moved me; or because his presence

seemed to carry back my mind to the days of my child-hood, reminding me of the pleasant fields and flocks round Lystra, and my brother Chrestus and my old nurse Trophime, and the shepherd Hermas ; but, be the cause what it may, certain it is that I was drawn to the man as if bewitched or fascinated, and taking out such money as I had (which was but very little) I gave it to the soldier. At the same time I asked the prisoner whether he had made any attempt to gain the interces-sion of Titus Annæus Seneca, a great philosopher in those days and the former tutor of the Emperor. " Nay, but the old bookworm has no power in these days with our Emperor," said the soldier taking my money, " and could no more rein him in now than a butterfly could rein in the dragons of Hecate ; besides, if he could, think you that a man of quality, such as the Emperor's tutor, would regard such scum of the earth as these Christian wretches ? However, whatever he be is no business of mine, and money should have money's worth ; so I give you five minutes with the prisoner ; but, mark me, no more."

I felt as one caught in a trap. Twice had I en-deavoured to depart from the chamber because I desired to avoid speech with this stranger, who knew Colossæ and my master Philemon ; and now of my own motion I had so wrought that I must needs have speech with him. So I sat down, and asked the prisoner his name. " My name was once Saul," he answered, " but I am now called Paulus and I was born in Tarsus." Hereat I stood up to go at once, but my limbs refused to obey me and I went not, but stood where I was, gaping and staring like one mad ; for I seemed to see before me,

next to Christus, the bitterest foe of my life; because
this Paulus had caused Philemon to be my enemy and
by his superstitions had slain my beloved Eucharis.
Yet on the other hand it was borne in upon me that
here was one that had seen Christus risen from the dead,
and I remembered as if it were but fresh in mine ears,
his invocation over me in the days of my childhood,
" The Lord be unto thee as a Father "; and I felt that
however I might endeavour, it was not possible for me
to hate this man, nor easy to resist the spirit that was
in him, for I was in his presence as one under a spell.
So, though my fears bade me depart, the hand of the
Lord constrained me to remain. While I thus stood
stammering, uttering something perchance but meaning
nothing, Paulus interrupted me, taking me by the hand
and saying, " I perceive that there is to be more discourse between us; wherefore I will only say this, that
this night my prayers shall ascend to the Father of our
Lord Jesus Christ in thy behalf. For the Lord hath
need of thee, and verily thou shalt be saved and redeemed from all thy sins. To-morrow, as thou hast
heard, I stand before the Emperor; but if (as I doubt
not) I receive deliverance from the mouth of the lion, I
am to discourse at sun-down concerning the mercies of
the Lord Jesus in the house of Tryphæna and Tryphosa,
hard by the Capenian gate. Prithee, my benefactor,
bestow on me yet another benefit, and promise that
thou wilt be there." " No " was in my heart, but
" yes " came from my lips before I knew that I had
framed an answer, and I left the chamber as one in
a trance.

§ 6. HOW I WAS LED INTO THE NET OF THE GOSPEL.

As soon as I was come forth from the presence of
Paulus I resolved one thing for certain, that, go whither
I might to-morrow, I would by no means go to the house
of Tryphæna ; for, in spite of all my former disbelief in
witchcraft, I began to believe that verily some kind of
fascination was being used against me to make me a
Christian against my will.   For a long time I dared not
lie down to rest, but sat reasoning with myself and endeavouring to call to mind the arguments of Artemidorus against the Christians ; yet ever and anon the
face of Paulus would appear before mine eyes, and I
seemed to hear him saying that the gods are immortal
men, and it came into my mind that, if indeed there
were but such a god as my beloved Eucharis or Chrestus, only immortal instead of mortal, how willingly
would I trust in him, how gladly face all peril and
endure all hardship for his sake !   And then I bethought myself of the saying of Paulus about his leader
Christus whom he mentioned as still living and bearing
witness to him, and how he seemed to see Christus
behind me ; and with that I leaped up crying for help
and screaming like one distraught ; and so timorous was
I that I lit a second lamp and sat down again resolving
not to sleep that night at all.   But presently sleep,
whether I would or not, fell upon my eyelids, and a
confused mixture of many visions passed before me,
Paulus and Pythagoras and Heraclitus, all beckoning to
me, and speaking about an " immortal man " and a

"mortal god"; and then such a chaos of words and sights that I grew dizzy, till at last I saw a small white cloud which grew larger and opened itself and inclosed all the former chaos, and on it was written "Chrestus"; but as I approached, it was not "Chrestus" but "Christus," and then "Chrestus" again, till the cloud burst with a loud sound as of thunder and disclosed my brother, bright and smiling as in old days, and on his breast he bore the token I LOVE THEE and he stretched out his arms to me. But when I ran to embrace him, behold, on his hands and feet the marks of grievous wounds, and the expression of his countenance was the same and yet not the same; so that I stood and drew back, and, though he beckoned to me, I fled. But he pursued after me and I still fled from him, and all around there were voices and faces of good and evil, the good helping my pursuer, the bad helping me; but, as he gained fast upon me, the priest of Cybele smote the ground, and, behold, a great yawning chasm, wherein was a multitude of skeletons with open arms waiting for me, and I leaped into the chasm, and the arms of the skeletons were clasping me round; when suddenly I awoke and found myself upon the ground, shrieking and struggling and my limbs all shivering and bathed in sweat; and by this time the night was well nigh past, and the first light of dawn was to be seen in the east.

So great was my terror that my first resolve was to depart at once from Rome. But then I bethought myself that, whithersoever I might travel, I could not avoid bad dreams; and, if I desired to avoid Paulus, no place was so convenient for me as the most populous of

all cities. So I concluded to remain where I was, but
to spend that day in Tusculum ; whither I accordingly
set out a little before noon.   But I had not gone a few
paces from the door of my lodging, before the slaves
of a certain rich Octavius, one of my patrons, came
suddenly behind me and, catching fast both my arms,
bade me return with them, saying their master entertained company that day unexpectedly, and much desired my presence to make them merry.   When I would
have excused myself, they replied that they were under
constraint to take no refusal ; for Octavius had threat-
ened them with a whipping if by fair means or foul they
brought me not.   Moreover, as they were to dine very
early, I must come with them at once, though it was
but the seventh hour, and thus they would be sure
of me.

So I went with them under a kind of friendly violence
and entertained the company after my power.   But
what I said and did I know not, save only that at the
beginning of the entertainment I overheard one of the
guests say to his neighbour that Tychicus (by which name
I was known in those days) was that day in admirable
fooling ; and his neighbour replied that truly Tychicus
would be the most wittily obscene buffoon in the whole
of the city, but for a certain unevenness in his jesting,
as if he were possessed with two spirits, a lewd spirit
and a surly spirit, " for," said he, " after keeping all the
table in a roar of mirth for two or three hours, if you
watch the fellow for a minute or so when he thinks none
are looking at him, he falls into a moroseness, or else
a kind of vacancy, as if he were a soothsayer and
saw visions."   When I heard this, I drank even more

recklessly than my wont, saying to myself that I would drive out that spirit of vision-seeing and give myself wholly to the evil spirit. And noting that it was near sun-down, so that I was free from the snares of the enchanter Paulus, I grew more and more furious in my revelry, exceeding all bounds in grossness and blasphemy so that the guests applauded amain and covered my head with crowns of roses.

When I was at last dismissed, the guests now retiring to prepare for a second banquet, it was full two hours after sunset. Now the house of Octavius was on the Cœlian hill (where now stands the Colisseum) so that I was in no way constrained to go near the Capenian gate in order to return to my lodging. But the Lord constrained me and it was as if my feet took me thither against my will. Again and again did I repeat to myself, "Fool, why goest thou into the snare with thine eyes open?" But I replied, "What harm in merely going through the street, since it is certain that I shall not enter the house?" Yet, as I drew near to the street, I perceived the folly of going whither I desired not to go, and I drew back and turned aside going towards the Prætorium, when of a sudden a fear fell upon me, and I felt a hand laid on my shoulder from behind, and I trembled from head to foot hearing the voice of Paulus: "My son, thou art not in the right way." Fain would I have made some excuse, or have fled at once without excuse; but neither could my tongue avail for words, nor my feet for flight. So I went on with Paulus even as a captive, and he took me by the hand and led me unresisting into a house where was a large congregation of the Christians already

assembled and expecting his presence ; through the
midst of whom I walked, crowned as I was with roses,
and dripping with unguents and staggering in my gait,
so that all gazed at me with wonder and some perchance
in anger.   However they all made way reverently for
Paulus, and for me with Paulus, he still holding me by
the hand.   Then Paulus ascended a bema or platform
and began to speak to the people.   At first I sat still,
as one hearing and yet not hearing, content to listen
but not knowing why I listened ; like a brute beast
not capable of understanding.   By degrees my senses
returned, and his words seemed to come nearer
and nearer to me till they penetrated my very soul ;
but I cannot recollect them so as to set them down,
except a few of the last sentences, and these not
exactly.

When I came to myself, he was speaking of the
mercies of the Lord, describing how he himself had
persecuted the faith yet had obtained mercy.   Who
therefore, said he, could not be pardoned, since he
had been counted worthy of pardon ?   Who was so
vile and sinful that must needs say ' I am not worthy
to draw nigh unto the Lord ' since he, Paulus, the
sinner and persecutor, had been embraced by the arms
of his mercy ?   " Therefore, say not within yourselves
' What new sacrifice shall I bring ? '   For the Lord Jesus
Himself is your sacrifice ; neither say in your hearts
' With what new purification shall I draw nigh unto
him ? ' for the blood of the Lord Jesus is your purification ; neither say ' What new deeds must I do ? ' or
' What new life must I lead ? ' for the Lord himself
hath prepared thy deeds that thou shalt do ; and as for

thy life, it is no longer thine own ; for behold thou art dead ; and the life that thou shalt hereafter live, is the life that Christ shall live in thee. Come therefore unto thy Lord and trust in him.

"Stumble not, O ye Jews, at the cross, neither say within yourselves, 'The Crucified cannot be the Christ ; he that died the death of a slave cannot be our King.' Nay, but I say unto you, because of the cross, and not in spite of the cross, the Lord Jesus is the Christ ; and because he made himself to be the servant of all, therefore is he now exalted to be King over all. Also, ye Gentiles, stumble not at the sepulchre of Christ, saying, 'It is not possible that one that is dead should rise again'; for verily these eyes have seen him, and your own consciences bear witness for me that I speak not as one deceiving you, but that I verily saw the Lord Jesus. And as many of you as believe, have, as a testimony, the presence of his Spirit in your hearts ; and as many as shall believe shall have that same Spirit dwelling among you, as earnest of the glory that is to come, bringing with it love towards God and good-will towards all men. Come therefore unto the Lord Jesus, and behold, the grave hath no power to make a gulf between you and him. Say not 'He is in the heaven far above us,' nor 'He is in Hades far beneath us'; for I declare unto you that neither heaven, nor earth, nor that which is beneath the earth, can part you from him ; fear not the gods nor the Gentiles, nor the reproach of men ; fear not the thrones nor powers of this world ; if Christ be for us who shall be against us ? Fear ye not therefore the fears of this world ; for behold, for them that are called of Christ, all things work together for good ; for I am persuaded that neither death nor life, nor angels nor principalities, nor things present nor things to come, nor height nor depth, nor any other creature shall be able to separate us from the love of God which is in Christ Jesus our Lord."

Now at first as I came to myself, and heard the voice of the Apostle discoursing of Jesus and of the life in Him, and of the joy and peace of it, being made conscious of my inward darkness and of the unattainable Light, I felt the burden of my miseries too great for me to bear. A shape of evil seemed to sit pressing down my soul, stifling her groanings and exulting over her unavailing struggles ; bidding me stop my ears against the voice lest it should disquiet my heart in vain, because having taken side with evil and having wilfully blasphemed, I was now his lawful slave, and regrets were unavailing ; and because I would not obey him, methought he was encompassing me all around with thick walls of an impenetrable dungeon, wherein I lay as in a sepulchre beneath the earth, fast bound, not able either to see or to hear. But suddenly, as if a great way off, I seemed to perceive a sound, though very faint, that " if Christ were for us none would be against us," and with that, a shaking of the walls of my dungeon ; and after that, came the other words of the Apostle each after each, battering at my prison, so that wall after wall fell with a great crashing noise ; and last of all there came that thunderous proclamation roaring around mine ears, that neither things present nor things to come, nor height nor depth nor any other creature should separate us from the love of God which

is in Christ Jesus our Lord ; and hereat my whole
dungeon straightway parted, like a curtain rent asunder,
and brightness burst in upon me as a flood, and the
Lord Jesus revealed Himself unto me as the Light and
Life of men.

THE END OF THE FIFTH BOOK

THE SIXTH BOOK

§ 1. OF THE TEACHING OF PAULUS.

WHO shall describe the marvels of the change when from the sea of sin a human soul is caught up into the life above, and lifted into the blessed brotherhood of the saints of God ? No fears, no doubts, no remorse ; but only a certain purifying fire of repentance within me, stimulating me to a life of virtue and to the helping of others, even as I had myself been helped. In addition to the delight of continual communion with my beloved teacher Paulus, my spirit was also refreshed by all the brethren of the church. For in them I found such a joy of fellowship as I had never before known, not like a common collegium where men meet merely to eat and drink and to be merry and to pay for the funeral of some deceased companion, and to give help to those of the collegium who may chance to be in need ; but the Christian collegium, if I may so call it, was far above all these, being bound together with a tie not to be loosened by death and so strong and passionate as I had never experienced nor even conceived, a veritable enthusiasm and insatiate desire for well-doing.

Marvellously great therefore was the change for one who had been but yesterday friendless, an outcast, despised of all men, now to find himself encompassed round with friends or rather brothers and bathed as it were in a flood of friendship. But the greatest help of all was the Lord Jesus himself, present in my heart by day and night, a constant fountain of inexpressible peace. Now also I heard once more and learned these words of the Lord which had first drawn my soul towards him at Antioch ; and other words I learned beside these, full of grace and healing. Many a time in Colossæ, and sometimes even in Pergamus and Corinth during the days of my darkness, I had caught myself unwittingly repeating to myself that most precious exhortation of the Lord Jesus to the weary and heavy laden, that they should come unto him and he would give them rest ; but then I had repeated these words as an unbeliever or as a doubter, striving to harden myself in unbelief ; now I repeated them with understanding, knowing them by experience to be true, and acknowledging that in him alone was rest. Notwithstanding the Spirit of the Lord, and the manifestations of the Spirit, came not unto me from the learning of the sayings of Jesus, but from the preaching of Paulus, who first revealed to me the power of the Lord unto salvation.

At this time I told Paulus the whole story of my life, and although I supposed that matters of love were scarcely fit for his hearing (as Epictetus had spoken of them slightingly, as beneath the attention of a philosopher) yet I concealed not either my former love for Eucharis or the bitterness of my sorrow for her death. He was moved by it more than I had thought possible, nor

did he rebuke me as I had expected. Hereon I described
to him the doctrine of Epictetus, who forbade me to
sorrow for her or for anything, or any person, because it
was necessary to preserve serenity of mind. But Paulus
shook his head, and said that it was not right that we
should in this way seek to escape from the troubles of
life by separating ourselves from others ; but that we
ought to rejoice with them that rejoice and sorrow with
them that sorrow, and that we should fulfil the law of
Christ by bearing one another's burdens. Yet he bade
me think of Eucharis as of one not dead but sleeping,
and not in the hand of Death but in the hand of the
Lord, " for " said he, " whether we live, or die, we are
the Lord's."

Again, when I spoke to him of my former doubts
concerning the ruling of the world, whether it were for
good or ill, he said that men had been placed in the
world as if in twilight, to seek and grope after God ;
but that now the day had dawned in the manifestation
of the Lord Jesus and in his rising again from the dead ;
" for " said he " this, and nothing else, is the salvation
of the world, resolving all doubts and shewing forth the
triumph of good over evil and of life over death."
And in all his doctrine he made mention of the
Resurrection of the Lord Jesus as being the foundation
of the whole Gospel and the seal of its truth.

As to the objections of Artemidorus (for I hid none
of them nor aught else, because of the perfect trust
I had in Paulus) namely, that the Lord Jesus had not
been sent into the world till after so many centuries,
and then to a most despised nation—the Apostle
lightened these doubts by teaching me more fully

concerning Israel; how the seed of Abraham, though
lightly esteemed of men, had been chosen of God to
proclaim his will; and how all things from the beginning, both the questionings of the Gentiles, and the
Law, and the Prophets of Israel, had prepared the way
for the coming of the Lord. But whereas Artemidorus
had said that there was no sin, and Epictetus also had
taught me that sin and crime were no more than
"erroneous opinion," Paulus now taught me quite
otherwise, that an Evil Nature was in the world from
the first, contending against the Good, and that the
Evil is the cause of all our sins and miseries; howbeit,
he bade me believe that out of our very sins the Love
of God worketh a higher righteousness, making evil
itself to be a kind of step of ascent to a greater good;
which belief I do still, and ever shall, hold fast. Touching any signs and wonders wrought by the Lord
(whereon certain of the brethren were wont to set great
store) he said but little, although he himself wrought no
small signs in the healing of diseases; for that which
drew him to the Lord was not signs nor wonders but a
love of him, and a trust in him, as being the spiritual
power of God manifested to the saving of the souls of
men. In the same way I also believed, and do still
believe, in the Lord Jesus, worshipping him not as the
worker of wonders and portents, but as the Eternal Love
of God, governing the world from the first, and in these
last days made flesh for us, that in him we might know
God, and love God, and be at one with God.

P

§ 2. HOW I RETURNED TO PHILEMON AT COLOSSÆ.

Even before I had been baptized (which took place on the seventh day after I had first heard the preaching of Paulus) I had resolved that I must at once return to Philemon. However, by the advice of Paulus, I went not straightway to Colossæ, but abode some days with him at his lodging, that I might be strengthened in the faith of Christ; and each day drew me closer to my new teacher. Those who knew him not might perchance have accused him of inconstancy; for his manner of speech and the features of his countenance changed every moment; and he was skilful as an actor to suit himself (in all honourable fashion) to them with whom from time to time he had to do, whether Jews or Greeks, bond or free, soldiers or courtiers, or whatever else. But the cause of his thus conforming himself to others in things indifferent was not inconstancy nor dissimulation, but a sincere love for all men and a power of feeling as others felt, so that his own nature disposed him without constraint to carry out that precept which was always on his lips, " Rejoice with them that do rejoice, and sorrow with them that sorrow." And beneath all this appearance of inconstancy there was a firm and solid resolution, the depth of which could not be known but by those who knew the depth of the love of the Lord Jesus. From Paulus (who knew Philemon well) I heard that my former enemy Pistus had fled from Colossæ some months ago, being convicted of theft, and after his departure his devices against me had been discovered and my innocence proved; hearing which I was the

more willing to return. Nor did the Apostle longer
delay me, saying that he doubted not but Philemon
would do what was right; but to make assurance surer
he would write a letter to him whereof I should be the
bearer.

I had not been an hour in Colossæ before Philemon
signified his desire to emancipate me without conditions,
at the same time lamenting that he had been led by the
practice of Pistus to suspect me without cause ; and for
the brief remnant of his life, he (no less than Apphia)
bestowed on me a truly parental affection ; which I for
my part endeavoured to requite with something of the
care and attention due from a son. Soon afterwards I
was appointed to the ministry, and I laboured in the
church at Colossæ to supply the old man's place, inasmuch as he became daily more infirm and less able to
preside over the congregation. Many difficulties in the
work began at this time to perplex me, because there
appeared in our little congregations divisions of opinion.
Some of the brethren were plain simple folk (slaves
most of them) delighting in wonders ; and these,
besides believing other portents, supposed that, after
their death, they would reign on earth with Christ for
many years wearing the same flesh and blood which
now they wore. Others (but of these only a few)
coming to the knowledge of Christ from the study of
philosophy, denied that there was any further resurrection, after the human soul had once been raised
up from the death of sin to life in Christ. Again,
others maintained Christ to be not very God, but only
the greatest of a great train of angels created by God ;
and some of these affirmed that Christ was not a man

at all (save in appearance only) but that he merely went
through the form of appearing to be born and to suffer
and to die. Many also attacked the Law of Moses
and the ancient Scriptures of the Jews; and these
(not understanding the doctrine of the Apostle concerning the progress of all things, and how the Law
was but as a slave to bring us to Christ) taking it for
granted that I must needs maintain the Law to be
perfect, and the doings of the Patriarchs to be perfect,
yea, and the letter of the Law to be perfect, endeavoured to bring the Scriptures into derision, by asking
whether the true God had nails and hair and teeth
and the like, as well as hand and voice and nostrils;
because, said they, the Scriptures declared that he had
the latter; and if the latter, why not the former?

Against all these opinions it seemed needful to contend, not so much inveighing against that which was
false, as rather pleading for that which was true. Many
times did I now desire that· my teacher, the blessed
Apostle, had been present to direct and guide me. But
then there came into my mind the saying of Epictetus
that "it is only a bad performer who is afraid to sing
alone," and how One greater than Epictetus had promised that he "would be ever with us." Yet I began
to lament (as did others also) that we had no writings
of the words and deeds of the Lord which might have
served as a lamp and guide to our feet. However,
in spite of these contrarieties, it was still a great
refreshment to note the work of the Spirit among all
such as believed in the Lord Jesus, yea, even among
some that erred in opinions. For not only did
all alike abstain from magic arts, and festivals, and

sacrifices to demons, and the like, but a wonderful change came also upon their whole lives : the thief no longer stole ; the lewd became chaste ; the cruel merciful ; the timorous and servile no longer feared aught save sin. To crucify slaves had become a thing hateful and abominable ; to expose children was to sin against God ; wealth and pleasure were despised ; and, in a word, such temperance, constancy and benevolence as are recommended by philosophers in their lectures to a small circle of pupils, these very virtues were practised by the whole multitude of the saints ; and this, not out of ostentation, nor " to preserve one's own serenity of mind " (as Epictetus would have had me think) but simply out of an insatiate desire to serve the Lord Jesus by loving and serving men. Nor could I fail to perceive how fruitful and blessed was the service of the Lord ; for that very peace and freedom of mind which Epictetus had held up to me as the chief object of life, and which I had found impossible to obtain by aiming at it, behold, now that I no longer aimed at it, but only desired to serve the Lord, this same peace of mind came as it were unasked into my bosom, peace deep, and calm, and past all power of tongue to utter or mind to understand.

§ 3. OF MY DISCOURSE WITH ARTEMIDORUS CONCERNING THE FAITH.

About this time died Artemidorus. Of late the old man had become infirm and bedridden, and I visited him often, and spoke much with him touching the

faith of Christ; and he received me the more willingly
because he had a great love for Epictetus (who was
now absent with his master in Rome), and he was wont
to say that I was now become a second Epictetus,
setting my superstition aside.   He retained all his
force of mind and keenness of understanding; and
still, as in old times, he would fain have judged the
Faith of Christ by the weakness of the weakest of
the brethren, and not by the strength which made
them strong.   For example, because certain of our
church (living from day to day in expectation of
the coming of the Lord) were wont to catch up,
perhaps too greedily, every light rumour of war or
famine or earthquake, as signs of the Last Day, on
this account he would call the Christians *misanthropi*,
enemies of Cæsar, and haters of the empire.   Again,
because others among us gave much time to fasting and
prayer, and in that condition discerned (or in some
cases perchance seemed to discern) visions of the Lord ;
or because a few, more superstitious than the rest,
abstained from eating flesh ; for this cause he mocked
at all the saints as dreamers of dreams and given to
foolish austerity and unprofitable abstinence.

   None the less, he willingly heard me speak of the
Lord Jesus, and sometimes himself questioned me concerning him.   One such conversation I remember, a few
weeks before his death, when, upon my entering his
chamber, I found him in a deep study : and, as soon as
he saw me, scarcely giving me time to salute him, " You
Christians," he said, " believe in a good God, who is all-
powerful ; whence then comes evil into the world ? "
" I will explain that," replied I, " when you can explain

whence arose the atoms which, as you say, made the Universe." He said, "Nay, my friend, I have no theories to maintain on this subject; but evil is opposed to your supposition of a good and powerful God." "Not more," I replied, "than atoms, existing from the beginning, are opposed to your supposition of no effect without a cause." Then he was silent, and said no more on that point. But producing my letters which I had written to him from Antioch (and it was at that time that he gave into my hands those papers the substance of which I have set down above) he urged against me more especially that which I had myself said, that the religion of Jesus was narrow, giving precedence to Jews, and compelling all men to be Jews in the observing of the Law; and he added that, however Paulus might affirm the contrary, this and nothing else was clearly the intent of Christus himself. But it was not difficult for me to shew that, howsoever Jesus had purposed that the Gospel should be preached to the Greeks through the Jews, yet his doctrine and kingdom had, from the first, been intended to include all mankind, without observance of the Law. I also repeated to him as many of the sayings of the Lord as I had been able to collect and to commit to memory; and hence I proved to him that he at whom Artemidorus had been wont to scoff, was neither juggler, nor magician, nor impostor, but a great Conqueror of the minds of men, and one whose doctrine and practice went down to the roots of life, and to the foundations of all things. And this indeed, when he had heard the account of his life and doctrine, Artemidorus did not deny, admitting himself to have misjudged in former times, and professing now to revere Christus as he would revere Socrates, or Epicurus, or Pythagoras; "but still," said he, "the acknowledgment of one great and good man more in the world, proves not that the world is divinely governed." Then I urged him again with a new argument, saying that it was very credulous to suppose that this wonderful Universe had come together by chance and without a Mind, whether the Mind had wrought through atoms or otherwise, and that if there were such a Mind, then those things that were done and said in accordance with that Mind would prevail (being in harmony with the universe) but those things that were not in accordance with it would come to nought; wherefore, since the words and deeds of Jesus of Nazareth had been already so very powerful (and that too without aid of force or cunning or any customary aids of great conquerors) it seemed certain that they were indeed in harmony with that Mind of the Universe to which Jesus had taught us to give the name of Father. To all this he listened patiently and attentively; and that he pondered these matters in his heart may be judged from the following rough notes which I found among his papers in his handwriting, dated about the time of our discourse together, that is to say a month or thereabouts before his death.

§ 4. OF THE DOUBTINGS OF ARTEMIDORUS.

"THE PROBLEM OF THE CHRISTIANS.

"This Christus lived in Syria less than forty years, and, after doing nothing worthy of mention, was put to death upon the cross by Pontius Pilatus, governor of

Judea. He made no conquests, no laws, and few disciples; and of these few one betrayed him. He wrought, it may be, some cures of a kind to startle the multitude (doubtless in accordance with nature, by working on the imaginations of men); but in any case none marvellous enough to persuade men that he was a prophet; for it is not denied that his own countrymen delivered him to execution. After his death, his disciples constantly affirmed that he had appeared to them, and in one case this was confessed by an enemy; but (saving this belief in his resurrection, and some kind of expectation that he would always be present with them as an ally) he bequeathed to his followers nothing except a policy that was no policy, but rather a dream, somewhat after this fashion :—

"THE DREAM OF CHRISTUS.

"The world is to be a commonwealth wherein the Supreme God is to be King, and all mankind the citizens. But God being the Father of men, mankind are to be to him as children, and to one another as brethren. Of this commonwealth the laws are to be as follows :—

"1. *The Law of Love.* Love (and not Force nor Cunning) is the strongest power in the world; and as little children take captive the hearts of their parents by force of love, so are the Christians to take captive the world by becoming as little children, loving all men and thereby constraining all men to love them in return. [Surely the vainest of vain dreams! In the fulfilment of which I will then believe when I see the sheep loving the wolf and thereby constraining the wolf to love them in return.]

" 2. *The Law of Giving and Receiving.* As by giving to Nature the husbandman receives a manifold return, so by giving to the Unseen Nature and Spiritual Harmony which Christus believed to exist—men shall receive an abundant harvest in return. Thus, by giving love, a man is to receive a return of love ; or giving pity, a return of pity ; or service, a return of service. [All this may be, and yet there may be no God. For doubtless, if a man give love to his fellow men, even though they love him not in return, yet he thereby enlarges his imagination of the Divine Love, and warms his heart with the fancy that he is now more perfectly loved by that Divine Person whom he has painted for himself out of the colours of his own mind. This dream may make some men happy, and more women ; but though a dream may give pleasure, it does not cease to be a dream.]

" 3. *The Law of Sacrificing.* All sacrifices of beasts are to be done away, the only true sacrifice being the sacrifice of the will, whereof the sacrifices of beasts are but as emblems. In the life and death of Christus (being a perfect sacrifice of the will) these Christians suppose the perfect sacrifice to have been offered up. Hence they regard Christus as the High Priest of mankind offering himself up for all men ; supposing that by force of sympathy with him, which they call ' faith,' they are able to be united with him and so to take unto themselves his sacrifice. [I deny not this doctrine of sacrifice to be less ignoble and superstitious than the notions of the common sort ; who vainly imagine

that they can bribe the Supreme by sheep and oxen.
But, even were it true, it seems too high and unsub-
stantial for the minds of the common people. Besides,
as there is no God, there can be no sacrifice, so that
this also is a dream, like all the rest.]

"4. *The Law of Forgiving.* It is supposed that, by
force of sympathy, every disciple of Christus has a
power of raising up men beneath him in goodness,
whom they call sinners. This 'sympathy' they call
bearing the sins of others, and the result of it is forgiveness; and Christus is said by them to have brought
this power into the world and to have bequeathed it
to his disciples. It differs, they say, from our 'forgiveness,' in that it means not the mere remission of
punishment, but the putting away of sin itself. [All
this is simply natural, and may be seen in any family
or assembly of human beings; wherein the better
always have a power of raising up the worse, and those
who are injured have power to set at rest the minds of
their injurers by forgiving them. Therefore all that
they can claim for Christus is, that he possessed this
power perchance in a singular degree, and discerned
how great a force it had over the minds of men; and
perhaps also that he (by some special and peculiar
influence) imparted it to his disciples.]

"5. *The Law of Faith and Trust.* No man, said
Christus, could be forgiven sins by him, except he had
'faith;' and in the same way his followers maintain
that without 'faith,' it is impossible to obtain the
forgiveness of sins, but by faith the worst of sinners
can be forgiven." [This again, so far as it is true, is
merely natural; because no offender can so much as

imagine himself freed from the consciousness of his
wrong-doing by the forgiveness of the man injured, if
he distrust the latter and esteem him as an hypocrite.
And without doubt this "faith"—as one may see even
in a dog that has faith or trust in his master—has not
a little power to confer magnanimity on men by raising
their minds to the level of a high idea of God, even
though that idea be but an empty imagination. But
here, as elsewhere, there is a deficiency of proof; for
what is wanted is, not superstructure, but foundation;
for I will not dispute the power of faith, if these
Christians will first give me somewhat certain to have
faith in.]

"ANSWER TO THE PROBLEM.

"This being the commonwealth and these the Laws of
Christus, the problem is, whence comes it that so many
thousands of men are drawn towards him, and thereby
led out of evil and vile courses into lives of virtue?
For other religions (and Onesimus justly urges this
argument) hold out similar hopes of Elysian fields, and
terrors of Hades, and purifications from sin; and some
also, like the religion of Pythagoras, pretend to join
men into brotherhoods; and almost all afford portents
sufficient to satisfy the natural credulity of men; yet
do they not succeed in persuading their votaries to lead
virtuous lives.

"The answer is, in my judgment, two-fold; first that
the Laws of Christus are in accordance with the
Harmony of things—by which however I am far from
meaning that there are gods, or any such things as sin,
forgiveness and the like, for all these things are probably

mere imaginations—but I mean that human nature is so framed as to be turned from the imagination of sin by the imagination of forgiveness and these other imaginations which Christus has devised; secondly, Christus himself appears to have been of a nature to imprint himself upon others to a degree much above the common; and his power over the minds of his disciples (as has been sometimes seen in the case of others, both teachers and law-givers and private men) instead of being diminished after death, was greatly increased.

"A third cause may be alleged by some, namely, that his disciples believed and cause others to believe, that he rose from the dead. But is this a cause, and not rather an effect? For we must surely ask, what caused his first disciples to believe that he had risen from the dead? Perhaps they did not believe it, but pretended to believe it, and deceived others. But this I do not think to be true in the case of Paulus; who was changed from an enemy to a friend by an apparition of Christus at the time when he was persecuting his followers. For this reason, and for others, I incline to believe that the first disciples did not deceive others, but were themselves deceived by apparitions, naturally arising from affection and imagination. Yet can I not deny that, on this supposition, the influence of Christus, being supposed to be so powerful over the minds of men as to force even an enemy to become a friend by the apparition of him whom he had persecuted, far exceeds anything that I have witnessed, or heard, or read; and it raises Christus to something almost above the nature of man.

"The sum of all is, that this commonwealth of Christus appears to me but a dream, though, I deny not, a noble dream. And even were it to prosper beyond expectation in the future, as it has already prospered in the past, yet could I not entertain it, having no belief in a god or gods. Yet thus much I admit, that, if I were able to believe in gods of any kind, I know not where among gods or men I could find anything more worthy of worship than this Christus, reasonably worshipped, without violence to nature; for if Plato was right in saying that 'there is nothing more like god than the man who is as just as man may be,' then certainly Artemidorus may say that 'if there were a god, there would be nothing more like god than Christus.'"

§ 5. OF THE LAST WORDS AND DEATH OF ARTEMIDORUS.

Thus wrote Artemidorus three or four weeks before his death; and from certain words that fell from his lips afterwards, I have hope that he came yet nearer to the Truth than this. However in his case I perceived (not indeed for the first time, but more clearly now than ever before) that it is not argument nor force of philosophy that brings into the Church of Christ them that are without, but it is rather the Spirit of Christ in the Church. For this Spirit, the Spirit of loving-kindness, and justice, and purity, and patience, not only binds us that are in the Church close together, but also causes them that are without to desire to enter in, while they wonder and admire at the concord of the brethren. In

this way the common people of Colossæ—rich as well
as poor, though more often the poor—coming by twos
and by threes to our assembly, were daily converted ;
but Artemidorus, being (as I have said) bedridden, could
neither know how great a change had been wrought by
Christ in the lives of the brethren, nor what a spirit of
power reigned over us in the meetings of the congregation, with which perchance he himself might have been
imbued had he been present among us.   Therefore when
I urged him a few days before his death, to believe and
to be baptized, though he was neither amazed nor in-
dignant, as of old, yet he shook his head, saying that
he was now too old and too sick to leap, at so short
notice, into a new philosophy.   "Nor," said he, "could
the gods themselves, if there be gods, take it in good
part that I, who have been, all my life through, a
perfect Mezentius, not merely offering no libations
to them but even denying their existence, should now
present to them as it were the dregs of the cup of this
life."   In this mood he continued even till his death.
Some of the brethren rebuked me afterwards because I
had not warned him of the fiery wrath that awaits
them that harden their hearts against the Lord.   But I
was not unmoved by the old man's answer to Archippus,
who had made some mention to him of the terrors
of hell.   To which Artemidorus replied that if Christus
were indeed a lover of truth, then he would of a
surety make some allowance for one who, all his life
long, had sought such truth as he could find, however
imperfectly, and who now, in his old age, was loth for
shame to say, "I will believe Christus to be god because,
if there be no gods, I thereby lose nothing ; and if he

be god, I thereby gain much." These words the old
man spoke to Archippus in my presence, when he was
now in extreme weakness, so that he could scarce move
his hand to bid me farewell; and on the morrow he
died, without making any sign at all of faith; only he
whispered to his secretary, a few minutes before his
death, to tell me this as his last message, that, whereas
he had charged me always to bear in mind the proverb
that " incredulity is security," now he perceived that
there was room for trust as well as distrust in the
life of man.

THE END OF THE SIXTH BOOK

THE SEVENTH BOOK

§ 1. HOW I CAME TO ROME TO- SEE THE BLESSED APOSTLE.

ABOUT six months after the death of Philemon, which took place in the same week as the Great Fire in Rome, word came to us that our brethren in the city were being called in question for their faith, having been falsely accused of many monstrous crimes and especially of having set the city on fire. Soon afterwards, in the month of January, we received most grievous tidings concerning them, how some had been cast into prison, and others slain with all manner of insults and tortures. The infection of this suspicion soon spread to Asia, first indeed to Ephesus, where it was soon allayed, but afterwards even to Colossæ, so that tumults were raised against us ; the more because of the earthquake which, in the summer of that same year, utterly destroyed Laodicea ; and in Hierapolis also and Colossæ many houses were cast down and many slain ; which calamities the common people imputed to us, the Christians, as if the gods had sent this plague on them because sacrifices had been withheld by our impiety. All that year I remained at Colossæ striving to confirm the brethren in

Q

the faith and to encourage the weak ; for though the
magistrates were not against us but rather for us
(knowing that we obeyed the laws) yet could they not
altogether resist the vehemence of the common people,
especially now that the fury of the multitude had some
pretext in the example of the Emperor. Wherefore
even against the will of the governors of the city, ten
or twelve of the brethren, having violent hands laid on
them by the rabble, bore witness to the Lord with their
blood. But, towards the end of the year, the cooler
weather setting in, and the memory of the earthquake
a little abating, the multitude began to cease from the
first heat of their fury ; when, behold, we received of
the brethren of Rome a truly piteous report, how the
Emperor was more incensed against us than ever,
causing such as were citizens to be beheaded ; but as to
the rest, crucifying some, burying others alive, casting
others to the wild beasts, or burning them, besmeared
with pitch, like torches. While we were all mourning
for their tribulation, there fell on us two blows of heavy
tidings, first that the blessed Apostle Petrus had been
taken and crucified, and then that Paulus also had been
put in bonds and was under accusation, and like to be
put to death. Then I could no longer restrain myself ;
so finding that all things in Colossæ now tended
towards peace, I left Apphia with Archippus (who had
come to lodge with us for a season, his house in Hierapolis being quite cast down by the earthquake while
ours was standing and not greatly damaged), and I
made all haste to Rome, hoping to find Paulus still
alive, and at least to have some speech with him before
he died.

. When I came to Rome, I went first to the house where the Apostle had been wont to lodge in times past, to make inquiry concerning him ; but it was not to be found, nor any of the houses near it, having been burned down in the Great Fire. Then I turned my steps to that part of the palace wherein I had first had speech with him ; but that also was burned down. For the whole of the former palace had been consumed by the fire ; and the Emperor was even then building for himself his new Golden Palace (as it is now called) on the Cœlian and Esquiline hills. Then I made endeavour to find the house of Tryphœna and Tryphosa where the church had been wont to meet ; but that also was not to be found. For indeed the fire had been far greater than I had conceived, and greater also (as I should judge) than any other fire within the memory of man, having wholly consumed four of the city wards, and partly destroyed seven more, leaving only three of the fourteen altogether untouched. So, what with the fire and the informers, the brethren had been driven out of the city ; and among these, Clemens and Linus. But, meeting at last with Asyncritus, I understood from him that the holy Apostle was in close keeping, in one of the dungeons of the New Palace. But whether his cause had been heard or not, and (if tried) what the issue had been, of this he was altogether ignorant. To the palace therefore I straightway betook myself, and finding there my old friend the actor Aliturius I frankly avowed to him that I was a Christian and that I was ready to die if I could but have speech with one of their number, named Paulus ; who then lay in one of the dungeons of the New Palace. He chid me for my rashness saying

that, if he himself had been such as he was when we
were last together, I had been a dead man; for what
prevented him from informing against me and gaining a
great reward? " But now," said he, " I also have known
something of this Paulus and (albeit I am myself no
Christian) I would fain do what may be done to aid
him and do you a pleasure." Then he took me to the
chief jailer, and by fair words, and large gifts, and
promises of close secrecy, I won him to consent that
if I would come thither on the morrow in the dress
of an actor as in old times, I should have speech
with Paulus.

§ 2. HOW I SAW PAULUS IN PRISON.

On the morrow, having gone to the palace, I was
straightway led down to the dungeon, and thence from
the outer prison into the innermost of all—rather a
barathrum, or pit, than fit to be called prison. As we
went down the steps, I questioned the jailer touching
the other Christians, whether any had been of late
condemned to the beasts, and whether the Apostle stood
in this peril. He replied that the prisoner was a
Roman citizen so that he was free from that death;
" and besides," said he, " the Roman people will not
have any presented before them to do battle with
beasts, except they be proper men and able to fight
for their lives, but this man was from the first lean and
sorry-looking, and now belike he is so worn with
imprisonment in the inner dungeon, and scant food to
boot, that I doubt we shall not find him alive." By

this time the man had descended the lowest step and
stood on the floor of the pit, turning his lamp on every
side, but making visible naught save pools of water, and
filth, and mire, and darkness without end. But presently, stumbling against something, I called to the
jailer, " Paulus is here " ; and he, bringing the lamp,
turned it so as to see more clearly, and said, " There
is no life in him."

Then I cried unto the Lord in my soul for mercy ;
for indeed, when the light of the lamp shone upon his
face, he neither spoke nor moved hand nor foot, and his
eyes were fast closed. But when I raised up his head,
and called him by his name, he opened his eyes and
looked on me, and I perceived he knew me. Then I
persuaded the jailer to take him out of this horrible pit
into the outer dungeon ; and we brought him out into
the court-yard, and the jailer departed, leaving us alone,
saying only to Paulus as he went forth, that it was the
last watch of the night and that the tenth day was at
hand ; which words I could not then understand.
When we were together, I took out bread and wine
mixed with water, which I had brought with me, and
besought him to eat and drink. He seemed loth at
first, but afterwards tasted a little, and his spirit was
revived, and strength came back to him, and he praised
God that he had vouchsafed to refresh him with the
sight of me once again. And turning to me with a
smile he said—playing on my name Onesimus, which
being interpreted means " profitable "—" Truly thou
hast been a profitable child unto me, and by this thy
kindness thou hast repaid him who begot thee in
Christ ; and yet I know not whether I should thank

thee or blame thee; for I was in the spirit when thou camest, and the Lord had sent unto me a vision full of delight in which methinks my soul would have passed away but for thy coming, so that by this time I had been with Christ. Yet doubtless it is the will of the Lord that I should be with thee a little longer."

Then he ate again of the bread which I had brought and drank also; and being now somewhat stronger, he sat upright, and laying his right hand lovingly on my head, he said with a smile, "Hast thou a grudge, my child, against the headsman, that thou wilt give him the trouble of taking off my head? for he and the jailer methinks had planned together that the prison should have spared them their pains; but now thou hast marred their counsel." "Surely," said I, "thou art not yet condemned by the Emperor." "Not by the Emperor himself," replied Paulus, "for he, as they told me, is on a journey to Greece; but by his freedman Helius, from whose lips 'Guilty' is a word of no less weight than from the Emperor's. In fine, it is now the ninth day since sentence was given that I should be beheaded; but the custom is, that the prisoner shall not suffer death till the tenth day, which, as the jailer but now said in thy hearing, is nigh at hand, or perchance already begun.

Hereat my eyes filled with tears, for pity of myself rather than of the Apostle, because I had come this long journey from Colossæ and would gladly have come ten times that distance to have speech with him, and to seek comfort and help and guidance from his lips, as from an oracle, yea, rather as from the Lord himself;

and now, behold, all my labour was for naught, and he, my guide and deliverer, and father in Christ, was to pass away from me at the season when my need of him was sorest. But Paulus comforted me, saying that he was glad, since the Lord so willed it, that he should die in the sight of men and not in yonder pit, and that he accepted me as an angel from the Lord bringing a message that he should bear public witness with his blood to the name of the Lord Jesus. Then he bade me tell him such tidings as I had to tell of the brethren at Colossæ and at Ephesus; and when I told him that both there, and in all Asia, the Lord was day by day adding to the number of the elect, he broke out into thanksgiving and praising of God, declaring that now he was well pleased to be offered up, for the work of his life was accomplished.

§ 3. HOW PAULUS RELATED TO ME THE STORY OF HIS LIFE.

After this he sat silent, but as it seemed to me praising God in his heart, and there was a wondrous light upon his countenance; and so he continued for some space musing and saying nothing. But I was in a great strait between two wishes, being on the one hand fearful to trouble or disturb him, and this too on the eve of his departure; and yet having a fervent desire to receive from him some last precepts for the guidance of the church. Presently however the Apostle himself broke silence thus: "Onesimus, my child, the hour approacheth when I shall bid thee farewell. If therefore thou wouldst ask aught of me, ask now; for the time is short." Then I betwixt the suddenness of the granting of my desire, and the multitude of the questions in my mind, could not find what to ask; but I exclaimed for sorrow, "Alas, my father, Petrus being now slain and thou also on the point to leave us, we shall be as sheep —— " At this he interrupted my words, putting his hand upon my mouth; "Nay, say not so, my child, that ye will be as sheep without a shepherd; for there is one Shepherd that hath promised that he will never leave thee nor forsake thee." I was silent, being abashed because of my want of faith; and he also sat for a while, musing and saying nothing. But at last he said, "The story of my life, and how the Lord guided me, yea, and constrained me against my will to follow him, this, having never yet related unto thee, I will now relate, or as much of it as the time may permit, that thou also mayst take courage, believing that even so will the Lord be a shepherd unto thee, guiding thee safe unto the end. Perchance also what thou shalt hear may enable thee the better to understand the mystery of mysteries, namely, how the kingdom of heaven is to be opened to all men, and how the Jews are for a time cast away that the Gentiles may be brought in, and so all mankind may be saved, even as the Lord ordained before the foundation of the world."

After a pause he began as follows: "Thou hast often heard those who wish not well to me, jest at my carriage and presence as being contemptible; and they say right, for so it is, and so it hath been with me from my childhood even to this day. For it pleased the Lord to chasten me in my tender years, making me weak of

vision, and well nigh blind. But it was turned to good
for me. For because of the infirmity of my eyes, not
being able to see such things as others saw, nor to take
pleasure in the pride of the. eye, and in the glory of
this world, and because also, whenever I went abroad,
I was despised and mocked at, for this cause I began
very early to bend my mind to take pleasure in knowledge and learning, and to think on the beauties of
things unseen, and on the strength of things that are
esteemed weak ; and I said often to myself ' Truth is
stronger than all things visible and shall prevail over
all.' When I grew older, this mind remained in me.
The love of women moved me not, nor gold, nor any
desire of pleasure ; but I had a fervent zeal for the
truth and for the Lord whose name is Truth, that his
name should be hallowed on earth, and that the people
of the Lord (for so I then deemed my nation, even
Israel after the flesh) should reign over the inhabited
world.

"The troubles and humiliations of Israel discouraged
me not, yea, rather they confirmed me ; for methought
the Scriptures shewed clearly that ever, in times past,
greatness sprang out of small beginnings, and triumph out
of humbleness. I perceived also that the Lord wrought
all his deliverances by means and ways unexpected
and strange to men ; not by force of arms, nor by
wisdom or cunning, nor by wealth, but for the most
part by faith contending against all these things, even
as David was caused to prevail by faith against Goliath,
and by faith Abraham was made to be the father of the
Lord's people. Therefore it disquieted me not that
Rome should be great and should rule for a season over

the Lord's inheritance ; for even thus Egypt and Assyria and Babylon and Persia and Syria had ruled over us, each in turn ; yet all these great empires had passed away, but the people of the Lord and the Law of the Lord still remained, and, said I, if we still have faith, we shall still remain and shall in the end be saved. Likewise I perceived that in every great deliverance there cometh first a transitory shadow of the deliverer, which is not the truth itself, but is of this present world ; and afterwards there cometh the true deliverer, which is of God ; and the will of this world is ever set against the will of God. For after this manner the world would have had Ishmael to be heir, but the Lord appointed Isaac ; and again, the world would have had Esau, but the Lord, Jacob ; and the world chose Eliab, but the Lord, David ; and even so, said I to myself, the world would have had in times past Egypt, Nineveh or Babylon, and, in these present times, Rome ; but the will of the Lord standeth fast, that he will have none other but Jerusalem to be his chosen City. With these thoughts did I comfort myself during my youth, saying, ' Though we be now under the yoke, we shall not always be thus.' Howbeit I perceived not that I should have gone yet further in my reasonings and I should have said, ' Israel after the flesh cometh first, but there is an Israel according to the spirit that shall come after ; and the world chooseth Jerusalem as it now is, but the Lord chooseth a new Jerusalem, even a city in heaven.' But this was not yet revealed unto me.

"As I grew up, when I looked around me to discern what it should be that should deliver Israel, I could perceive nothing except the Law. Men, as it seemed to

me, might pass away, yea, prophets could not be always
with us; but the Law remained, and would remain, a
safe guide for ever.   Therefore I gave all my mind and
my labour and leisure both by night and by day to the
study of the Law and the Traditions; wherein if aught
seemed to me unfit for the times, or imperfect, I would
stifle all such whisperings and murmurings of my soul
with such words as these, 'Doubtless the Law is perfect;
for if it be imperfect and in error, we must needs be
without a guide; and without a guide the people goeth
astray, and Israel is lost, and the promises of the Lord
are made of none effect; but this cannot be.'   Therefore it seemed to be the mark of a wise man and one
that loved Israel to see no blemish in the Law, yea, to
see perfection, though my understanding discerned im-
perfection.   So by degrees the Law took such a hold
upon me that it seemed all one with truth itself, and
instead of saying, 'Truth is great and shall prevail,' I
began to say, 'The Law is great and shall prevail.'
Then my parents, perceiving that I was wholly given to
the study of the Law, determined to send me from
Tarsus to Jerusalem, there to be brought up at the feet
of Gamaliel, one of the most learned of the Scribes.
And there in Jerusalem I remained many years, per-
fecting myself in the knowledge of the Law, and
endeavouring thereby to gain righteousness.

" As I grew more learned in the Law, so did I grow
in contempt for them that were unlearned.   I perceived that there were many, both men and women,
that had not leisure nor opportunity for the observance
of the more minute Traditions of the Law; and some
of these were troubled in their souls, full of doubts and

questionings, desiring forgiveness and deliverance from
sin, but not attaining to it ; others were even cast out
of the synagogue for light offences ; and this unlearned
and ignorant multitude was despised by the teachers of
the people, as if they were brute beasts to be restrained
by bit and bridle ; and I also despised them likewise.
Yet sometimes when I saw a rich man that had leisure,
highly honoured in the synagogue, and a poor man shut
out for neglect of some lighter matter of the Traditions,
which perchance he had no leisure to observe, my heart
would say, 'Surely these ways are not God's ways.
Surely to trust thus in the Law is not faith.' But then
I would still quench all these questionings, as before in
Tarsus, saying, 'If these ways be uneven, which is the
even way ? And if we are not to obey and trust the
Law, what shall we obey, and in what shall we put our
trust ?' By such answers as these I hardened my
heart ; and as an ox struggles against the goad of his
master, even so did I resist the Lord, who would have
goaded me into the path of truth.

"When I came to have to do with the followers of
the Lord Jesus, or Nazarenes as I then termed them, I
hardened my heart still more, and esteemed them
accursed because of the cross. For I said 'Whosoever
is crucified is under a curse. Wherefore this Jesus, whom
the Nazarenes call Messiah, is accursed, and his followers
also. Moreover if this sect prevail, the Teachers of the
people will be despised, and the unlearned will have the
upper hand, and the Law (which is the Truth) will be
trampled under foot ; wherefore the Truth itself as it
were proclaimeth that these Nazarenes are liars and deceivers.' So I hardened myself like a flint against them.

Yet by degrees as I learned more and more of the life
and manners of the saints, their zeal in well doing, their
long-suffering and patience, their purity and justice, and
above all, the steadfastness of their faith in God through
the Lord Jesus Christ, then, even in the midst of my
course of persecuting them, I could not forbear sometimes
from reproaching myself in such words as these : ' This
man whom thou art dragging away to prison hath
attained to a righteousness beyond thy compass ; this
woman, whom thou threatenest with death, hath a faith
in God surpassing thine.' With such self-chidings did
the Lord still goad me toward the right road ; but I still
kicked against the goads and hardened my heart against
him."

§ 4. HOW PAULUS CONSENTED TO THE DEATH OF THE
BLESSED MARTYR STEPHANUS.

Here the Apostle ceased for a space, as if he were
unwilling to make mention of somewhat that came
next to speak of ; but anon, as though all thought of
bitterness was swallowed up in the remembrance of the
marvellous mercies of the Lord, he continued with a
kindling countenance and speaking more quickly than
before. Now, although I treasured up each word that
fell from his lips, yet because of his manner of speech
being as much Hebrew as Greek, and very brief,
abrupt, and vehement at all times, and now more
than ever, I was not able to set down his words exactly,
though indeed I wrote them on my tablets a few
hours afterwards. Wherefore it must be understood
that the exact words, both before and in that which

follows, are not his. But the substance I will set down with all faithfulness, and it was to this effect.

"The more closely I joined myself to the Pharisees against the Nazarenes, and the more I saw of the cunning, and baseness, and hardness of heart of those inferior instruments by whose aid our chief priests and elders were wont to execute their designs, the more was I troubled with doubts. Sometimes when I lay down to rest at night, after a day spent in persecutions in the company of these base companions, the words of the Prophet Isaiah would rise up against me in the darkness, ' Wash you, make you clean ; cease to do evil, learn to do good ; your hands are full of blood ;' and once, when I was sitting down to meat, methought I saw blood upon my hands. All the more did I frequent the temple and offer up many sacrifices and purify myself with daily purifications that I might wash away all sinfulness if perchance there were any stain of guilt upon me. But still I was not at ease, neither had my soul rest. By degrees, the Temple itself, and the sacrifices in the Temple, instead of taking away my burden, began to add thereto. For of the multitude who came together thither, very few appeared to come worthily ; some being strangers come from afar to see strange sights ; others desiring to expiate evil deeds or to pay vows, but not with any sincere love of righteousness ; and many more because it was the custom, and not because they loved the worship of the Lord ; not a few also with purpose to make gain, trafficking in beasts for victims or serving as money-changers. All this I noted daily, and it troubled me more and more, because I perceived that many were hardened in ill-doing by their

worship and by their sacrifices, and their feet stood in
the Temple of the Most High, but their hearts drew
nigh unto Satan ; and again the words of the Prophet
rose up to my mind, ' Sacrifice is an abomination to me ;
bring no more vain oblations.'

"But when I said to one of the elders that it were
well if the money-changers and sellers of victims could
be put away from the holy place, and if the stir and
tumult of the Courts of the Temple could be diminished,
he said that I was of too tender a conscience, and that
it would not be possible to obtain such a temple as I
desired, clean, and pure, and spotless in all points,
unless I wished to join myself to the Nazarenes who
dreamed of some magic temple not made with hands,
wherein some invisible sacrifice of the imagination was
to be offered up, and not the blood of bulls and goats.
These words (although I knew it not at that time) sank
deep into my heart. For though I abhorred all thought
of imitating the Nazarenes in any matter, yet could I
not refrain from pondering in my mind the thought of
some new Temple, not made with hands, nor liable to be
polluted nor destroyed by the hand of an enemy, but
imperishable, incorruptible, undefiled. Being in this
perplexity, I thirsted for some new revelation from
the Lord, and besought him that he would send some
prophet or deliverer who should make all things clear.
But then the word of the Lord brought back to
me that which had been revealed to me even in my
childhood, namely, how each deliverer of Israel was
wont at first to be despised and rejected; and fear fell
upon me lest, even if the Messiah himself should come
before our generation had passed away, the Pharisees

should not acknowledge nor receive him. But, all this while, it never so much as entered into my heart that the Messiah was already sent, and already despised, and already rejected by the rulers of the people ; but I had my eyes fixed on some deliverance yet to come.

" None the less, yea, rather the more, did I persecute the Church of Christ, giving my voice ever in favour of violent courses and advising that the common sort among them should be less regarded, but the leaders sought out with all diligence and slain. So it came to pass that by my advice the servants of the chief priests laid hands on the blessed Stephanus (concerning whom I have often spoken unto thee in times past) and set him before the Council, and accusation of blasphemy was brought against him ; and I sat with the Council when he made his defence. The words of his speech were as a two-edged sword cleaving my heart asunder and strengthening all my former doubts against me. For he declared unto us how, even as Israel had rejected other deliverers, so had they rejected Jesus the Messiah, and that this was fore-ordained by God ; as also that the Temple of the Lord was not to stand for ever, but that there was to be a new Temple not made with hands. So he showed how Joseph and Moses had saved the people, albeit they had been at first rejected ; and how Israel had made a calf and turned to idolatry ; and how Moses, being permitted to make the earthly tabernacle for the hardness of their hearts, had, none the less, made it after the pattern of a better tabernacle not made with hands ; and how the Temple itself had not been made by David, but only by Solomon (who in his old age went after other gods) ; and with that he cried aloud that no earthly Temple was fit for the Most High, using the words of the prophet, ' Heaven is my throne, and earth is my footstool ; what house will ye build me, saith the Lord ? '

"Hereat the men of my faction, and especially those from Cilicia and Asia, cried out that Stephanus blasphemed, and they rent their garments and would have stopped his mouth with their uproar ; but he rebuked us, saying that as we had persecuted the prophets, so had we murdered the Holy One. Hereat the uproar waxed still louder ; but I sitting speechless all this time, and not able to take my eyes off his countenance, perceived that, of a sudden, as if one had plucked him by the sleeve, he turned round and ceased from rebuking the multitude, and stood still, looking upward very intently as if he saw somewhat. Then a great splendour shone upon his face, and he stretched out his hand towards heaven saying, ' Behold I see the heavens opened and the Son of Man standing on the right hand of God !' At this I could not forbear turning round also, and gazing upward to the heaven above me, if perchance I also should see somewhat there. But I saw naught (for my eyes were not yet opened) and anon arose another general shout that the prisoner was worthy of death, and all cast dust in the air and rent their garments again. So the whole multitude arose, and I with them, not knowing whither I went, nor do I remember what further happened, till I saw Stephanus on the ground, covered with blood, in a loud voice beseeching the Lord that this sin might not be laid to the charge of us his murderers ; and, behold, the clothes of them that stoned him were lying at my feet, in token that I was the chief doer of this deed."

§ 5. HOW THE LORD APPEARED TO PAULUS.

"On the night after the blessed Stephanus died, I had no rest, nor for many nights after. Dreams and visions visited me in my sleep. Sacrifices and ablutions I made without ceasing, but they brought me no peace ; neither did my prayers find answer from the Lord. They that were rich praised me, and I was held in honour by the rulers of the people, but I said in my own heart, 'Doth not the Lord, the God of Israel, cast down the wisdom and power and riches of this world and raise up the lowly and meek ?' By night methought I saw the face of Stephanus covered with blood and praying for me ; and the hand of the Lord was heavy on my soul filling me with fears and thoughts of evil. Yet still, like the stubborn ox, kicking against the goads of the Lord, I resolved that I would not think on idle dreams, as I called them, but that I would give myself with a single heart to the persecution of the Nazarenes. So I gladly obeyed the High Priest who besought me at this time to go to Damascus, bearing letters to the chief men of that place, that I might have power to imprison such of the Nazarenes as I could find there.

"We journeyed slowly ; for the burden of the Lord was grievous upon me, and my eyes (which were infirm by nature) were now, more than ever, dimmed and dazzled, so that I could scarcely endure the light of day. Likewise by night evil dreams departed not from me. Now also, methought (which had not been so before), I began to hear a strange voice (yet as it were

in my heart and not in my ears) as if some one reasoned
with me, accusing me that I had slain Stephanus without cause; insomuch that sometimes I could endure no
longer to listen in silence, but made answer to the voice
aloud; but presently, it was as if no voice had spoken,
and one of my companions overhearing me, reproached
me in jest, because, said he, I discoursed aloud with
myself, preferring my own speech to theirs.   Therefore
that I might not hear these voices, I ceased not speaking
with my companions, reasoning with them (though none
reasoned against me) and proving to them from the
Scriptures again and again (though none denied it) that
the Law must not be set aside and that the Temple must
abide for ever, and that this Jesus was a deceiver of
the people.   But ever and anon there would come into
my ears (yea, even in the midst of my speaking) such
words as these : ' What if the Law were indeed fore-
ordained to prepare the way for Faith ?   What if there
should be indeed a new Temple, prepared of God, not
made with hands ? '   Then would I weary my companions with the superfluity of my reasonings and
disputings, waxing fiercer and louder than before in
defence of the Law and against the Nazarenes.   They
that went with me, falling in with my humour, ceased
not to revile the deceivers of the people as they termed
them ; and one among them speaking of Stephanus (of
whom all this time I had made no mention) said that he
had been a hypocrite and a deceiver even in his death,
gazing up to heaven as if to persuade us that he saw
a vision, and framing his face to assume a divine
appearance of gentleness and peace, and all to delude
the people.

"Hereat my heart was stirred within me and I was moved to say that I did not feel assured that Stephanus (however deceived) was acting deceitfully at that moment when he was on the point of death; but as I feared lest this might cause my companions to suspect that I favoured the Nazarenes, I restrained myself and assented (against my conscience) to the man that had spoken thus. So I answered, 'Thou sayest well; this Stephanus was a deceiver.' Then, because I felt that I had lied, straightway there swelled up within me a violent desire to cry aloud 'Stephanus was no deceiver;' but still. I rejected it as a voice from Satan, and strove to turn the discourse to other matters. But in vain; for now, even as if they were desirous of set purpose to thwart me, my companions would speak of naught else but Stephanus, and how he bore himself, and what he said, and of the manner of his death, and of his vision.

"By this time we were come unawares within sight of Damascus; and I looking afar off upon the pleasant gardens that encompassed the city, rejoiced greatly because here, I said, I shall have rest from my weariness, and here these voices of Satan will cease from troubling me. But even as I spake thus within my soul, the Voice came to me much louder than before, and not once but many times: 'Wilt thou yet continue this course of blood? Wilt thou again shed innocent blood? Wilt thou yet kick against the goad of the truth?' Then I made answer 'Yes I will continue;' and these words I repeated again and again. Then suddenly the hand of the Lord fell on me, my body seeming on fire as well as my soul, and my eyes not knowing whither to turn for pain, and at last I could no longer contain myself for the sore agony of my doubting, but said aloud (yet not so that my companions could hear), 'If now that deceiver Stephanus were no deceiver, if'——— and behold, I looked up to heaven as Stephanus had looked, and lo, a brightness indeed, as of the glory of God; and a voice no longer in my soul but in my ears also, penetrating to my soul, and saying, 'Saul, Saul, why persecutest thou me?' Then I fell upon my face, knowing who it was that spoke, yet constrained to ask as though I knew not, and I said, 'Who art thou, Lord?' And he said 'I am Jesus of Nazareth whom thou persecutest. It is hard for thee to kick against the goad.' Then said I 'Lord, what wilt thou have me to do?' And he made answer saying, 'Arise, go into the city, and there it shall be told thee what thou shalt do.'

"So I arose: but behold, I was wholly blind. Being led into the city by my companions I lay some days still under the heavy hand of the Lord, pondering many thoughts and doubting whether it would please the Lord to restore to me my sight; and during all this time I spoke many things not according to my own knowledge, for I was no longer master of myself. Among other matters the Lord caused me to make mention of one Ananias, one of the chief among the Saints in Damascus (whom I had purposed to have slain) saying that it was the Lord's will that he should come to me and make me whole. Whereof when the rumour came to the ears of Ananias, he, being also moved by a vision of the Lord which he himself received, came to me and laid his hands upon me, and straightway my senses returned to me, and

presently I began to see a little, and in no very long
space I was made whole and received my sight as
before."

§ 6. HOW PAULUS WAS PREPARED FOR THE PREACHING
OF THE GOSPEL.

" When I was recovered of my blindness, some of
the brethren in Damascus would have had me go up
to Jerusalem that I might be instructed in the faith
by those that had been disciples before me. But the
Lord suffered it not, but bade me go into Arabia ;
where, for the space of two years, I remained, giving
myself wholly to prayer, and to the reading of the
Scriptures, and pondering the purposes of God. And
here it pleased the Lord to reveal many mysteries unto
me and more especially the mystery of the New Temple
and the heavenly Jerusalem. And the grace of the
Lord was poured out upon me very abundantly, working for me good out of evil, enabling me to discern
the truth the more clearly perchance because I had
once fought against it. For as I had ever been wont
to say, ' If the Nazarenes be right, then are the Jews
wrong, and if Jesus be the Messiah, then are the Law
and the Temple destined to pass away,' so now, believing that Jesus was indeed the Messiah, I had the less
difficulty in believing that the Law must needs pass
away, and all things must be changed.

" At the same time it was revealed to me in the
spirit that the outward fashion of all things must
change but the will of God abideth for ever ; for in

spite of death, and sin, and all the devices of Satan, the purposes of the Highest are unchangeable ; which have been, and shall be, fulfilled, in many diverse shapes, yet ever remain the same ; and how the redemption of the world through Christ and the casting away (in part and for a time) of Israel, together with the bringing in of the Gentiles, were not by chance— as if the purposes of the Unchangeable were changed— but fore-ordained before the foundation of the world ; even as it was also fore-ordained that Adam should fall, and Abel should be slain, and that Ishmael and Esau should be rejected to the intent that Isaac and Jacob might be chosen ; in all these things I now discerned the unchanging purpose of the Lord triumphing over Satan from the first, and out of sin and death drawing forth life and righteousness. Also, as regards the death of the Lord Jesus upon the cross, I no longer felt shame at it, nor passed lightly over it in my doctrine (as some do still, my Onesimus) ; for I perceived that it was a sacrifice fore-ordained, yea, the only true sacrifice and oblation for the sins of men, whereof all former sacrifices had been but shadows.

" Likewise it was revealed to me that mankind must rise from the death of the flesh and be born to the life of the spirit. For as man was first made and sinned in Adam, so man was afterwards made again and born to righteousness in the Lord Jesus ; the first Adam was the shadow, the second, the truth ; the first Adam was of the earth and of this world, the second Adam was of the spirit and of heaven. And as all men are bound to Adam by the bonds of

flesh, so must they be bound to the true Adam by the
bonds of the spirit, that is by trust or faith and by love,
whereby men must be so knit to the Lord Jesus that
whatsoever hath befallen him must also befall them. For
all flesh, being redeemed in Christ, is made one with
Christ. As therefore the Lord Jesus suffered and died and
rose again and reigneth in heaven, so must the children
of men, even all the nations of the earth, suffer and
die according to the flesh, but rise again according
to the spirit, and reign in spiritual places, perfected
with him. And this hath been the eternal purpose
of God from the foundation of the world.

"Moreover, lest I should despise the past, and reject
the Scriptures, or lightly esteem the Gentiles, or stumble
because of the many generations of darkness which
have been since the world was created, all of which
knew not the Lord Jesus, for this cause the Lord
revealed unto me that he for the most part worketh
by slow means, and teacheth by slow degrees ; first
the elements, or teaching for babes, then for youths,
then for full-grown men ; and this is true for every
soul of mankind, yea, and for every nation also.
Wherefore I no longer despised the Gentiles, albeit the
Lord had suffered them for many generations to go astray
after idols ; nor did I begin to despise the Law of Israel,
although I no longer esteemed it as before. For it
was revealed to me that, though the Law had been
ordained only for a time, and because of the hardness
of our hearts, and could make nothing perfect, yet
did it prepare the way for perfection in Christ. For
by the grace of the Lord it was given to me to
understand that all things in heaven and earth, whether

past or present, whether among the Jews or the Gentiles, yea, even the beasts of the field and the very dust of the earth beneath our feet, were all created for the glory of God, to testify that he, the Highest, is the Father of men, and that men must be conformed to his divine image.

"Wherefore, since the will of the Lord standeth fast, take comfort, dear Onesimus, child of my bonds and heir of my labours, and overcome evil with good. Shut not thine eyes against evil, but fight against it with a stout heart. Whensoever thou lookest upon it triumphing in high places; or setting itself up as having dominion over the earth; or creeping into the Church, causing therein errors, schisms, and deceits; yea, and when also thou lookest upon it in thine own heart, prompting thee to despair because of thine own ill courses in old days—then do thou contend against it in the name of the Lord Jesus, and in his name thou shalt surely overcome it. Say not in thine heart, 'Rome is against us,' but say rather, 'Rome that now is, shall be like unto Babylon and Nineveh, which once were, but now are passed away.' Look not upon the outward things which are but for a moment, but upon the things which are not seen, which are eternal; even as I also look not upon these my manacles and fetters, and upon this poor wasted flesh nigh unto destruction, nor upon the filth and foulness of yonder pit; but instead of this earthly flesh, I see the heavenly body wherewith my Lord shall shortly clothe me, and instead of this visible darkness, mine eyes behold the invisible glory of the Eternal Majesty on High, wherein enfolded, amid the blessed company of the saints above, I shall for ever magnify the unsearchable riches of the mercies of God.

"And now, since thou knowest whither I go, why wouldst thou, dearest Onesimus, that I should longer delay my departure ? For I have been these many years like unto a servant making all things ready for a journey, that, when the master shall knock, he may be prepared to go forth to a pleasant land. And behold, the Master knocketh, and the door is now open, and shall I not gladly go ? "

§ 7. THE LAST WORDS OF PAULUS.

When the Holy Apostle had made an end of speaking, I was ashamed of all the questionings which had disturbed me at Colossæ ; and in his presence I felt myself lifted up above all doubts. Yet again, looking to the future when I should be alone, I said, " One other question I would gladly ask of thee," and he bade me " Ask on," and I proceeded thus : " Thou saidst, but now, that all men and all nations, yea, and all created things, are made subject to ignorance, and error, and death, and sin, to the intent that they may be raised from the lower to the higher ; even as children are led up from the restraint of nurses and guardians to the freedom and knowledge of manhood, and as Israel also was led from the law to Christ. Now therefore I would that thou shouldst resolve me this doubt : As it is the nature of every child of man to pass through error to the truth, and as Israel also hath erred, may not we also err, even we the Saints of God ? And certain of the saints who

say that they have seen the Lord Jesus in dreams and
visions or other ways, may not they also sometimes err ?
Yea and in the Traditions of the Acts and Words of the
Lord, amid much that is true, may there not also be
somewhat that is false ? "

Hereat he smiled and said, "Thou hast well
questioned me. Assuredly we, even the Saints, may
be, nay, must needs be, in some error. For whereas
hereafter we shall discern all things as they are, seeing
God face to face in heaven, on earth we can but see
them darkly, as it were through a mirror. Yet be thou
ever prompt, my dear Onesimus, to make distinction
between those cases where to err is to lie, and hurtful to
the soul, and those where to err is not to lie, and therefore not in the same way hurtful. For I also, not many
months ago, was in error concerning the time of the
coming of the Lord. For as a peevish child is im-
patient till the day shall dawn, though the sun be not
risen nor like to rise, even so I desired that my Lord
should come before his time, while I still lived, and that
I should be snatched up into the clouds to him, before
this generation had passed away. But now I perceive
that the day of the Lord is not yet, nor will be perchance during this generation nor the next, nor perhaps
for many generations yet to come. Herein therefore I
erred, but inasmuch as this error was not against my
soul, to err in such a matter was not to sin.　·

"But now let me tell thee what kind of error
corrupteth the soul, and warreth against righteousness.
Whoso supposeth that to abstain from swine's flesh
maketh expiation for impure thoughts, or that a man
may be envious and a slanderer if he do but observe

Sabbaths, I say unto thee that such a one walketh in the darkness of error that wholly cloudeth the soul and shutteth out the light of God. For these opinions or beliefs are against the perfect Law of Love; against which whatsoever opposeth itself is not of God but of Satan. From such errors as these flee thou, and fight thou, with all thy power; but the other errors none can altogether avoid, nor be thou overmuch troubled concerning them. As I myself was in error touching the day of the Lord, so doubtless art thou touching some other matters, and so are and so will be, many others of the saints, liable severally perchance to several errors. Yea, all earthly knowledge of heavenly things must needs be, in some sort, error, because they are seen as it were by reflection through an imperfect glass; for the perfect God none hath seen nor can see in the flesh. Wherefore doubt not but thou art assuredly in error; yet be not on that account disquieted, provided that thou strive to attain more and more of the truth. Neither forget thou that the Spirit of the Lord Jesus Christ shall be with thee to guide thee into all truth, and to turn darkness into Light before the feet of the Saints, from generation to generation, that all men may grow in the knowledge of the Lord, and in the understanding of his unsearchable ways.

"Be not thou therefore, O my son, shaken in thy faith, if in the Traditions of the Acts and Words of the Lord some things be diversely or inexactly reported; only strive thou earnestly to keep pure and undefiled that truth which is the source and foundation of the rest; I mean, that Jesus of Nazareth the Son of God hath manifested to us the love of the Father through himself, and that he, having verily risen from the dead, reigneth in heaven and helpeth his saints on earth, purposing to conform all nations of men to the Father and to destroy death and sin through his cross. Believe this, my son, and cause others to believe this; and then thou needest to concern thyself little with genealogies and minute disputings of words and diversities of traditions, nor even about sundry visions and dreams, whether they be of the Lord or no; for the foundation of the faith consisteth not in knowing how, or to whom, or when, or in what places, the Lord hath manifested himself or shall manifest himself, but in believing that he is verily not dead, but liveth. All this I say, not as if thou shouldst be careless or slothful about the attainment of the exactness of the truth, so far as lieth in thee; but place not letters before words, nor words before things, nor any kind of knowledge of things, no nor even prophecies nor visions themselves, before Love. For verily I say unto thee, the time shall come when prophecies shall fail, tongues cease, and knowledge vanish away, but Faith, Hope, and Love shall never pass away but shall abide for ever, and the greatest of these is Love."

The sound of the unloosing of the prison-bars now fell upon my ears, and presently the jailer entered saying, "The night is spent, and the guard ready." I besought him that I might accompany Paulus to his death, but the jailer would not allow it, saying that I must remain with him in the prison, for he should lose his place were it known that I had been with the prisoner. When I would have urged him further, the Apostle suffered it not, saying to me with a cheerful countenance, " Nay, my son, tarry thou with our friend here ; for thinkest thou that thy father cannot walk alone, or fearest thou lest he stumble in the darkness ? Nay, but if the night be spent, the day must needs be at hand ; therefore fear not." The man marvelled, not understanding that the Apostle spoke of the day beyond the grave ; but he said, " Thou goest to death bravely ; however, there is no need of haste if thou wouldst have meat and drink to be thy *viaticum*." " I thank thee," replied Paulus, " but I have other *viaticum*, whereof, since there is no need of haste, I would gladly partake with my son ; suffer us, therefore, if it may be, to be alone yet a brief space longer." Then when the man had retired, Paulus said to me, " Now, my son, because the time is short, let us make haste to be with Christ a while, and with all the company of saints, both the blessed ones that have gone to rest before us and those that have remained below." Then he took of the bread and wine which I had brought ; and when he had broken and blessed, we ate and drank, and the Apostle called on the Lord in prayer. What words he uttered I know not ; for I was as one in a vision, and the walls of the dungeon seemed to have fled away, and as he continued speaking of the Lord in heaven, who is above all thrones and powers, and of the glory that is to come to us with him above, I seemed to pass beyond earth, and upwards from the lower heaven, even till the highest of all, even to the region of everlasting joy, where thou, O Eternal, dost feed Israel for ever.

When I had come to myself, I was still kneeling, but the holy Apostle standing before me, with his hands upon my head, blessing me ; and he touched me on the

shoulder saying, " I go, Onesimus." " Nay, my father,"
replied I, "let us abide here evermore in heaven." But
he made answer, and these were his last words—" Thou
hast a work yet to do, Onesimus, and a battle yet to
fight for the Lord; yet be assured of this, my child,
that wheresoever thou mayst be on earth, thou shalt
verily abide with me in heaven, for I am Christ's and
Christ is thine."

THE END OF THE SEVENTH BOOK

THE EIGHTH BOOK

§ 1. OF THE DEATH OF NERO, AND HOW ROME WAS DIVIDED AGAINST ITSELF.

AT thy bidding, dearest Epaphras, I once more take up the pen; having been minded before to have concluded this book with the end of the life of the blessed Apostle Paulus upon earth. But indeed thou sayest well that all unwittingly I have been writing, not so much the story of mine own life (which had a fit end methinks when I was first brought to the knowledge of the Lord Jesus and began a new life in Christ) nor yet the life of the blessed Apostle, but rather the history of the manifestation of the power of Christ; wherefore thou biddest me continue this history, passing over smaller matters in my own life, and speaking of such greater matters as concern the Church of God; and this, by God's grace, I will now endeavour to do.

When I returned to Colossæ and to my labours in the church there, endeavouring to keep the brethren in the right path, in accordance with the doctrine of the blessed Apostle, at first I had small success. For whereas even before, the Jewish brethren had been bitter against me, now, after my return, their bitterness had increased, yea, and was daily increasing. Hereof the main cause was the troubles of their brethren which were in Syria. For now of late the fires of those discontents which had been as it were smouldering, even from the time of Cumanus the Proconsul, nearly twenty years ago, and then in the time of Felix, about ten years ago, broke forth into flame. During the same year in which I had gone to Rome to see the Apostle, the Emperor Nero had sent Titus Flavius Vespasianus to have command over the legions in Syria; and from that year onward for nearly five years, even to the time when the Holy City was destroyed, naught but wars and rumours of wars ran all through the world, and more especially through Syria. Throughout all that time the Jews were shamefully oppressed, thousands, yea, tens of thousands, being sold (even before the siege of the Holy City) to 'be slaves in Rome, or scattered through the cities of Asia. These and countless other injuries set the whole nation—yea, even many of those that believed—against all Gentiles, whether belonging to the saints or not; and more especially did they rage against the memory of the beloved Apostle Paulus, some saying that he was no true Jew, others that he was not really an Apostle as the rest of the Apostles, and others even calling him "the enemy." So there was for five years and more a great battle raging in the Church, whether the saints should observe the Law of Moses or no; and for some time it seemed not unlikely that the Jewish faction would prevail and that the Gentiles would be compelled to submit to the Law.

During all these five years the minds of all men were marvellously moved, and the empire was divided against

itself, and many among the saints thought that the Lord
would daily appear. At first indeed the Church began
to rejoice because their chief adversary, the Emperor
Nero, was taken away.   I was in Corinth, as I remember,
in that year, ministering to certain of the saints (whom
I had known formerly in Rome), who had been sent by
the Emperor to work at the great canal, which he desired
to have made between the two seas near that city ; and
while I was with the prisoners, a trireme came sailing
past within bowshot, decked with flags and garlands.
One of the guard, that kept the prisoners, cried aloud,
" What tidings from Rome ? "   And answer came back
across the water, " Nero is no more."   Then all held
their breath because none could believe such happy
tidings, and when the voice came again from the trireme,
" Nero is dead," then all the prisoners, yea, and the
guards too, raised a shout for joy, and within a very few
hours, they all were free and the business of the canal
at an end.   Not unlike the joy of these prisoners was
the gladness of the whole Church of Christ when he
whom they called the Beast was taken out of
their path.

   But anon came divisions, nation against nation and
army against army fighting who should be emperor ;
and first one and then another rose up and passed away,
and all was chaos, nothing solid or sure. But there
was heard again the old prophecy that " One from the
East " should come forth and rule over the empire.
Some said that this was Vespasianus ; others (and this
began to be commonly believed more especially among
the Jews and the Jewish faction of the saints) that
Nero, being raised from the dead, would come again

from the East across Euphrates with all the kings of
the East, to make the rivers run with the blood of his
enemies ; and this even from the first, straightway after
the death of Nero, was commonly believed in Rome by
the baser sort, insomuch that many deceivers arose
pretending to be Nero, and his effigies were set by
unknown hands in the public places, and the rostra
were crowned, and sacrifices offered in his name ; and
thence this belief spread quickly through the empire,
and it is commonly believed even to this day, namely,
the fourth year of the Emperor Domitian wherein I
now write. So it came to pass that even after the
death of Nero, the minds of men were still in division
and discord ; and the Jews of Syria, yea, and certain of
the Jews also among the faithful, had expectation that
still their nation would prevail, because Rome seemed
divided against itself ; and as long as this opinion held,
so long the Jewish faction had the upper hand in the
Church.

§ 2. OF THE JEWISH FACTION.

But presently came tidings that the legions were
gathered together against Judea, and then that they
were encompassing Jerusalem round about, and afterwards that the Holy City was closely beset, and that
the brethren had fled forth, but that the Jews that
stayed therein were at discord among themselves, and
in great straits, insomuch that they were driven to feed
one on the other for lack of food. But still not many
of the Jews among the faithful believed that the Holy
City would be taken ; for they supposed that the Lord

from Heaven would stretch out his hand to save the place which he had chosen. So when the tidings came at last that the Holy City had been indeed taken and burned, and the Temple also, and that all the sacred furniture of the Temple had fallen into the hands of the Romans, at first none would believe it; but when it was no longer possible to doubt, many began to believe that the end of the world was now at hand, and to some it seemed as if, with the passing away of the Holy City and the Temple, the old world were passed away and a new world already begun.

From this time forth began the Jews to sever themselves into two distinct parties. Some on the one hand, seeing the will of the Lord in the taking away of the Old Jerusalem began to fix their thoughts on Jerusalem that is above, even the spiritual city, the Bride of Christ; and as they could no more fulfil the Law according to the letter by offering sacrifice in the Temple, they now began to turn themselves more from the letter to the spirit, and from the sacrifice of bulls and goats to the sacrifice of the Lord Jesus; and so it came to pass that this party joined themselves more closely to the Gentiles that were in the Church. But upon the other and larger faction of the Jews the destruction of the Holy City had an effect altogether contrary; for being embittered against the Gentiles even before, now, in the extremity of their rage, they made no distinction of Roman or Greek, believer or unbeliever, but hated all alike. Hereat none could marvel, that knew how great had been their sufferings and oppressions; thousands slain with the sword, thousands on the cross, thousands with famine, tens of thousands sold for slaves or condemned to the mines and quarries; those that were suffered to live, burdened with taxes, often dispossessed of their lands, and their lives made miserable with penalties and insults, so that to be a Jew seemed now the same thing as to be an outcast and laughing-stock for mankind.

Hence, among some even of the more honourable of the Jews, now to cease to be a Jew seemed all one with beginning to be a coward and a renegade; wherefore they preferred to be more Jewish than before; and, because they could not now observe the Law in such matters as appertained to the Temple, on this very account they observed all other matters of the Law more diligently than before; and, in a word, the Temple being gone, the Law became unto them both Law and Temple also. In former times the unbelieving Jews had spoken against the Church of Christ and blasphemed the brethren, but only on certain occasions; but now they began to make a rule and habit of cursing us with formal curses, so that it became a part of their worship in the synagogue. Of Nero, the deceased Emperor, they ceased now to speak reproachfully, because they esteemed him as an enemy to Vespasianus, or at least, to the saints; and Poppæa, his concubine or wife (a woman of no virtue nor purity) they praised; but the Emperors Vespasianus and Titus were in their eyes as monsters, to be smitten with the plagues of God. Such a spirit of blindness fell upon the greater part of the Jewish nation at this time; wherefore seeing they saw not, and hearing they could not understand, nor be converted to the Lord. Such of the Jews as took a

middle course—who were commonly called Ebionites
—neither wholly separating themselves from the
Church of Christ, nor yet desiring to cast in their
lot with the Gentiles, were sorely exercised at this
time; and many were the defections and apostasies
among them; and the Gospel with them was a Gospel
of sorrow rather than of joy. Hereof some judgment
may be formed, and some knowledge of the history
of the Church in Syria from a certain letter written
to me in the seventh year of the Emperor Vespasianus by one Menahem, a foremost teacher among the
Ebionites, of which letter I will now set down some
parts.

§ 3. OF MENAHEM, THE EBIONITE.

After many lamentations for the evils of Israel, and
especially because the Holy City had been destroyed
by " Babylon " (meaning Rome) whereby the sacrifice
had been made to cease, the letter turns aside to
describe the manner of the worship of the Temple in
times past and especially the presence and glory of
the High Priest: " Alas, how was he honoured in the
midst of the people in his coming forth from the
sanctuary! He was as the morning star before the
sun hath risen, and as the moon at the full, yea as
the sun shining upon the Temple of the Most High,
and as the rainbow giving light in the bright clouds.
When he took the portions of the priests' hands, he
himself stood by the altar compassed round with his
brethren, even as a cedar of Lebanon compassed round
with palm-trees. He stretched out his hand to the

cup and poured out the blood of the grape, a sweet-
smelling savour unto the Most High King.   Then
shouted the sons of Aaron, then sounded the silver
trumpets, to be heard for a remembrance before the
Most High.   And the people besought the Most High
by prayer before him that is merciful, till the solemnity of the Lord was ended.   O Lord, if thou didst so
much hate thy people that thou must needs cast them
down, yet shouldst thou at the least destroy them
with thine own hands and not give them over to
Babylon.   For what are they that inherit Babylon ?
Are their deeds more righteous than ours that they
should have the dominion over Sion ?"

After this Menahem reproached me in his letter that
I had made myself one with " him " (meaning Paulus)
" who professed to be a Jew and was no Jew ; " and he
affirmed that Jesus had not come to destroy the Law
but to confirm it, and that we blasphemed God because
we made Jesus to be even as God, whereas he was a
man and of the sons of men, howbeit the deliverer and
Messiah.   Thence, passing again to the condition of his
nation he added this hope that " the hand which now
had power "—meaning the Emperor Vespasianus—should
be wasted suddenly, and that " Babylon " (that is to
say Rome) should be cast down, and that the spoils that
she had taken from the nations should be carried back
to the cities of the East in the day of vengeance of the
Lord.   After these things, said he, a time should come
when men should hope much but obtain naught, and
labour, but not prosper ; for the world should be turned
back again into the old silence for seven days, even as
in the first beginning, so that no man should remain ;

and, after that, the Judgment should come, and the Lord Jesus should judge the earth and reward his brethren in Israel. But still the strain of trust died away in sorrow, and the thought of the Deliverer was lost in the thought of Israel, and the letter came to an end in these words : " Our psaltery is laid in the ground, our song is put to silence, our rejoicing is at an end ; the light of our candlestick is put out, and the ark of our covenant is defiled ; our priests are burned with fire, our Levites led captive, our virgins and wives defiled and ravished, our righteous men are carried away, our little ones destroyed, our young men brought into bondage, and our strong men become weak ; and the seat of Sion hath now lost her honour, for she is delivered into the hands of them that hate us."

After this manner wrote Menahem the Ebionite, a good man and devout, and one that loved the Lord Jesus and was himself of a gentle and meek disposition. Wherefore if even in so gentle a nature the thought of Jesus was swallowed up in the thought of the Holy City, much more was this likely to happen with others of his countrymen. And so indeed it was. For each year of troubles now seemed to cast a new veil of ignorance on the hearts of the Jews so that they might not understand the Scriptures, nor discern the will of God, nor be brought into the Church of Christ.

§ 4.　HOW THE CHURCH WAS GUIDED AT THIS TIME BY THE SPIRIT OF GOD.

Out of all these evils and troubles one good at least was gained, that there was no longer any danger lest the Church of Christ should become a mere sect of the Jews. For now to all the believers of the uncircumcision, the destruction of the City of Jerusalem seemed to be a sign sent from God that the Law was at an end, and that all things were to be made new in Christ, yea, and wholly new : and it became a common saying that the vesture of the Church was not to be made up out of the rags of the vesture of the Law, patched and botched up to serve new needs ; but that it was to be a wholly new garment, woven afresh in one piece, without seam or rent. As for the Jews, they that stayed in the Church, finding themselves now constrained to choose between the old garment and the new, gave themselves with a more single mind to the Gospel ; but the greater part went out from us, as I have said. They also that were called Ebionites, who had once had much power in the Church so that they had persuaded many, began now to be lightly esteemed ; and whereas in former times they alone seemed to be the Church, and the rest heretics ; now the contrary came to pass, and the Ebionites themselves came to be thought heretics—insomuch that the name Ebionite became a reproach among the faithful— and the doctrine of Paulus the Apostle was considered to be the doctrine of all the Churches. From this time forth therefore there was no more fear lest the Lord Jesus should be regarded as a mere prince or prophet

in Israel. In old days many had said that he was but
as John the Baptist and some (more especially in
Ephesus) had been baptized with John's baptism and
no other; but now all men believed that John was far
inferior to Jesus, and the traditions of the Church began
to teach this more clearly and fully than before. Also
because men now perceived that the Kingdom of the
Lord Jesus was to include all nations of the earth, and
indeed to consist of Gentiles rather than Jews, for this
reason there were sought out such parables and
discourses of the Lord as taught and explained the
calling of the Gentiles into the Church. And all through
the Church it was everywhere believed that Jesus was
not a mere prophet, but King of kings and Lord
of lords.

When great multitudes of Greeks and many other
nations had now been brought into the Kingdom of
Christ, they began, as was likely and reasonable, to seek
out traditions concerning the nature, birth, and parentage of the King and Prophet in so great a Kingdom.
The common people among the Gentile brethren believed
as a thing of course, that he was divine and of divine
parentage. "For if," said they, "Trophonius and
Heracles have been called gods, and if we have been
wont to give the name of gods to the Emperors, even
such as Caius and Claudius and Nero, how shall we deny
it the Lord Jesus the King of kings?" Herein the
minds of the unlearned were doubtless led to a right
conclusion, though a philosopher might justly find fault
with the method of it, and might understand differently
the "divine parentage" of which they spoke. Nevertheless, from this desire to do honour to the Lord Jesus,

there crept into the Church some error. For some began to deny that he was man at all, or born as men are born, affirming it to be monstrous and incredible that a divine being should pass through a mortal womb. Others—but these were but very few in the Gentile churches—favoured the old opinion of the Ebionites that Jesus was merely human, although superior to any other of the children of men.

Between these two errors, some denying that the Lord Jesus was divine, and others denying that he was human, the Church was marvellously guided by the hand of the Lord, so that the greater part of the brethren held fast the true belief, namely, that he was both human and divine. For as the most part of the Gentiles revolted against the doctrine of the Ebionites, who would have had Jesus to be a mere prince or prophet of the Jews, so did the common sense of almost all the brethren perceive, as by a heaven-sent instinct, that, howsoever he might be divine, he must also needs be human and able to suffer human-like, or else be of no avail to bear the sins and sorrows of the children of men. Thus by the Spirit it was revealed even to the simplest and meanest of the brethren that in Christ Jesus God and man are joined together.

About this time also began the Churches to commit to writing the traditions of the acts of the Lord ; and, not long afterwards, certain of the longer discourses of the Lord, having been written down in Greek, were joined to the other tradition and came to be commonly read in the churches ; but this happened for the most part toward the end of the reign of Vespasianus, or not much before. For as long as the disciples and apostles of the Lord themselves lived, it had seemed to the saints that there was no need of books, having as it were the living words of the Lord Jesus among them. Moreover before the destruction of Jerusalem, the saints for the most part lived in continual expectation of the coming of the Lord, wherefore, hoping soon to have heard his voice from heaven, they were the less careful to record exactly the words he had spoken on earth. But now, during the reign of Vespasianus, when the Church had rest, and peace was everywhere, and the Lord seemed to delay his coming, and one by one the disciples of the Lord fell asleep, and the accounts and traditions of the words and deeds and especially of the birth and rising again of the Lord began to be multiplied with great diversities and not without many errors, then it was revealed to certain of the saints that the time was come when the traditions must be set forth in writing. But all this came to pass at a time when I was far away in Britain; whereof the reason will be set forth in the next chapter.

§ 5. HOW I CAME TO PHILOCHRISTUS, A DISCIPLE OF THE LORD IN BRITAIN.

About the seventh year of the Emperor Vespasianus, it pleased the Lord, in a manner altogether unexpected and marvellous, to reveal to me the names of my parents. There was a certain Philochristus, a Jew by birth but not one of the Jewish faction, a man of some learning, who had studied Greek letters at Alexandria; and he had been a disciple of the Lord Jesus, having himself seen the Lord in the flesh. This man I had met

many years ago at Antioch, and, being drawn to him by
his love of truth and the simplicity of his nature, I had
recounted to him the story of my life, telling him the
place and exact time wherein I had been found as a child
at Pergamus, and withal shewing him (for so the Lord
would have it) the very token that had been hung round
the neck of my brother Chrestus, which I then wore.
About this time therefore I received a letter from
Philochristus (who was then in Britain at Londinium),
telling me that he had found my former nurse, one
Stratonice, who had come to Britain as a slave in the
household of Pomponia the wife of Aulus Plautius the
legate, and who now belonged to the saints that were
in Londinium.   This Stratonice, it seemed, had chanced
to speak to Philochristus about her former mistress, how
her twin sons were taken from her by the guile of some
runaway slave, she being then in Asia, in the last year
of the Emperor Tiberius (mentioning the exact year
when my brother and I had been found) ; and when
Philochristus further questioned her whether any sign
or token had been on the children, she replied that one
bore round his neck just such a token, and with the
same inscription, as I had shewn to Philochristus. She
added that the slave, who had been persuaded thereto
by one that desired to make a way to an inheritance
through our death, had confessed his guilt three or four
years after the deed, and that my mother (whose name
was Euelpis the daughter of Nicomachus, an Athenian
by birth) had, since that time, made continual search
for us, at Pergamus and elsewhere, even till the day of
her death, which had happened in the first year of the
Emperor Vespasianus ; but my father (whose name was

Clinias the son of Aristodemus, also an Athenian by birth) had died many years before.

Ever since I had spoken with the priest of Asclepius at Pergamus, I had been assured in my mind that my mother had not willingly deserted us; yet even now it was joy to know for certain that foul practice, and not our mother's fault, had cast my brother Chrestus and me upon the world; and a great desire seized me to have some speech with my old nurse, Stratonice, concerning my parents before she died. So finding an occasion when I could conveniently leave Colossæ, I journeyed to Britain to Philochristus, meaning to return in a short space. But after I had satisfied my heart's desire, learning all the story of the goodness and love and sorrow of my beloved mother from Stratonice (who lived but three months after my coming to Britain) Philochristus persuaded me to tarry with him yet longer, first for a few months, and then for a year; and, in fine, a door being opened to me of the Lord, I laboured with him in the Church of Londinium for the space of seven years, in peace and great joy. For I was drawn toward the old man more than I can describe, because he was wholly given to the Lord Jesus and abhorred vain quarrels and disputations and (which was not so in all the saints) he added to his love of Christ such a love of letters and learning that (next to my beloved master Paulus) he, more than any other, seemed to join together that which is best both in the Jews and in the Greeks.

From the lips of this my beloved teacher I received the tradition of the words and deeds of the Lord pure and uncorrupted; and it was no small strength and

refreshment to hear the very sayings of Christ himself
from one whose love of truth appeared in this saying
of his, a saying often repeated in his doctrine, that " he
loved to think of the Lord Jesus as Son of man, and
also as Son of God; but he loved no less to think of
him as the Eternal Truth, whom no lie could serve nor
please." Moreover, because he discerned the divine
nature to consist not so much in the performance of
fleshly wonders as in the working of spiritual works,
for this cause he never was led to magnify (as I had
heard some magnify) the mighty acts of Jesus in the
healing of the diseases of the body; but he spoke the
more of his divine power in casting down mountains of
sin, and in the uprooting of error, and in satisfying the
hungry soul with bread, and in cleansing the spotted
soul from all the defilements of Satan. Therefore in
all his discourses, without any straining after new and
convenient traditions, and without any fear and avoid-
ance of old traditions as being not convenient, he spoke
of the Lord Jesus as being verily a man in all points,
sin only excepted ; subject, as men are subject, to birth
and pain and death; but, none the less, as being the
Beginning and the Goal of human life, the Eternal Love
of God, spiritually begotten of God before the foundation of the world. In this doctrine I rejoiced, and this
doctrine I strove to teach ; and it was a great delight
that here were no Greek factions nor Jewish factions,
nor disputations about traditions, or prophecies, or aught
else ; but all was peace and harmony, as if in some
haven, shut in and sheltered by the hills, wherein the
mariner, resting from long tossing on the deeps, can
scarce hear the roaring of the sea without.

But after seven years had thus passed away in peace
it being now the second year of the Emperor Domitianus,
it came to pass that new troubles fell upon the Church ;
and, the Bishop of Berœa having borne witness for the
Lord with his blood in a tumult in that city, I was
called to the charge of the flock there ; and the voice
of the Lord bade me go. So bidding farewell to the
beloved Elder Philochristus with much sorrow, well
knowing that I should not again behold him in the
flesh, I set forth with his blessing upon my journey,
intending first to go to Rome and there to tarry some
days, and so to Berœa.

§ 6. OF THE CHURCH IN ROME, AND OF THE NEW GOSPELS.

When I came to Rome I was well received of the
brethren, and I tarried there two months, observing the
manner of their worship, and the teaching of the catechumens and the discourses of the elders to the faithful.
But I seemed at first to be listening to a new Gospel ;
so great a change had fallen on the Church since I had
last tarried in the great city, about fifteen years before.
This appeared, not only in their worship, but also in
the pictures and sculptures wherewith they had begun
to adorn the tombs of those that fell asleep in the
Lord ; for in these I perceived that those very beliefs
whereof I had written to Artemidorus as being
currently reported among the faithful but not yet
added to the Tradition, were now accepted by all. For
example, when I entered into one of the places where

the congregations commonly assemble themselves for worship—these are quarries, after the manner of galleries, hewn out of the rock under the earth beneath the city, commonly called catacombs, and used for entombments by the faithful—I perceived there the figure of a certain prophet, with a scroll in his hand, pointing to a Woman which bare a child in her arms, and above the child was a star ; and I questioned my companions whether this was the Lord Jesus, the Son of the Virgin Mother, and they said "Yes," but when I went on to speak of the Virgin as the Spiritual Sion, which is the Church of God, then they said, "Nay, but it sheweth the mother of our Lord according to the flesh, according to the saying of the prophet, 'Behold a virgin shall conceive and bear a son, and shall call his name Immanuel.'"   Then asking concerning the star, I said that I supposed that it represented the brightness of the Messiah, even as it was written in the Scriptures that "a star should come out of Jacob."   To this they assented, " but," added one, " it is also well-known that a star, visible to the eyes of men, did verily shine forth in the days of Herod, being seen of many nations, and especially in the East, insomuch that then was fulfilled the saying of the Psalms that the kings of Arabia and Saba should bring gifts."   "Are these things then," said I, "contained in the Tradition of the Acts of the Lord ? "   Then he that had spoken replied, " No, not in the Tradition, but in a certain supplement which is now beginning everywhere to be read in all the churches, and it is said to have been put forth by the interpreters and disciples of one of the Apostles " : but another, correcting him, said that one of the Apostles himself had

T

written it, not indeed Petrus nor Jacobus who were
unlearned men ignorant of letters, but in all likelihood
Mattheus, as having been in his earlier days a tax-
gatherer and therefore ready with his pen.

Going on a little further I saw on the walls another
picture of men supping at a table, and the food two
fishes and some loaves. When I asked what this meant,
they told me that it signified the banquet of the kingdom of God wherein all the faithful partake of the body
of the Lord who, said they, is our Bread of Life, and
also our true ΙΧΘΥC ; and " of the two fishes," said
they, " the one denoteth Baptism, whereby the faithful
enter into Christ, and the other the Lord's Supper,
whereby they are made partakers of the Lord's body,
so that they remain in him and he in them." " And is
this also," I asked, " in the Tradition ?" " Neither in
the Tradition," said they, " nor in the Supplement, but
it is a symbol." Then I took courage to speak concerning that other parable of a banquet, wherein I had been
wont to teach how the Twelve had been bidden by the
Lord Jesus to minister both of the Bread of Life and
of the Fishes, asking them whether they interpreted this
also spiritually and not according to the letter, even as
they interpreted that other story of the ΙΧΘΥC. But
hereat their countenances changed, and they said, " Nay,
but this story is written according to the letter in the
Tradition of the Gospel." Then I told them how
Philochristus the Elder had related to me that the
Lord Jesus himself, in speaking of these matters, had
rebuked his disciples because they understood him
not, saying unto them, that when he spoke of leaven,
and of bread, he spoke not of earthly bread or leaven,

but of spiritual leaven and spiritual bread. But they replied that " it was not so written in the Tradition now, and that Philochristus (albeit to be reverenced as a faithful disciple of the Lord) was not to be too much trusted as a remembrancer of the Tradition, because he had lived now many years apart from the rest of the saints, not having experience of that which had been from year to year newly revealed to the Church, so that he knew naught save what he himself had heard and seen of the Lord Jesus, and this in all likelihood faintly and imperfectly remembered by him, as being well-stricken in years, not much less than fourscore and ten." It came into my mind that to be thus all alone, remembering and teaching the words of Christ which he himself had heard (apart from controversies and colours and glosses of those who were disputing rather than remembering) was perhaps rather a help than a harm to Philochristus. However at that time I said no more.

On the morrow, coming somewhat late into the congregation in the midst of their worship, I heard them singing a psalm which, because there arose hence a question afterwards between myself and the brethren, I will here set down ; and as near as I can remember, the words were these :—

1.

" *O Pilot of our bark*
What though the night be dark ?
What though the tempest rave ?
Thou still canst hear and save.

2.

" *Tossed by the troubled sea,*
 O Lord, we cry to thee,
 And through the murky night
 What figure meets our sight ?

3.

" *Lo, pitying our fear*
 The Lord himself draws near,
 Walking upon the wave
 His helpless ones to save.

4.

" *In terror of his face*
 Vanish the clouds apace,
 His footsteps on the deep
 Lull every wave to sleep.

5.

" *The winds obey his will,*
 The raging storm is still ;
 Then turn we to adore
 And lo, at hand the shore."

Now these words or others like unto them, had been
well known to me for a long time, because some such
psalm had been brought to us at Colossæ from Ephesus
(from which city many psalms and hymns had come to
divers churches) and it was commonly sung in the
churches of Asia; and indeed, even among the ancient
poems of the Jews, there is a psalm not much unlike
this, wherein the mariners cry unto the Lord in their
trouble and he delivereth them out of their distress,
for, saith the psalm, " He maketh the storm to cease
so that the waves thereof are still "; and another psalm
saith, " Thy way is in the sea and thy path on the great

waters." But, often as I had sung these words, it
had never so much as entered my mind to interpret
them according to the letter; for even as the Greeks
or Romans compare the state to a ship and the ruler
to a pilot, even so had we been wont to speak, in a
figure, of the Church as being a ship tossed upon the
sea of troubles and persecutions, and of the Lord Jesus
as her pilot in the storm ; and I had also heard mention
made, when I was in Britain, of some new hymn
shewing in a figure, how the blessed Apostle Petrus
denied his Master, and describing how he adventured
to walk, in his own strength, upon the troubled sea of
temptation ; but his faith failed him so that he began to
sink, and he had been drowned in the deep waters of
sin, but that the Lord stretched out his hand and saved
him ; but in this and other such psalms and hymns
there was never a thought of any real boat nor of a
real storm of wind and waves.   Therefore, the worship
being now ended, when a certain Philologus, one of
the brethren, accosted me asking my judgment of
this psalm, as if I should have censured it, I replied
(not without some wonder at the strangeness of his
question) that the psalm was a good one, and that none
could find any fault in it.   But Philologus replied,
"If therefore, O Onesimus, you allow of this miracle
of the Lord, why contend you against these other
miracles of which the Gospel makes mention ? " I said,
"Nay, but of what miracle do I allow ? "   He said,
"Even that miracle and no other, which is clearly described in the psalm, how the Lord Jesus walked upon
the waters to save the holy Apostles ; yea, and one of
the new Gospels affirms that the blessed Apostle

Petrus adventured himself to walk upon the waves; but his faith failed him so that he began to sink."

Hereat I was speechless; and Philologus, as if he were ill at ease by reason of my silence, bade me follow him and two or three of the other elders into another chamber in the place where they were assembled. Here were depicted divers wonders, first, the sending down of the manna from heaven for Israel, and also the gushing forth of the water from the rock; and said he, if Moses wrought these wonders, must not the Lord Jesus have wrought others still more wonderful? Then said I to them, " Moses not only caused bread but also water to arise for Israel; and again the prophet Elisha, even when dead, had power to raise up a dead man; wherefore, if indeed the Lord Jesus desired to surpass Moses and Elias in wonders according to the flesh (and not, as I believe, in wonders according to the spirit) he must needs have caused water, as well as bread, to spring up for the multitude, or else perchance honey or wine; and he must needs also have raised up from the dead some one that was on the point to be buried or already buried; but is any such relation as either of these to be found in any tradition concerning the Lord Jesus ? " They said there was not; and methought they were somewhat at a stand. But presently Philologus corrected them saying, " Nay, my brethren, say not ' the Tradition containeth not these things ' but rather ' These things are not known to us at present,' for although it hath not yet been revealed to the Church in any Tradition that the Lord Jesus hath produced water or wine, or raised up a dead man from the tomb, yet is it possible that he may have wrought these very works, and in time they may be made known to the Church, even as the walking on the waves was not made known in the first Tradition of the Acts of the Lord, nor were other mighty works ; " and here he made mention of many unknown to me such as the catching of a mighty draught of fishes, and the finding of a fish with a coin in the mouth of it.

Hereat I ceased from further speech. For I perceived that my questioning had the contrary effect to that which I had intended. For I had hoped to lead Philologus and his companions to see that the spiritual works of the Lord Jesus were greater than those wonders according to the flesh, of which they made so much. But instead thereof, Philologus had been made by my words more greedy than ever of fresh wonders, and was now ready to believe anything if it were only wonderful enough. So I held my peace, and only besought Philologus to lend me copies of the written books of the Gospels such as were now read in the churches.

§ 7. HOW I LABOURED IN BERŒA.

Having given myself during many days to the reading and meditating in the three books of the Gospels, I found much less addition of wonders and other doubtful matters than I had expected, and least of all in that book which was said by most to have been written according to the teaching of Marcus ; only in rendering the Hebrew into the Greek there had been a few errors ; and in some two or three passages, figures of speech appeared to have been interpreted according to the letter. But the other two books, though they contained most excellent traditions, very full and ample, of certain words of the Lord, had added supplements touching the birth of the Lord Jesus and his childhood and youth, and also concerning his manifestations after his rising from the dead, which were not known to me. So, after much debate with myself, I concluded to write to Philochristus, sending to him the three books and asking his judgment concerning them. This done, I bade farewell to the brethren in Rome and betook myself to Beroea where the Lord had prepared for me an abundant work.

Many days I continued labouring in Beroea and hearing naught from Philochristus ; yet was I not without some guidance from the Lord. For day by day, ministering to the unlearned among the brethren, I perceived that the presence and the power of the Lord among them were not let or hindered by what 1 deemed their errors. The three books of the Gospels were beginning at this time to be commonly read among them, and I saw that the multitude willingly believed all things written therein, especially concerning the birth of the Lord Jesus, and concerning his manifesting of himself after death by divers signs and tokens, as by eating in the presence of the disciples, and by giving his body to be touched. Now remembering what the blessed Apostle Paulus had enjoined on me, that I must by all means seek to attain as much of the truth as possible, though there must needs be some error, I was minded at first to restrain the brethren in Beroea from the public reading of these new traditions. But one of the elders of the Church dissuaded me, saying in the first place that the truth was uncertain ; and in

the second place, that, if the people believed not these
traditions, and especially the tradition concerning the
birth of the Lord, they must needs fall into error, not
being able to receive the doctrine that the son of Mary
and Joseph was verily the Son of God begotten before
the worlds and taking flesh as a man for our sakes.
" Either therefore," said he, " they will believe that
he was merely man and not God ; or else that he was
not man at all, but a phantom, born of no human father
nor mother either ; as certain sects in Asia believe."
And he added that the Lord seemed to allow this new
doctrine, if doctrine might be judged by the fruits
thereof ; because all that believed it were full of zeal,
and patience, and love for the brethren, and all virtue,
ready to lay down their lives for the Lord. So I,
considering that it was one thing to strive towards
certainty, and another thing to restrain others from
their opinions, being also myself uncertain, suffered
the new gospels to be read in Berœa without hindrance,
and the more willingly because the three Gospels now
brought in began to drive out many other writings of
Gospels which sprang up about this time, or even before,
full of wonders and portents, and not preserving the
truth of the life of the Lord Jesus. So in a very short
time the three Gospels were brought in, and multiplied
by transcribers, and were read in all our assemblies, and
the catechumens were also instructed in them.

And now, after I had been about one year or more
in Berœa, I received from Britain a letter written by
Philochristus, which was most welcome ; but withal
another letter most unwelcome, written by the new
Bishop of Londinium, saying that the blessed Elder

Philochristus had fallen asleep in the Lord, and that
this his letter, written some months before, had only of
late been found among his papers, wherefore it had
been long delayed in the sending.   So, when I opened
and read it, I seemed to be receiving his message from
beyond the grave, guiding me on the path in which I
should go ; and these were the words of the letter.

§ 8. THE LAST WORDS OF PHILOCHRISTUS.

" PHILOCHRISTUS TO ONESIMUS, GRACE AND PEACE IN
THE LORD JESUS CHRIST.

" I received with your letter, my dear Onesimus, the
three books of the new Gospels ; concerning which
having purposed to write to you some months ago,
as soon as I had read them, I was hindered by long and
grievous sickness.

" They contain relations of certain matters whereof I
neither saw nor heard aught, while I followed the Lord
Jesus in Galilee ; nor have I heard aught of them from
the disciples, nor from the Lord's brethren, nor from the
mother of the Lord.

" Nevertheless, albeit I heard no such matters, yet is
it possible that they may have been revealed to the
disciples after my coming to this island in the reign of
Caius Cæsar.   And this, I confess, hath not a little
moved me, that during my sickness the three Gospels
have been very diligently read by those who are here
labouring with me, and by them have been interpreted
to the unlearned ; and everywhere they meet with
great acceptance, and the Church is edified by them,

insomuch that they had already begun to be read in the assemblies of certain of the churches when it pleased the Lord to raise me up for a short time from my sickness. Notwithstanding, thou sayest truly that in all things we must not willingly consent to error, though some error be a necessity ; and therefore my counsel is that thou take early occasion to go to Ephesus where thou mayst question John the Disciple of the Lord. For if neither he nor I know aught of these new traditions, then it is likely that they are not according to truth ; but if he consent unto them, then are they, without doubt, true.

" Not without much prayer and meditation, having striven to put myself in thy place, my dear Onesimus, have I written these words ; which do thou take to heart, as my last message, because my mind forebodeth that I shall not write unto thee a second time. I know well thy sincerity and thy unfeigned love of the truth ; yet bethink thee that it is the kernel of the truth that thou shouldst seek and not the shell ; and if the kernel be sound, be not thou troubled over much though the shell may shew some blemish. For put this case that John the Disciple of the Lord be no longer in the flesh, or that thou find no occasion to see him, or that in other ways thou be frustrated of thine endeavour to search out the truth. What then ? Is it needful or fit that thou shouldst therefore journey from Ephesus to Antioch, or to Nazareth, or to Bethlehem, or to Jerusalem, to inquire of these matters ? Nay, but a pastor of the flock should abide with the flock. The exact truth, it may be, thou shalt never find out in this life ; but thy duty towards thy brethren thou canst certainly find out. This therefore find out, and do. I say not that thou, in thy doctrine and preaching, shouldst teach or even assent to these new traditions; but what I say is this, that if the worship of the Lord Jesus be enwrapped (among the unlearned) in some integument of doubtful tradition which commendeth itself to the brethren—because they cannot easily believe that he worked mightily in the spirit, except they also believe that he wrought mighty works according to the flesh—then I say it needeth not, nor is it fit, that thou shouldst spend all thy time in rending this integument asunder, but rather that thou shouldst labour to teach the main truth, which is, that our Lord Jesus Christ was verily a man, and verily the Eternal Son of God, in whom all mankind hath died to sin and is born again to righteousness.

"But thou sayest that 'A time may come when these traditions shall be found to be false; and then as much as they now draw the unlearned to Christ, so much, and more also, shall they then drive the unlearned from Christ. For, being unapt to distinguish, and apt to reject all if they reject a part, the common people, finding a part of the tradition of the Acts of the Lord to be false, will cast aside the whole as a mere fable.' Well and wisely is this said, and providently also according to thy nature, my dear Onesimus; yet have I faith in Truth, according as it is written, that 'Truth is great and shall prevail'; and whensoever the danger whereof thou speakest shall press upon the Church, I doubt not but the Lord, who is also the Truth, shall raise up teachers that shall have skill to sift the true from the false; yea, and if, even now, thou seest this danger, or if thou obtainest certain knowledge that these traditions are false, I deny not but thou shouldst speak openly against them. But until thou shalt obtain such certainty, wait thou patiently upon the Lord, and do with all thy might the works which he hath appointed for thee to do.

"Remember, my son, that thou art called to be a bishop and champion for the souls of men, to deliver them from the mouth of the lion; and the battle presseth sorely against the army of the Lord. Play thou the man therefore, and be no mere pedant nor seeker after the antiquities of small matters. Even in this year, as thou thyself dost write, many of the Saints have borne witness with their lives to the Captain of our Salvation. Whilst others therefore are fighting among the vanguard and pouring forth their blood for the Lord, be not thou content to lag behind in the rear with the baggage; nor, from being a soldier of the Lord, stoop thou to be a mere camp-follower. Lovest thou the Lord? I know thou lovest him with all thine heart. Then be content. The Saints of the Church in Berœa whom God hath committed to thy charge, do they also love the Lord? Thyself hast confessed as much. Then again I say, Be thou content. 'But,' sayest thou, 'they err in certain traditions concerning the Lord.' Well, then, they err. But which is better, that they should love the Lord and be in some error, or that they should be free from error and void of love? Better to have wheat with tares than no tares and no wheat. Let both stand till the harvest; and in the day of winnowing of the Master, a separation shall be made. Farewell, Onesimus; and again I say unto thee, as from the Lord,

in whose presence I hope to stand when thou shalt read
these words, Play thou the man and prevail, in the love
and trust of the Lord Jesus Christ; and the Lord shall
be with thee and bless thee."

When I had read the letter of the blessed Philochristus, I was confirmed in my purpose not at once to
quit the city of Berœa; and the more because at that time
the saints began to be sorely persecuted; insomuch that I
had no leisure to be absent, no, not so much as for a few
days, during the space of two whole years; so busy was I
in comforting the afflicted and strengthening the weak,
and ministering to the widows of them that bore
witness for the Lord. And as I strengthened, or strove
to strengthen, others, so also and much more did they
strengthen me, when I perceived their constancy and
fortitude, and noted how, amidst all their sufferings,
even the unlearned (yea, some of those on whom I had
been apt to look with some pity for their superstitions),
were lifted up with a divine magnanimity such as no
philosopher could surpass. And at this time I began
more clearly to understand that which Philochristus had
said (and Paulus before him) touching the distinguishing of things great and small. For I now perceived,
as never before, that the love of Christ was the main
thing, and that whoso could love him and cling to him
should be first in the Kingdom of God, and that I
myself (though I were bishop in Berœa) should come
far behind many of the simple brethren, halting as it
were into heaven, while they should come borne upon
wings.

But now, two years having passed away and the
Church being now at peace, the advice of Philochristus

hath come again to my mind that if I crave after certainty concerning the additions to the Tradition, I should go to see John the Disciple of the Lord at Ephesus. For the holy Apostle still lives, although stricken in years and infirm, not having been able for these many years to preach the Gospel. Yet is there a tradition or doctrine at Ephesus (as I have heard say) differing much from the three Gospels, and taught by the disciples of John and especially by one, John the Elder, a man of Alexandria (one that has travelled much, and is well versed in the philosophy of the Alexandrine teachers, but much more in the deep things of the Spirit), whom I met many years ago in Antioch. These lines I now write in the sixth year of the Emperor Domitianus, purposing shortly to set out for Smyrna, and thence to Ephesus, to see John and to obtain concerning the Traditions such certainty as I can. Howbeit the Spirit in me forebodeth that I shall not obtain certainty after this manner, neither shall I come again to Berœa, but the Lord hath some other purpose concerning me.

§ 9. OF MY JOURNEY TO SMYRNA, AND HOW THE LORD HATH HELPED ME EVEN TO THE END.

Verily the Spirit deceived me not; for being now about to bear witness for the Lord Jesus with my blood, I add these last words to this history, no longer free, nor amid friends, but in a dungeon, expecting shortly that I shall fight with wild beasts for the Lord in this city of Smyrna, wherein now I write. For coming hither about the time of

Passover, I found the people of the city in no small disturbance, because of a great earthquake, and the drying up of the springs, and also incensed against the Proconsul because he had awarded some prize in the games against their judgment. Wherefore the people on the one hand were moved against the Christians, as being causers of the earthquake, and the Proconsul for his part was the more ready to listen to them so as to turn their wrath from himself on us. So when I was, without any disturbance, preaching the Gospel to the Saints on the first day of the week, behold, the Irenarch came suddenly upon us with great violence, and after loading me with fetters he dragged me (with one of the presbyters called Trophimus) before the Proconsul; who straightway bade me swear by the Fortune of Cæsar and reproach Christ. When I refused, he said to me, " I will consume thee with fire, except thou repent." Then Trophimus made answer, somewhat bitterly, " Thou threatenest me with fire which burneth for an hour and, after that, is extinguished; but thou knowest not the fire of the judgment that is to come which is reserved for the ungodly." Hereupon the multitude that were in the Stadium, cried out, " Away with the Atheists." Others bade let loose a lion upon us. But the Proconsul gave orders that we should be taken to the dungeon and there kept for a night and day; and after that, if we would not repent and offer sacrifice saying, " Cæsar is Lord," we were to be cast to the wild beasts; for the show was appointed for the day after the morrow. So with many reproaches and blows from the officers, goading me onwards that

I might come the quicker out of the multitude—who were gathered round, cursing and threatening, and ready to have torn me in pieces—I was dragged along the streets to the prison, and there my clothes were rent from off me,' and I was cast naked, more dead than alive, into the barathrum or pit which is in the centre of the inmost prison, there to abide till the time came that I should fight with wild beasts.

Amid the darkness and mire and stench of that noisome den, it pleased the Lord that I should be tempted of Satan that I might prevail over him with the strength of the Lord. For when I knelt down to call upon the Lord, being always used to make mention of Chrestus and Eucharis in my prayers, behold, I found myself bereft of the tokens of them both, whereon were written TRUST and HOPE; and then a terror fell upon me and a shuddering that was not of the limbs but of the heart (so did my very spirit seem to shiver within me) and a voice of evil whispered in my ear saying, "*Trust* no more," and then again, "Thy *Hope* is dead;" and methought monstrous shapes moved around me, making my flesh to creep; and I was on the brink of a bottomless gulf wherein I must needs fall, and Satan was waiting below, ready to swallow up my soul.

Then fell I upon my face and I called upon the Lord in my sore trouble, and besought him that he would send me help from heaven; and I repeated over and over again his comfortable words, how he bade us not fear them that could slay the body, and how he promised that, though we should be slain, yet not one

U

hair of our heads should perish; and I bethought
myself of my beloved teacher Paulus, how he also had
lain in just such another dungeon for nine days and
nights, and with what a constancy he had held fast to
the faith of the Lord Jesus; and I also called to mind
the last words of the elder Philochristus, how he had
bidden me play the man and fight the good fight for
Christ. Now up to this time I had been still wrestling
with Satan and trembling lest, coming upon me a
second time, he should gain some advantage over me;
but now, taking courage, I besought the Lord, as in old
times, for Christus and Eucharis, that they also might
obtain mercy and be with me in Christ.

Then it pleased the Lord Jesus my Saviour to turn
my thoughts wholly upon him, and upon his passion
which he endured for men upon the cross; and gazing
thereon I was rapt up with him above the stir and
tumult of earth; and methought I saw, looking down
from above, how all the past had worked together for
me for good; and how all my wanderings and gropings,
yea, even my sins, being washed away by the blood of
him who suffered, had become helps instead of hin-
drances, helping me to love much because I had been
much forgiven. Then also I saw how the Lord in his
mercy had taken from me the hope of Eucharis, and
the trust of Chrestus, yea, and the love of my dearest
mother, that so he might guide me up unto himself, the
source and object of all trust and hope and love. So
being filled with all certainty of joy I besought the
Lord once more for them, and for the mother whom
I had never seen in the flesh, that they also as well as
Eucharis (who had received the seal of baptism) might

attain to the resurrection of the just, and I prayed that, if it were possible, I might receive from him some sign or vision that it was well with them.   And so it was that, as soon as I had thus prayed, I was lifted up in the spirit with the cross of Christ yet higher than before, and the Lord shewed me a vast sea of death, and beneath the sea of death, a sea of sin ; but beneath the sea of sin and of death I saw a great gulf of life and love, which swallowed up the sea of sin and death, so that they vanished away.

How long I remained in the Spirit I know not ; but when the Spirit left me I was lying in the courtyard of the prison ; and around me were standing some of the elders ministering to me, and bidding me be of stout heart ; for, said they, in two hours hence must thou needs fight with wild beasts in the amphitheatre for the Lord Jesus Christ.   Then I spoke to them strengthening their hearts, and telling them of all the glories of the vision which the Lord had revealed unto me, and having obtained pen and paper I have written down the vision, and how the Lord helped me ; to the intent that others also, in time to come, vile and sinful, and defiled, and faithless, may take courage from this history, perceiving how even the weakest and vilest may be made pure and strong in Christ.

As I write these words, knowing that in the third hour of this same day I shall bear witness for the Lord beneath the jaws of the leopards, how small and petty seem to me now the matters of which I once doubted ! Better is it to be a fool (as the world counteth folly) and to love the Lord than to have all knowledge and to be without love.   He that loveth his brother hath all

things and knoweth all things; and, if he lack aught,
behold, all possessions and all knowledge shall be added
unto him. Behold, the voice of man calleth me to
arise and to go forth unto death. But I obey not
his voice but thine. Thou callest me, O my Redeemer,
and I come.

§ 10. *CONCERNING THE PASSION OF THE BLESSED MARTYRS TROPHIMUS AND ONESIMUS.*

*For the edification of the saints it hath seemed good
to us, the Elders of the Church in Smyrna, to add to
this history a brief relation concerning the passion of
the blessed martyrs Trophimus and Onesimus, to the
intent that others, taking them as their ensamples, may
be encouraged to testify with like boldness for the Lord.
The manner of their going forth from prison was of
a strange difference; both rejoicing, but Trophimus
threatening the people with the wrath of God, and saying
to the Proconsul, "Thou judgest us; but God shall judge
thee." Likewise to the Asiarch he said, "Note well our
faces that thou mayst remember us in the judgment-day,
when we shall laugh, and thou weep." Hereat the
people, being angered, demanded that they should be
scourged, passing through two rows of venatores: but the
blessed martyr Trophimus rejoiced that he should have
received this further torment for the Lord Jesus.
Onesimus also shewed no less cheerfulness and constancy; but he walked silent and with eyes fixed and
uplifted, as if intent on the glory to come.*

*But before they should make trial of the leopards,
Satan had prepared a fierce wild bull to assail the*

*martyrs of the Lord; and first Trophimus was tossed,
and fell crushed and, as it seemed, lifeless.   Then
Onesimus was also tossed; but he arose, as if in a
trance; and seeing Trophimus lying crushed, he drew
near, and took him by the hand, and lifted him up,
himself being all the while in an ecstasy; as was
apparent from certain words which he spoke to a young
man, one of the catechumens, whose name was Symmachus.
For when Onesimus was recalled by the usual gate, while
the leopards were making ready, this young man
Symmachus received him and ministered to him; and
at this time he heard the blessed martyr say, as one in
a dream, " I marvel when we shall be led out to that
wild bull," not knowing what he had already suffered;
nor could he believe that he had suffered till he perceived
the wounds and bruises on his body.   Coming to himself he
thanked the young man Symmachus for his kindness and
blessed him.   Also it pleased the Lord to move the mind
of a certain centurion, named Hipponax, who, having
before despoiled the blessed martyr of some slight tokens,
now came to him restoring them; upon which the blessed
martyr, mindful even of the smallest matters, thanked
the soldier courteously and placed them around his neck.
And by this time also Trophimus was fully recovered,
and eager to bear witness for the Lord.   So, the Lord
having appointed the time for their release, they are led
out to the leopards.   Then Trophimus, running forward,
provoked one of the beasts to attack him; and straightway springing upon him, the beast with one bite drew
forth such a stream of blood that all the people, mocking
at him (as if he had been baptized in his own blood) cried
out saying, " Saved and washed, saved and washed ";*

and Onesimus also was struck down by another of the leopards, and dragged hither and thither by the beasts. But when the beasts had been taken away, and the blessed martyrs cast on one side to be slaughtered after the usual manner, then the people clamoured that they should be set in the midst of the amphitheatre that their eyes might enjoy the spectacle of the slaughter. So both stood up and moved, of themselves, to the appointed place. Here Trophimus, being very weak with loss of blood, fell on the ground; but Onesimus, standing up, stretched out his hands, looking to heaven as if he saw a vision; and the shouting of the multitude and their scoffing and cursing became less, and at last there was a deep silence, all the people expecting what he should say or do; but the blessed martyr, taking in his hand that which he wore round his neck as if it were some memorial of the Lord, held it up to heaven and cried aloud, " O Lord my Hope and my Trust, thou lovest me, yea, and thou shalt love me, for thou art the Eternal Love." And having said these words he laid himself down by the side of Trophimus and having embraced him, he bade the gladiator strike his throat; and the sword fell twice and no more; and so Trophimus and Onesimus, blessed martyrs for the faith, fell asleep in the Lord Jesus, to whom be glory and honour for ever and ever. Amen.

THE END OF THE EIGHTH BOOK

AN ADDITION

CONTAINING THE DISCOURSE

OF

LUCIUS OF CYRENE

WHICH WAS OMITTED FROM THE THIRD BOOK

AN ADDITION

CONTAINING THE DISCOURSE

OF

LUCIUS OF CYRENE

" It is known unto you all, my brethren, that whensoever we bring forward proofs from the mighty works of our Lord Jesus Christ, desiring thereby to show that he was the Messiah, our adversaries are not thereby persuaded, but the Jews say that he was a magician, and the Greeks that he was an impostor. Wherefore it is meet that we resort to stronger arguments than these, opening the Scriptures and proving from them that Jesus is the very Messiah. For jugglers, say the Greeks, and magicians, say the Jews, can perform mighty works at will; but it is not possible for a juggler, nor even for a magician, so to be born and also to live all his life and to die, so as to fulfil all that is written in the Law and the Prophets. Wherefore it is fit that we should diligently search the Scriptures that we may prove that the Lord Jesus was born and lived, and died, in accordance with the word of prophecy; for thus shall we establish the truth so that it cannot be shaken.

"First therefore concerning his birth, the Prophet saith, 'Who shall declare his generation?' Now of any common mortal this could not be said; but it is predicted concerning him whose generation is a mystery, in that he is the only Son of God. Moreover another prophecy saith, 'A virgin shall conceive and bear a son.' Now if the very heathen assert no less than this about Asclepius, and Heracles, and Romulus, and a hundred others, who were no true sons of God, but only sons of demons, how much more must it be true of our Master and only Saviour that he was veritably born of no human father, but was the Son of God! And it hath been shewn to be in accordance with the saying of the Prophet.

"Likewise when the Prophet Daniel speaks of 'one *like* unto the Son of man,' doth he not hint at the very same thing? For, in saying '*like* unto the Son of man,' and not '*the* Son of man,' he declareth thereby that Jesus was man, but not of human seed. And the same thing he doth express in mystery, when he speaketh of 'this stone which was cut out *without hands*,' signifying that it was the work, not of man, but of the Father and God of all things. And again, when Moses saith that 'he will wash his garments in the blood of the grape,' doth not this signify what I have often told you.—albeit enwrapped in obscure terms, after the manner of prophecy—I mean, that he had blood, but not from men: even as God, and not man, hath begotten the blood of the vine?

"Now I know indeed that certain of the Rabbis, interpreting amiss the prophecy of Isaiah concerning him that was to be born of a virgin, affirm the words of

the Prophet to have been fulfilled in the time of
Hezekiah ; for they say that the prophecy was, that
'the riches of Damascus and the spoils of Samaria
should be taken away from before the king of Assyria ;'
and that this was to come to pass before the child, born
to the Prophet from the Virgin whom he took to be his
wife, had learned to cry 'my father and my mother ;'
and accordingly they say that the prophet took the
prophetess to wife, and that she bore a son, who being
yet an infant, Damascus and Samaria were destroyed.
But we affirm that the prophecy is not thus written ;
but it is, 'he, namely the child, *shall take away* the
power of Damascus and the spoils of Samaria.' Now
who will dare to assert that, in the days of the King
Hezekiah, any infant among the Jews, 'before he had
power to cry, my father, or my mother '—for mark this
addition—conquered two so great nations ?

" Assuredly no one will assert this. But the meaning
of the prophecy is as follows. The evil demon who
dwelleth in Damascus, and who also may be well
termed in parable Samaria, was overcome by Christ as
soon as he was born. For I have heard (and it is by all
means to be believed, for it is according to the words
of Holy Scripture, which needs must be fulfilled) that
certain Magi, who dwelt in Arabia—and none of you
can deny that Damascus was, and is, in the region of
Arabia, although now it belongeth to what is called
Syrophœnicia—came from the East to worship Christ at
his birth, thereby shewing that they had revolted from
the dominion of Satan. Now it is said that these Magi
came first to Herod, who was the sovereign of the land
of the Jews, but who by the Scriptures (on account

of his ungodly and sinful character) is called king of
Assyria. Nevertheless they gave not their gifts to him,
but going forth from his presence, they gave gold, and
frankincense, and myrrh,—which were as it were the
spoils of Damascus,—to the child Jesus in the manger:
and so it came to pass that he who was born of the
Virgin, while still a babe, 'took away the power of
Damascus and the spoils of Samaria, from the presence
of the King of Assyria.'

"Next as to the place of his birth, even the Gentiles
do bear testimony that there shall come forth from the
East one that shall obtain dominion over the Empire,
and this is known throughout the whole world; nor do
the prophets write otherwise, saying, 'Behold a Man,
the East is his name.' And that our Christ was born
in Syria, that is in the East, is confessed of all. But
further, touching the city in which he was born, some
have been wont to affirm that he was born at Nazareth
because he lived there many years from a child. But
that he must needs have been born at Bethlehem is
clear, because it is written, 'And thou, Bethlehem
Ephratah, though thou art the least among the hundreds
of thy people, yet out of thee shall come a governor
who shall feed my people;' and that he was to
appear first in the south (for Bethlehem is in the
south) and not in a northern city, such as Nazareth, is
clear also from another Scripture, which saith, 'God
cometh from the south.'

"Moreover, which of you knoweth not that the Lord
Jesus is the Bread of Life? Therefore, when the
Bread of Life was to descend and to find a house and
home among men, what city in Israel was more fit for

him than that one which is called Bethlehem, which
being interpreted, is 'the House of Bread?' Lastly,
it is known to all of you that Mary, the mother of
Jesus, being of a royal race, was descended from David
the king, who was of the city of Bethlehem ; wherefore
it was the more fitting that the Son of David should
be born at the same place. Also I have heard some
say that there is a certain cave in Bethlehem wherein
he was born ; and to this day the cave is shewn ; and
they affirm that it must needs have been so, because
it is written, 'he shall dwell in a high cave of the
strong rock ;' but because it is commonly reported that
he was born in a manger, and because I purpose to
speak of none but such things as are certainly believed
among us, for this reason I affirm nothing on this
matter.

"But (that he might not be inferior to his servant
Moses), as Moses was persecuted by the Egyptian king
Pharaoh, so was Jesus by Herod, the King of the Jews ;
and, even as Israel sojourned for a time in Egypt, so
must the Redeemer of Israel sojourn in the same
country, that it might be fulfilled as it is written,
'Out of Egypt have I called my son.' His mighty
works also, which he wrought on those that believed in
him, are they not written in the books of the Prophets ?
namely, that in that day the ears of the deaf should be
unstopped, and the eyes of the blind opened, and the
dead should be raised up, and the poor should have the
gospel preached unto them : which all are recounted in
our tradition, even to the raising of the dead. For as
Elisha the prophet raised up the son of the Shunammite,
even so did the Son of God raise up the daughter of

Jairus; and, whereas our adversaries say that this was
but a small matter, doubtless this is but one among a
multitude of like marvels. Again, whereas they
assert that Moses was superior to Jesus in that he gave
unto the people manna in the wilderness, to this I reply
that even so did the Lord Jesus prepare a table for his
people in the wilderness; yea, and as Moses gave water
from the rock, even so did our living Rock grant unto
us living water from his own side, yea, wine instead of
water, pouring forth his blood to be the drink of many,
and affording his body to be the Bread of Life unto all
mankind.

"When thou wast born, O mighty One—before
the Morning Star wast thou begotten—and when the
Star of thine uprising was seen, then all the host of
heaven worshipped thee and the sun and the moon
did thee homage, and the Sons of the Morning sang
for joy together at the brightness of thy glory;
for thy Star did far outshine all earthly light, appearing as a token of the destruction of the kingdom
of Satan, according as it is written, 'A star shall
shine out of Jacob, and a sceptre from Israel, and
shall destroy the corners of Edom.' Then did Edom
tremble, but the poor and simple rejoiced. To thee
also the Wisdom of the East did obeisance, the kings
of Arabia and Saba brought gifts. Thou also didst
feed the hungry, and heal the sick, Satan fled from
before thee and thou didst cast his demons into the
abyss; thou didst guide thy disciples through the
paths of great waters; when they cry unto thee, thou
hearest them; thy voice stilleth the wind, and thy
path is on the deep. To thee the Law and Prophets

do bear witness that thou art the very Christ. Yea, Moses and Elias stand at thy right hand and at thy left, to bear witness unto thee, that in thee must needs be accomplished all things that are written in the Law and the Prophets.

"But concerning the manner of the death of the Lord Jesus, that it is prophesied a hundred times both in the Psalms and in the Prophets, what need is there that I should speak unto you? For ye yourselves know these Scriptures. But as concerning his rising again on the third day, it is written, 'I will lay me down and rest, for thou wilt raise me up;' and again, 'Let us go unto the Lord; he hath smitten and he shall revive us; on the third day he shall raise us up, and we shall live in his sight.' Moreover, brethren, let me also declare unto you, as many as have fathers or mothers according to the flesh who have fallen asleep not having known the Lord Jesus that ye sorrow not for them as if they were lost; for it is written, 'The Lord God remembered his dead people of Israel who lay in the graves; and he descended to preach unto them his own salvation.' And this saying, 'he descended,' what meaneth it except that he went down, even into Hades to break the bonds of Satan, and to preach his Gospel unto the fathers who lived in times past, even unto all the righteous, that they also might have hope of salvation? Wherefore also, when he arose from the dead, a multitude of the saints arose from their graves with him, being delivered from the captivity of death, according to the saying, 'He led captivity captive, and gave gifts for men.' But last of all, after he had risen from the dead, having manifested himself during many days to his disciples, it was necessary that he should ascend into heaven, according as it is written, 'Lift up yourselves, O ye gates, and be ye lift up, ye everlasting doors, and the King of glory shall come in.'

"Now therefore, beloved brethren, called of God, heirs of everlasting life, having the Lord Jesus, in his birth and mighty works, and in his death and rising again, thus visibly set forth as it were before your eyes by the Prophets and the Psalms, what remaineth but that ye should watch, and pray, and shew forth all patience, esteeming lightly the joys and sorrows of this present world, and making little account of your worldly possessions (for great possessions are great temptations) ; but be ye possessed with a new Spirit, even with the Spirit of the Lord Jesus Christ, filling your hearts with an insatiable desire of doing good, comforting the sorrowful, feeding the hungry, healing the sick, and preaching the good news of Christ; and covet no man's wealth, nor slaves, nor apparel ; but covet ye every occasion of well-doing. Thus shall ye make yourselves ready for the day of the Lord when, the number of the elect having been at last completed, the Lord your Saviour shall come again from heaven in great glory, and ye shall reign with him in joy unspeakable.

"The Grace of the Lord Jesus Christ and the Love of God and the Fellowship of the Holy Spirit be with you now and always. Go in peace."

NOTES.

x

NOTES.

MANY of the dialogues and some of the descriptions in the preceding pages, are borrowed from ancient authors; who how-ever wrote in most cases after the times of Onesimus. For example, whereas Onesimus lived at Colossæ about 60 A.D.; Epictetus probably flourished a generation later; Maximus of Tyre, the defender of polytheism from the social side, who is represented above by the fictitious Nicostratus, wrote under the Antonines; Ælius Aristides, the eulogist of Asclepius, who is represented above by Oneirocritus, was born about 117 A.D.; Apuleius, from whom is borrowed (p. 17) the description of the ergastulum, and also (p. 180) the description of the dancers of Cybele, wrote in the second century after Christ; Celsus, the sceptic, who is represented (pp. 122-7) by the sceptical Artemi-dorus, wrote at the beginning of the second century; and lastly Justin Martyr and Irenæus, from whom are mainly borrowed the discourse of Lucius of Cyrene, wrote severally about 150 A.D. and 170 A.D.

"A confession of anachronism then?" Yes: anachronism. But if only such sayings have been selected from these authors as express thoughts that were, at least in their germs, con-temporaneous with Onesimus, then the life of St. Paul's convert is really far better illustrated by this systematic anachronism than by the most felicitously invented dialogue of modern scholars. Artemidorus, Nicostratus, Philemon and Oneirocritus

represent thoughts that must have been in the air throughout
Asia as early as 60 A.D., though they did not find expression
in extant books till some time later. So also of Justin and
Irenæus ; it may safely be asserted that the tendency to see
in each of the acts of Jesus the exact fulfilment of some prophecy, and in each prophecy the prediction of some act of
Jesus—the next step being to believe and then to assert, that
that act must consequently have occurred—permeated the
early Christian church at least as early as the date of the com-
position of the Introduction to St. Matthew's Gospel, and long
before it found expression in the pages of Justin and Irenæus.

In the following notes on special passages, it has not been
thought necessary to give a separate reference for every quotation, but only in those cases where the words of some ancient
author seemed in danger of being supposed to be modern.

Book. Sect.

i. 6. This description of the slaves in the ergastulum is
from Apuleius.

i. 7. "The cross has been the tomb," &c., a quotation
from Plautus.

ii. 2. Epictetus was probably a child at this time.

ii. 2. The remarks of Nicostratus and Heracleas are taken
from Maximus of Tyre.

ii. 2. The remark of Heracleas on the ancient transformations is taken from Pausanias.

ii. 3. The whole of this description of a festival is from
Maximus of Tyre.

ii. 4. For the story of the fighting-cock and the rest, see
Friedländer's work on the *Religion of the Ancients*
(French translation), vol. iv., 180.

ii. 4. Oneirocritus, describing his sickness and the favours
of Asclepius, here repeats the sentiments of
P. Ælius Aristides, born about 117 A D. (see
Friedländer, *ib.*, 181-4).

Book. Sect.

ii. 4. Pliny esteemed it right to build temples, &c., of gods in whom he disbelieved.

ii. 6. The account of the descent into the cave of Trophonius is borrowed from Pausanias, who himself went down.

ii. 6. "I could not restrain myself from laughing": this detail is borrowed from Pausanias.

ii. 7. The whole of this travesty of Socrates is taken from Lucian's *Halcyon*.

ii. 7. "Sobriety and incredulity," &c.: see note on iii. 4.

iii. 3. Philip is reported to have raised a dead man (Euseb. *H. E.*, iii. 39): but the account given in the text is borrowed from the account of the revivification of the Archbishop of Bordeaux, written out for the Author by one who heard it from the Archbishop himself.

iii. 4. "Sober incredulity," &c.: a translation of the proverb, Νᾶφε καὶ μέμνας ἀπιστεῖν· νεῦρα ταῦτα τῶν φρενῶν.

iii. 7. "With whom I do not agree; neither would I," &c.: this statement about the diversity of opinions concerning the nature of Christ, is a quotation from Justin, *Dial.*, 48.

iii. 8. The "Tradition" here mentioned by Onesimus in the beginning of this section, is the matter common to the first three Gospels. It may be roughly represented by the Gospel of St. Mark, excluding the verses after Mark xvi. 8, which are recognised by all scholars to be an interpolation. For fuller information on the nature of this "Tradition" the reader may consult the article on Gospels in the new edition of the *Encyclopædia Britannica*.

iv. 1. The description of the voyage is from Lucian.

THE DISCOURSE OF LUCIUS OF CYRENE.

Page.

297. For the importance attached to prophecy, see Irenæus (*Against Heresies*, ii. 4) : "If, however, they maintain that the Lord performed such works simply in appearance, we shall refer them to the prophetical writings, and prove from these both that all things were thus predicted regarding Him, and did take place undoubtedly." Justin Martyr also takes the same view, I. *Apol.*, 30.

297. "Who shall declare his generation?" This passage is similarly applied by Justin Martyr, *Dialogue*, 63.

299. "*He shall take away*," &c. So Justin (*Dial.*, 77), "But now the prophecy has stated it with this addition : ' Before the child knows how to call father or mother, he shall take the power of Damascus and spoils of Samaria.' And you cannot prove that such a thing ever happened to any one among the Jews. But we are able to prove that 'it happened in the case of Christ." And he then proceeds to interpret Damascus as referring to the Magi, and Assyria to Herod, as in the text.

300. "Behold a Man, the East is his name," Zech. vi. 12, according to the Septuagint, quoted by Justin, *Dial.*, 106.

301. "He shall dwell in a cave," &c. : quoted by Justin Martyr from the Septuagint version of Isaiah xxxiii. 16 (*Dial.*, 70).

303. "The Lord God remembered his dead people of Israel," &c. This passage is quoted by Justin Martyr (*Dial.*, 72), who accuses the Jews of cancelling this and other passages of the Scriptures. It is also quoted by Irenæus (*Against Heresies*, iii. 20) as from Isaiah, and (*ib.* iv. 22) as from Jeremiah. But it is not found in our Scriptures.